Behind The Lines

THIRD EYE CENTRE
1989

BEHIND THE LINES

An Anthology of New Scottish Poetry and Prose

Published in September 1989

ISBN 0 906474 88 4
Edited by Carl MacDougall
Illustrated by Willie Rodger
Designed & Typeset by Adrian Tyler

Published and distributed by:
Third Eye Centre
346–354 Sauchiehall Street
Glasgow
G2 3JD
Tel: 041–332 7521

U.K. Trade Sales:
Lund Humphries Publishers Ltd
Park House
1 Russell Gardens
London
NW11 9NN

Behind The Lines is financially assisted by the
Scottish Arts Council

Printed by:
E.F. Peterson & Son
12 Laygate
South Shields
Tyne & Wear
NE33 5RP

Third Eye Centre (Glasgow) Ltd, an independent Arts Centre with charitable status, is subsidised by the Scottish Arts Council and Glasgow District Council.

Behind The Lines

For trouts are tickled best in muddy water.

Samuel Butler (1612–80)

BEHIND THE LINES

Contents

Poems

Stories

Poems

INTRODUCTION

Carl MacDougall

Writers' Groups, Clubs and Circles have existed for some time, but the last five years has seen a remarkable growth in Writers' Workshops throughout Scotland.

Glasgow Writers' Club is the oldest in Britain, and, as far as Scotland is concerned, the workshop movement started when Glasgow University's Extra Mural Department ran informal writing classes in the late Sixties. In the winter of 1969 they began a creative writing workshop; nine groups now meet every week, attended by over 250 people throughout the West of Scotland.

Some workshops began under similar umbrella organisations, such as the Workers' Educational Association, and now manage their own activities; others began as writers' groups and joined an existing network, such as the Glasgow University Extra Mural Department. Some began as workshops and are now affiliated to the Scottish Association of Writers' Groups. Many were started by writers in residence to a college, university, library or town and when the writer's term expired the groups carried on, sometimes with another writer, but often on their own.

Many groups do develop with the help of a professional writer, who acts as a tutor, either on a regular or an irregular basis; others have the service of a writer in residence; but more often than not writing groups meet and develop on their own, bringing a writer in to judge a competition, do a reading, look at their work, or, more usually, all three. The emphasis is almost always on new work, usually on poetry or short fiction, and on developing individual writers' skills, rather than finding a market for their work or manoeuvring their way into existing markets. As a result, this movement is beginning to develop a new breed of writer and a new method of publishing. What looks like an embryonic publications network is being established between groups and though it would be fanciful to say this was any kind of underground movement, this work rarely finds its way into the established markets.

Ten years ago, when I edited WORDS magazine I was constantly surprised by the number of eloquently finished pieces we received from unknown writers. When we began, there was no regular outlet for story writers, apart from the fifteen or so pieces that were published in the annual SCOTTISH SHORT STORIES volumes, and it was generally assumed short stories were not being written. The few magazines that exist now do, in the main, publish short stories, though new writers find it difficult to break into these diminishing markets. Existing outlets hardly seem to have bothered many writers' workshops and even the established annual anthologies such as SCOTTISH SHORT STORIES and NEW WRITING SCOTLAND largely pass them by.

Like every writer, the workshop members want their work read, but reckon they are writing for a different audience. They are mainly interested in reaching people whose experience is similar to their own and since cheaper printing has brought publication within the range of most groups, they have set about producing a few hundred copies of booklets containing their own work, which they sell locally, to friends and neighbours. At present this is a trend rather than an established practice, but there has been a sufficient number of well produced booklets over the past few years to lead us to believe the trend is continuing.

Story telling has always belonged to the people. It is a genuinely popular traditional art which has been lost only in the last few generations. The writers in this book and others like them are reclaiming what was always their own; even though the printed word now generates a gargantuan industry which seems able to give huge financial rewards to a few and has little or nothing to do with the individual or the languages a large percentage of people in this country would either recognise or consider their own.

There is something noble and endearing in how writing manages to survive in spite of continuing and obvious discouragements. It is virtually ignored by most of the media, though token representations are being extended now that books appear to be fashionable. It cannot hope to benefit from the big money sponsorship that most musical, some theatrical and even a few art events manage to attract. And as far as this publication is concerned, it soon became obvious that there was nothing glamorous and little appealing to a potential sponsor here, that the return would be small and probably not at all obvious, even though we were looking for what, in sponsorship terms, was a very small amount of money.

Such sponsorship as literature attracts tends to discourage new fiction; the big money literary prizes certainly discriminate against experimental work, usually going for a safer, middle of the road choice. Writers may find their books in the short lists on merit, but it is usual to find the judges have argued over compromise rather than standards before picking their winner.

Of course, there is a reading public and a writing public and it seems that folk like me who thought they were one and the same were very wrong, since many contributors and would-be contributors are more interested in having their own work published than in seeing what published writers are writing. Magazines and anthologies have tried for years to tap into the reading public, with some success, but the prejudices against new writing can also come from the reading public, and the safe option is to give them what everyone knows they like. I am not alone in urging would be writers to read. Some writers in residence I know have offered reading lists, and it is certainly true that editors can usually tell readers from non-readers. If you are watching an assembly line of earthenware chanties, the chances of coming across a Ming vase are fairly remote.

Some workshop anthologies obviously include pieces which are there because everyone who turns up deserves to have something published. It is an unfortunate trend of human nature that we compare ourselves to the worst. We watch a bad play on television, think we could do as well and proceed to write another bad play, rather than compare ourselves to Bleasdale, Byrne, Potter and the like, see what they do, ask how they do it, try to do the same ourselves, or maybe even improve on it. The same is true in other forms of writing.

Some writers tend to standardise work by putting a heavy emphasis on publishing, and often on a certain type of commercial publishing. Others can be imitative of recent trend setters and there are some where the demands need to be known in advance, the length of the story required and so on, which produces a considerable number of stories of 2,000 – 2,100 words, big enough to fit the BBC's MORNING STORY slot. Many pieces are written to be read aloud, usually to one's friends in the group, which makes the writer uncertain, or even unable, to try something new, something other than formula, standardised, inoffensive work.

This collection comes from the belief that what it contains deserves a wider audience. There are over 50 contributors and few have appeared elsewhere. More than half the contributors are women. Many writers show a welcome readiness to tackle difficult themes in a convincing and realistic way. There is a refreshing sense of humour in much of the work as well as an ability to distinguish between personal experience and insight and to use personal experience as the starting point for fiction rather than the result of it. And there are even a few writers here who have learned to use their imaginations as a tool of discovery rather than invention. It is often difficult to assess a voice from one or two poems or from a single story, but the work here is offered as an introduction and as such will hopefully provide an incentive for further investigation.

Submissions were invited from over ninety writers' groups in Scotland and the initial letter was deliberately unspecific about what sort of contribution should be sent. This was because I knew that many people who attend writers' workshops write reminiscences, historical pieces, journalism and so on and I hoped that people would submit what they thought was their best work, irrespective of language, subject, length or category. I wanted the submissions to determine the shape of the anthology and that has happened. There were only a couple of submissions in any category other than poetry and prose and none in Gaelic. In fact, less than half the groups we contacted submitted work and some were represented by a single submission.

In spite of these difficulties, I hope others will persist. It is important that new writers are encouraged and that while the practice of self-publication has a noble and honorable pedigree, writers need to develop their work and the more outlets there are, the better opportunities there are for new developments.

Finally, I would like to thank Third Eye Centre, Chris Carrell and his staff for their encouragement, patience, help and support. They have made my job a lot easier than it might have been. I would also like to thank Willie Rodger for his finely crafted and vivid illustrations. Thanks also to the contributors, who have waited far longer than was reasonable for this wee book. Some of this work was accepted three years ago and it is heartening to see that since then many contributors' work has appeared elsewhere. I would like to thank all contributors for their commitment and their patience; in every case they responded with kindness, warmth and enthusiasm. They taught me a lot and I am very grateful.

Behind the Lines is intended to be an introduction to the writers and their work. If you care about the future of writing in this country then I am sure you will welcome this book and find a cause for rejoicing in its pages.

ROSA MACPHERSON

Hungry

Violet hadn't always had difficulty remembering. She never had trouble with dates: battles, proclamations; things like that. But recently she had found that her memory was becoming elusive. Obscure things: like when exactly to blend the custard-powder with the warm milk, so as to avoid lumps, baffled her. Or whether she had taken her medication that morning, or simply confused the image with last night's memory . . .

Was the dog whimpering with hunger or greed?

The first World War ended in 1918, the second began in 1939. That meant twenty-one years of peace: coming of age. There was nothing wrong with Violet's arithmetic.

On her twenty-first birthday someone had sent her a bunch of beautiful carnations; small pink-budded carnations . . . or were they roses? She still had the card with her name printed on the pink-padded cover: Happy 21st. Violet! Coming of Age! It was printed in gold letters, captured in a golden love heart.

Perhaps the dog was thirsty.

Someone had told her that the flowers would have lived longer if she remembered to change the water. Only when it was too late had she carefully picked a brown-edged head from a stem and placed it in her First Communion Bible. A souvenir of her birthday.

Now she decided to look for it. It would be upstairs with all her other souvenirs, in the drawer with the broken handle. One day she would have it fixed, and wonder how she managed to put up with it like that for so long.

But now she simply eased the drawer carefully, pulling it gently from side to side, until it opened far enough for her to put her hand in and feel for the Bible. She felt the smooth cellophane cover immediately. It was yellowing now but Jesus and the children still smiled happily; not caring that the dove above them was no longer white.

Violet smiled. She gently caressed Jesus's face and recalled the words: You are now a soldier of Christ. Or were they said at her Confirmation? She frowned momentarily then smiled again, opening the book.

A photograph of herself fell onto her lap and she gasped, delighted. There she was, seven years old, her red cheeks visible, even in black and white. She held the white Bible in her seven-year-old hands, as if it were a wedding bouquet.

She remembered the day: her daddy had kissed her and her mother had frowned and said: "Watch her veil; don't crush it."

Suddenly the dog whined again and placed his large heavy paw on her knee. He looked straight into her eyes and she was sure he was trying to tell her something.

The Bible forgotten, Violet put her arms around the dog's furry neck and whispered: "My little Love."

The German Shepherd responded with a wag of his tail.

"My little Love, show me how much you love me. Come on. How much do you love me?"

The dog sat back on his hind legs, poised as a circus poodle.

"You do love me, don't you?" she laughed.

The dog continued in his pose but whined repeatedly.

"All right. I'll get a can of dog food for you. Just be patient, for goodness sake."

Violet walked to the kitchen and checked inside her shopping bag.

"Why you greedy dog, you. You've been fed already. Out you go!"

Violet pointed sternly towards the now-open door, and the dog, lowering his head, slunk slowly into the garden.

"Now, what was I doing?" she thought aloud, as she bit absently at her ragged thumbnail.

"Oh yes, I must've been making the bed."

When Violet walked back into the bedroom and saw the Bible lying there, she kicked off her shoes and sat on the bed. She laid her Communion photograph aside with barely a glance, and flicked eagerly through the pages until she came to the flattened carnation, as brown now as a dead autumn leaf.

She lifted it gently, sniffed it and smiled:

The delivery man said, "Miss Violet Bradley?" and I nodded my head and he said, "Happy 21st. Miss Bradley. He must really love you . . . "

He handed me the flowers and went away."

Violet held the flower a moment then placed it between the pages once more. She lay back on the bed, resting her head on the pillow.

"Happy 21st. Violet," and she closed her eyes.

Suddenly she sat upright on the bed, remembering again: It was Stanley who sent me the flowers! Who'd have thought it? Stanley! You were so handsome, Stanley. And all those flowers and chocolates you brought me.

Oh Stanley. In those days . . . I was happy, Stanley. I remember.

Violet swung her legs over the side of the bed and began to search for her shoes. Did I kick them off?, she wondered.

Suddenly she heard the front door slam loudly, and a voice cried out, "Violet."

She muttered silently and continued to look for her shoes.

She walked barefoot into the kitchen.

"Oh you're home," she said and looked out of the window, towards the watching dog.

"How have you been today then,?" he asked, and she replied "Fine," without looking away from the window.

"What's for dinner?"

She did not answer but looked at the curtains and decided they needed changing.

"Did you buy anything for my dinner, Violet?" he asked, immediately exasperated.

But still she ignored him.

He looked at the empty cooker, then checked the larder. He looked inside her shopping bag, then walked over to her:

"Did you take your medication?"

She shrugged his resting hand from her shoulder.

"I'll make some scrambled eggs," he sighed.

She continued to watch the dog, while he prepared the meal.

They ate in silence.

Afterwards he said: "I think you should see the doctor again, Violet. Your memory's getting worse. Poor Fred hasn't even been fed. He's starving again."

He brought the whimpering dog back into the kitchen.

She sat glumly at the table and chewed at her ragged thumbnail.

"Feed him, will you? I'm going out for a drink and something decent to eat."

He walked off slowly towards the front door.

Suddenly Violet rushed down the hall behind him.

He turned, startled.

"There's nothing wrong with my memory at all Stanley. Nothing at all."

She slapped him hard across the face. Then she turned and ran towards the bedroom. She grabbed the white Bible and tore at the pages until she found the decayed flower. She crushed it in her hand.

Stanley grabbed his jacket and walked out of the house, slamming the door behind him.

The sound seemed to startle Violet, and she wiped the sudden tears from her eyes. She left the torn petals lying on the floor.

She walked back to the kitchen, but stopped suddenly, seeing the dog in front of her.

He sat obediently, offering her his paw.

"So you're hungry again, Fred? I've forgotten to feed you again?"

The dog continued to beg.

"You're a bad dog, Fred. You don't deserve any dinner."

The dog cowered as she walked to the table and pulled out a chair.

"There was a time I didn't need reminding to cook his meals, Fred.

I remember it as if it were yesterday," she added, and absently chewed at her ragged thumbnail.

JANET PAISLEY

Long Haul

The rain hung across the Shap as he made the run down into Carlisle. Like a grey heavy curtain it spanned the valley. He hit it with a smack, felt it part round the cab, heard it drum on the roof. The daylight dulled to a yellow glow. Reaching forwards he flicked wipers and lights on. Mac didn't mind the rain. He felt good on the downhill run. All the way from Aberdeen and as many runs as a man could make in twenty years. But he still felt good.

It was a long time since they'd taken that sudden steep drop and run it smooth. A long time since he'd had to climb down the gears and sweat on it. But it was still downhill. It was still his rig leaping forward to bite on the grey asphalt as the ground dropped away in front. A longer, smoother, speedier descent with the frail dimpled crash barrier a continuous reminder.

He always took the run down the Shap on an empty stomach just before lunch. There was nothing like the keen edge of fear to sharpen up an appetite. Nothing like knowing there was twenty tonne of Swedish pine at his back and if it went bad he'd maybe, just maybe halt the cab. But he'd have a thirty foot trailer jack-knifed up his arse. And a load that would keep travelling on.

He picked her up outside of Carlisle. She stood by the access road. Bare-headed, impervious, rain making rats tails in her hair. So he broke his own rule. On a full tank and a full belly he thought — what the hell. First time in twenty year. In the cab she shook her hair like a dog. Water spat onto the back of his hand, left round blacker spots in the wheel. He felt good still.

"Where to?" His idea of a joke. She shrugged. But he'd known it wouldn't matter. She'd been on the road a long time. They all had.

"South," she said. He watched as she stuck a battered hold-all under her feet and raked in her pocket for fags. Then he swung back out into the motorway traffic. Maybe it was the rain had made him act generous. It thrummed still on the roof of the cab, closing them in. Pasted photographs over the windscreen smiled down at them. Madge — at the door of the house. The two boys. He nodded at the pictures.

"My kids." His voice seemed loud and the silence empty. She didn't offer her fags when she found them. She didn't seem to listen either. He wondered if she knew what it was like — having family.

"Kids?" She said. "Sure. I had kids." The match head crumbled, left bare stick and a pink streak on the side of the box. He slid a pack from the dash, tossed them to her.

"Wet," she said. The damp box was rammed back in the pocket of her sodden coat.

Funny she should have kids. His own two grinned down at him. Not often they grinned, except in photographs. Obligatory then. Madge was grinning too. He didn't see much of them. Not on the road. Not with the house to pay for. Maybe he shouldn't have mentioned them. It was kind of uncomfortable to have them in the cab, grinning. Made him feel a queer

need to explain, apologise. Funny she should have kids too.

"Exeter," he said. "That's where I'm headed."

"Fine." She blew a thin stream of smoke at the windscreen and watched it spread across the glass. Strange kind of life, he thought, just travelling up and down the roads. Everywhere someplace you'd been and nothing to go back for. He was curious.

"Someplace special is it? Down South?" She looked at him then. First time since she'd got in the cab. Her eyes were grey — like the rain. She could have been any age.

"Land's End." She made it sound like nowhere. It was his turn to shrug.

Land's End was for tourists. For long haired weirdos with back packs or bikes. Doing it for charity. He turned his attention back to the road. They were running out of the rain. It had thinned to a fine drizzle. He gave the lights to an overtaking container and settled down for the afternoon run. But it wasn't the same. Irritation prickled in his shoulders. The smell of damp clothes drying out filled the cab. He should have left her standing at Carlisle with her silence and her unconcern. Now he was shut in, cramped by the physical presence of her. She ought to know the ropes, ought to at least talk. His eyes flicked back to the photographs.

There was no comfort for him there. Mr. Money was all he was to the kids. Think of them, think of their wants. And Madge. He wasn't sure anymore what he was for Madge.

"For them is it?" Her voice startled him. "For them," she repeated. "Long distance. For the money?"

"Oh. Yeh." He nodded the lie. The grey eyes were on his face. He corrected himself, sheepish to be caught out. "Hell, no. Guess I just like it."

"'Sa good enough reason. For anything."

He eased his foot back, shook his head as a station wagon cut in too close, too soon. First of the blips, rushing to be home.

"The only thing," he said.

"Only thing you like? . . . Or the only thing you do?"

"Both," he said. He'd caught it from her. He must've caught it from her. Christ she should still be at Carlisle.

"Stupid Bastard!" He yelled, laying on the horn to make up for the one he let go. The blip that had tried the bumper swop slacked off then picked up speed. He eased back on the pedal. There'd be no race'n chase. It wasn't his style. But he could play her game. He didn't have to talk. It was his rig. Miles of grey road dashed under his wheels, heading North. His shoulders felt stiff. The seat didn't fit his back anymore.

"Been driving long?" she asked. Another driver would have answered the hours for that day. But he was proud of his twenty years. He'd chalked them up one by one. With enthusiasm at first, then steadily and now he worked towards what he held as a triumph. Twenty five years on the road. It was a target like a date ringed with red on a calendar. A target he reached for with a feeling of glee.

So he forgot he had meant to stay silent and he talked. As he talked all his pride in his skill shone on his round face. He talked of his rig as a lover would talk of his woman. He exulted in the power under the boards and his control of it. The throb of the engine, the hiss of air from the brakes, a thirsty tank gulping diesel, the sing of tyre on tar — these were the things that put music in his life.

The woman's grey stare stayed on his face as he talked, watching the light in his eyes. He staggered over sudden shyness.

"You'll be thinking I'm soft in the head," he said. But she was feeding on his pleasure.

"No, no," she protested. "I think you're lucky. To be so alive." They laughed together — as though they shared some illicit secret. Mac felt himself spread out to fill the cab again. And he told her stories from years ago. Long and short. Sad and funny and strange.

The road ahead shrank to the beam of the headlights. Beyond was a black gullet lined with lighted teeth. At Stoke-on-Trent he took the slip road for the A34. It was coming close on dinner time and he avoided eating in the giant service stations that straddled the motorway like dinosaurs. He liked the closed-in warmth of the Transport Cafe survivors.

Just beyond Stafford he pulled onto the ash-park at Kate's Kitchen. He let the engine growl twice before he switched off. A habit he passed off as feeding fuel to the carburettor for an easy start. But he knew he just liked to leave with the roar ringing in his ears.

"Dinner," he said. She climbed down and tugged her hold-all free from under her seat, joining him as he walked to the lighted cafe.

Inside Kate's the air was heavy with the smell of constant frying and tasted of bacon fat. Eggs spat on the griddle. The round tables were covered with plastic gingham cloths, yellowed at the edges, and set with salt and pepper, vinegar and squeezy containers of brown sauce that were never quite clean. In one of the side booths he caught sight of Big Ben with the Fixer tucked in beside him. The woman followed a step or two behind so that he had to stand aside to let her squeeze in at the table first. The other two drivers glanced at her and Big Ben nodded but they paid her no more attention than that.

"Thought they'd pensioned you off," he said to the Fixer. Fixer looked seventy, thin and lined.

"Naw," he said, "Been trying deliveries but nothing doing. Got to feeling like a yo-yo on a short string."

"We'll pass a coffin trundling North one o' these days," Big Ben grinned, "Be him!" His whooped laugh disturbed the greasy air of the cafe and his broad shoulders shook heavily so that the table rattled. The young girl who'd come over to take their orders yawned her boredom.

Mac recited his list from memory. It read like the entire menu. The biggest meal he ate all day and it never varied. The girl made quick pencil marks on her pad then waited, tapping the pencil stub like a drumstick on the paper as she glanced at the woman.

"Just tea," the woman said. Mac screwed his head round.

"You'll have the same as me," he said. He screwed back to the girl. "She'll have same as me." The girl ticked out a two and walked off. Beside him Mac felt the woman shift in the seat.

"I'll get it," he said. She didn't reply. Ben coughed. Mac felt his spine begin to prickle. "Hell, you have to eat," he justified himself.

A pall of discomfort had crept up on him and touched them all. Then Fixer launched into one of his long tales. This one about short haul which made a change and took the scunner out of Mac's back so he felt easy with them again, like usual. When the food came he dove at it hungrily. The woman was hungry too and ate almost despite herself. He felt pleased then. Let them think what they liked. Just because you broke one rule. Didn't mean you had to change your life.

The Fixer gave a short foxy laugh.

"And d'you remember coming in through that door, Mac, with your handbrake in your hand," he slapped his knee and chuckled. "You want to have seen his face, Ben. A picture it was, a picture."

Mac grinned through a mouthful of food. That was the first time he'd met Fixer. And the time he'd learned where he got his nickname.

"Bloody lucky you was here," he said. The Fixer accepted the compliment as due.

"We were all held together with string in them days," he said. "String and wire and a helluva lot of luck." Ben stood up. He towered over the table.

"I'm off," he said, "Before the violins start. See you." The Fixer rose to follow him out.

"Me an' all," he said, "I've sat my spell. Mind how you go, Mac." Mac nodded. He'd run into them again, a week, months, a year from now. He sipped at his black stewed tea and watched the woman push her empty plate away.

"You was hungry then?" She nodded.

"Haven't ate much the last couple of days."

Outside he checked the ropes for slack, tightening where it was needed. He worked steadily, content now he was fed and could rest up. The ropes were wet and stretched as he pulled them on. He worked up from the driver's door towards the rear. As he came round from the back he saw her leaning against the nearside door. Despite the dark he could feel the grey eyes on him. His spine tingled again. He loosed off the rope and pulled on it.

"I stop over now," he said, "Down the road a bit. You might pick up another lift here. If you wait, like." He tied off the rope, not looking at her. He could tell she hadn't taken her eyes off him. His fingers felt like thumbs.

"'Sall right."

He moved down to the last rope. Beside the cab where she stood. He'd noticed in the cafe her hair had dried and curled round her face. The wet rope was stubborn under his fingers. He stifled the irritation that grew in him.

"You can if you like," she said.

He looked at her then. Her face was close to his. So close he could make out the dark pupils in the greyness of the irises. But her look stayed with his. He had to turn away. He was having trouble tying the rope back.

"For the dinner," she added. He shook his head.

"You don't owe me," he said. He slapped the wet loop home, walked past her round the front of the cab and climbed in. The passenger door clicked open. Her head, then her face, then her body was back sliding into the seat behind him. He relaxed. On his home ground now, the wheel under his hand, leather at his back. His eyes flicked up to Madge's photograph over his head.

"Besides," he said, "no offence like. But how'd I know if you're clean."

He could just hear Madge if he had to explain he'd given her something. Jees, she made enough fuss if he spilled fag ash on her good carpets. The picture was unbearable. He blotted it out and switched on the engine. Unaware, the corner of his mouth smiled at the growl of the throttle.

A few miles down the road he drew into a lay-by and switched off again. It was black outside. Into the sudden silence fell the song of the motorway. On the right of them it rose out of the ground. Pegged on concrete stilts. Passing lights whined through the night. He liked to sleep where he could hear it.

Inside the cab he clicked on the light. Reached for the newspaper. He was hardly settled when the first drops of rain spattered on the roof. It had caught up with them. He could tell from the size of the drops it would be a downpour. In minutes it thrummed on the cab. The windscreen became a waterfall. He could hear the drip, splash, drip from under the trailer over the skittering sound of rain bounced high off the tarmac.

Beside him the woman shuffled in her seat, searched in her hold-all. She was changing her clothes or some such thing. He clawed his attention back to the newspaper. The door clicked open. Rain spewed into the cab. He glanced over, past the humped towel that crouched on her empty seat. Saw the flash of her naked back as she dropped to the ground. Heard her gasp as the rain stung on her skin. The cab door slammed shut on the night again.

The newspaper crumpled on his lap. He caught sight of her, white and exposed, slip down the bank into the field beyond. On the grass she made a quick scan round. Then she raised her arms to the sky. And turned her face up to the rain. He knew she must have her eyes shut. The force of the rain would feel like the cut of a thousand steel spines on her flesh. His fingers raised of their own accord to wipe the mist of his breath from the window. Quite unaware, he hunched over her seat and the waiting towel to watch. He felt as though he gazed on some primeval right of worship. Awed and amazed.

Now her hair streamed with water. She began to wash herself. Soap frothed in the hair of her armpits. Rain washed it away. She soaped over her breasts, her stomach, her thighs. White bubbles collected in the dark patch below her belly before the rain rushed them, scudding down her legs. The she hurried back to the cab. She reached for the towel left on the seat. Buried her face in it. Moaned and trembled with the chill of the rain.

Mac could not turn away. It took some conscious effort to raise his jawbone and close his mouth. He swallowed hard on the immovable lump in his throat. When she looked out of the towel, her eyes met his. He knew from the way they crinkled at the corners that her mouth, hidden under the towel, was smiling. Even though she trembled and her teeth chattered. She rubbed the towel over her breasts and her legs. But her eyes, greyer than ever and candid, never left his.

"I'm clean now," she said.

Her skin was cold, pimpled with goosebumps but her mouth was warm and hungry on his. Her nipples tasted of soap and the rain and she arched up against him drawing heat from his skin as he dragged the clothes off him with her helping as well she might. The cabin steamed and the windows fogged but Mac was back on the downhill run where it swept him along and sucked him down and his gut was shoved back to his backbone and fear curled high in his stomach. It was long and slow and sudden and frightening. And from nowhere it reached him. The dream of a sudden steep drop. It waited still. And he drove headlong towards it.

It was the whine of the motorway Mac heard first. It started to jump about seven. Blips on a heart monitor — speeding up. Sounding faster and faster to become a continuous solitary shriek. Fear dried his mouth and he woke. The seven thirty song settled itself steady in his ears. Then he heard the birds and her breath. The weight of her leg across his reminded him.

She was still asleep, looked younger asleep. Sometime they must have gotten onto the bunk behind the seats. They were cramped together. He would not be able to move without waking her. He knew this was going to be one of the big embarrassing moments of his life. He eased his leg from under hers and reached for his shirt. He had his head in it, poking out the top when he knew she was awake and saw the same grey eyes as yesterday, like she was dead already, looking steady at him.

"Time we was off," he said, squirming into his trousers under the blanket and thankful that he could dodge over into the driving seat before she spoke. He had the rig out, swung round the roundabout and bowling into the motorway traffic before she climbed down in front beside him. He was easy now. He was home.

"Them kids you said you had," he looked over at her. "You just up and leave 'em?" She was staring out the windscreen.

"I said my goodbyes." The grey eyes were fixed on the glass. Behind it was the pall of smoke, the flash of fire. And the charred black flesh on the grass under the blanket she had ripped aside. The scream of the traffic froze her. She couldn't remember who had screamed. But it went on, and on. Even with her hands over her ears, it went on. She shrugged, smiled with her mouth towards Mac's face.

"I said my goodbyes."

He wished he could. He looked up again at the prisoned smiles of his sons. At Madge. Her lips were parted a little, showing her teeth, like they were bared. They made him feel tired. An intruder in his own home. The perpetual lodger. And because she was still, and quiet, and contained he began to tell her about them.

"Maybe you should stay home," she said after a while.

"That would be nice," he scorned, "That would be great. Mend this, fix that, mind your feet, move your butt. Give us a pound, give us a lift." His breath steamed down his nostrils. "Maybe they'd appreciate me!"

"Maybe," she said. It was a question. He didn't know the answer. Some day he'd have no choice but find out. But not yet, not for a while yet.

They had breakfast at Bristol. It was a meal Mac never liked. He was always eager to be up and off, back on the road while the day was fresh. He'd gotten quite used to having her in the cab. Her quiet spells, when she stopped listening or seeing him, didn't trouble him now. He just rolled back into being alone with himself and his rig. It was good to be comfortable and think his own thoughts. This was the last leg of his run and he soaked up every good mile of it.

The sun had come up with the morning. Grey fields became green.

Colour picked out roofs and houses. By the time he turned off the M5 for Exeter the road was dust dry under the wheels. Up ahead was the junction. And the Plymouth road. He pulled the rig over and pointed.

"That's the A38," he said, "To the left. I go straight on." He watched as she tugged the hold-all from under seat. It caught and she twisted in the seat to pull it free. Then she had it in her hands and was reaching for the door catch.

"You could stop on," he rushed the words out, "Get me back up the road." The door was open. A smile ghosted across her mouth.

"We're going different roads now," she said. The she jumped. He was looking at blank space. At the empty field beyond. He leaned over, gaped out the open door at the top of her head.

"Hey," he shouted, "What the hell are you going to do at Land's End?" Her face turned up to him. The grey stare froze on his eyeballs.

"Jump off," she said. The door slammed shut.

He had to stop at the lights. In the mirror he saw her trudge down the Plymouth road a way, prop up the hold-all and sit down on it. When the lights showed green he roared the rig straight through. Crazy woman, he thought. Real crazy. There was nothing to make of her at all. But he had his peace back. The cabin was his own again. He kept his eyes away from the passenger seat that rode empty side by side with him all the way to Exeter.

He parked up in the woodyard, had his sheets signed and left them to unload her. It was hot now, the sun high in the sky and lunchtime. He settled for a beer at the first place he ran across. Exeter reminded him of Aberdeen. Only wider and warmer. More foreigners too.

He remembered one time he'd gone in the pictures, the big cinema on the main street. A crowd of them had sat down in the row behind. They might have been French or Dutch. It was all Greek to him. They'd chattered away through the film, laughing at the jokes they'd discovered on the sides of the matchboxes. One of them had tapped him on the arm, passed the box over for him to read. It wasn't a very funny joke. They'd thought it was hilarious. He wondered if they'd laughed with him or at him.

He swallowed the watery beer. There were always groups of foreigners on Exeter's street. Might have been students at the University. Maybe just tourists. He left the last inch in the glass, it had no taste anyway, and went back for his rig. He'd make time and catch lunch up the road. The beer had sickened his appetite.

He drove out of town through the wide streets, round the green parks. Back the way he had come. The space in the cab beside him yawned wide and empty. Had she gotten a lift yet? He didn't see the road anymore. He saw her in the field. In the rain. And afterwards, she had clung to him like he was life itself. Madge never came on to him like that. His knuckles whitened on the wheel. Maybe she'd still be there, sat on her hold-all, waiting.

The junction was up ahead. The lights were going to red. His mouth tasted of soap and rain. He braked up and looked down the Plymouth road. The space where she'd sat was empty. But she'd not have gone far. Nobody went all the way to Land's End. Nobody.

He glanced up at the pictures above his head. His sons sneered. Madge snarled. And his rig was in the wrong lane. His hand whipped out at the photographs — tore them down. He ripped them through and through. The cabin closed round him. He wasn't going anywhere. It was the road that moved. He dropped the torn pieces out the open window. Green shone on his face. He slammed in the gear, swung the rig over. A horn honked. The artic strained. It was a long haul back to Scotland and Aberdeen. And uphill all the way. In the wake of his wheels littered pieces of photograph danced in the dust.

ELLEN McMILLAN

Relative Strangers

Alice lay in the darkness holding the bed covers tentatively, ensuring they never made contact with her tummy. The room was in darkness and she felt so uncomfortable, so very afraid. Whenever she let the bed clothes drop, the combined pressure and weight made her aware of the second heartbeat. As faint as a pulse but so loud to her it seemed as though she could actually hear it. It was a life within her, she knew it, and the thought made her body sweat. She wanted to cry but anxiety wouldn't let her. She yelled inside her head and felt none the better for it. She couldn't bear to touch her tummy for fear of some positive sign of life; even the speculation terrified her. It wasn't the thought of telling her parents she was pregnant which terrified her, but of admitting to them, or even to herself, who was responsible.

Even the thought of the party, her parents' stupid bloody party, made her gulp. After all, if they hadn't decided to have a family get-together she wouldn't have been in this position. She wasn't even late but she knew she carried a life within her; why else would she feel so ill that her insides wouldn't settle? Again her body was covered in a film of sweat. She wept quietly.

They had laughed at her at the party because she had some spirits to drink. All the relatives thought it funny that she was so quickly drunk — they always let her sample their drink because she was safe and at home, and so she should have been. She was nearly the right age to drink in pubs anyway. Oh, it was funny the way they'd carried her to bed and, laughing, dumped her on top of the bed; even she had laughed at it. Her auntie had had such a job trying to take Alice's clothes off because her arms were flopping, as was her head, like a typical drunk. And when her aunt left she had slept.

In her dreams she had felt herself being pulled and torn by some strange, animal-like creature she couldn't quite identify. It tore at her and with its rough bristled skin it kept tearing at her face. Scratching at her face with its teeth and in her conscious moments it looked like her Uncle Joe, the family drunk. The animal kept saying things like 'Shut up!' when she wanted it to stop and pulling her lips together made her sleep. But the animal kept on tearing. At one stage she thought she'd die. Vaguely she remembered seeing the figure of Uncle Joe leaving the room, like a thief on tiptoe. Somehow it hadn't mattered then — she was only too glad to stop the animal from killing her and she'd fallen asleep again.

In the morning she had felt terrible and so dreadfully sore. The family hadn't yet got up, but Joe lay on the settee with his mouth open. His face bristly and unshaven. Even at this stage she had thought it was a dream. In school girls always talked about sex, but she refused to accept that her dream of the previous evening could have any possible connection with the subject. In the bathroom she'd felt sick, but not morning sickness, just the sickness that accompanies a feeling of lying to yourself. The toilet bowl felt cool on her face as she'd lain prostrate and felt the sting of her tears on the surface of her skin, before they dropped into the clear water below. Before the bathroom mirror she had examined the skin of her face and the minute scratches belied the dream story her mind was only too ready to accept.

She had, with the vigour of a soldier polishing his boots, scrubbed at her body in the bath, half believing that it would have made her feel clean. It only made her feel painful. In her bedroom she'd gently creamed her face to cool the stinging scratches and vehemently piled all the furnishings she could lift behind the bedroom door, as though preventing intruders, until Joe left. Her parents had called her to say goodbye to Joe, but finally gave up and left. They eventually concluded she was in a typical teenage huff and left her until she decided to come out. Her mum was in a bad mood because Alice was rude to her brother Joe, and looked at her accusingly for having the temerity to stage a tantrum when her Uncle hadn't left yet.

They didn't even bother to ask her why. But she could not have told them anyway. Her Uncle Joe was forty three years old. Drunk and unshaven at the best of times, but they always made excuses for him. His wife had left him, he was a poor soul, what else could a man do but drink? He didn't have a family even. Oh, she'd heard them all. Every excuse was put forward to make him seem like the victim. Nobody mentioned that his wife had left him because of his drinking. Her parents had argued over him many times, her dad saying Joe should put a stop in it while her mother defended her little brother, saying he drank to hide his inability to socialise.

When Joe had left, Alice took the soiled sheets and put them in the refuse shute without so much as a flicker of guilt because of their newness. Her mum looked bewildered, but Alice refused to make any excuses for their absence.

That was three weeks ago or just over and every day she'd wanted to tell someone. But she didn't. At times she'd felt her dad watching her and once or twice she'd wanted to run to him and tell him, while he held her and told her not to worry, as he had when she was a child. He had always told her not to worry; nothing's as bad as it seems was his motto in life, but she couldn't bring herself to see if it still applied.

And so she lay in bed and listened to the heartbeat she was sure was the life within her body, every night when everyone else slept, trying whenever she remembered to lie on her side and keep the clothes off her tummy. During the day, strangely, she could almost put it out of her mind. But, even as a child her fears had seemed to heighten at night in the darkness. If there wasn't a baby, she would be so pleased. Nobody need ever know and she could sleep again without lying until her tiredness overtook her thoughts of what to do if there was a child inside her. This was Alice's last thought before she once again fell wearily into a sleep.

In the morning she had to drag her legs to make them walk. On its own this sign would have meant little, but her tummy felt swollen and very firm. These were signs of menstrual tension, and normally these two symptoms made her irritable, but not today. She wanted to rejoice. It didn't matter that she wasn't pregnant she thought, as she dragged her weary legs to the bathroom. She wanted to laugh out loud for the first time in weeks. At the wash basin she thanked God, she didn't have to tell anyone. Only she and Joe would know.

JANETTE WALKINSHAW

Occupational Therapy

"A greenhouse is like a womb", said Henry.

"Now, now," said the nurse. "We'll have none of that kind of talk." She pushed Elsie forward. "I'll leave you for an hour, Elsie," she said. "I'll come back for you at half past three."

"I haven't a watch," said Elsie.

"It doesn't matter. You stay here till I come for you."

She left. Elsie closed the door behind her. Loose panes rattled gently.

The impression was of size, and light, brighter than the grey day outside, and not the clamminess she had expected, but dry and pleasantly warm.

The staging held rows of pot plants, some of which she knew to be geraniums. Under the eaves massed tomato plants grew out of the earth, their bunches of fruit beginning to redden. It all stretched away from her to the far gable like the art teacher's perennial lesson in perspective, only he, so many years ago, had used a battlefield of rearing horses and fallen bloody lances.

Henry was watching her, while his fingers tamped earth into a flower pot.

"You know about greenhouses, do you?" he asked.

"My grandfather had one."

She had chosen the greenhouse because she thought it would be quiet. Despite their promises, the hospital wasn't peaceful. There were too many people. When she didn't answer the nurses, they reported her to the doctor and he came and made her talk about why she didn't want to talk. He'd made her discuss her grandfather's greenhouse. Somehow, it wasn't altogether clear to her how, she had pleased him, though it upset her, dragging out of remote memories still more detail for him to analyse and add to her deadweight of self-knowledge. The doctor called it a useful session and had approved of her doing occupational therapy in the hospital's greenhouse.

"Been here long?" asked Henry.

"Oh, weeks. Going home soon."

She looked around again. There was no one in the place except her and Henry.

"Most women do knitting," he said.

"They let me choose anything."

He shrugged. "All one to me. Only, women usually do knitting."

He heaved a bag of potting compost onto the bench and slit it open with his thumbnail. He showed her how to lift the compost in handfuls into a seed tray, breaking up the lumps, patting it firm. She copied his movements, liking the dry peaty feel of the stuff.

Crumble, spread, pat. They worked in silence, save for an occasional word of apology when their hands knocked each other as they lifted the soil from the bag. Elsie relaxed. She glanced at Henry for his approval and he nodded to her.

Lift, crumble, pat. One seed tray. Two seed trays. Three. As she filled each one he took it from her and added it to the row, and gave her an empty one.

Crumble, spread, pat.

Her new summer dress was white with pink commas printed on it. They had bought her a pink cardigan to go with it. She read once, long ago, that well-dressed women didn't wear cardigans. They were for children and old ladies. But it seemed to her if she protested about the cardigan, that might cause another talk with the doctor, and today she felt she couldn't face that, so she was wearing it.

Her feet felt clumsy in her outdoor shoes. She had worn slippers for the last six weeks.

"The theory of a hot-house," said Henry, "is to provide a protective, nurturing environment where growth may take place without stress. It is no coincidence that psychiatric hospitals such as our own have a greenhouse as part of the occupational therapy programme. The atmosphere of warmth and quiet is conducive to rehabilitation."

She finished filling a tray and waited for him to take it, but he ignored her.

"Namely," he continued. "Womb-like."

"Well," said Elsie. "I thought it would be nice and quiet."

"In due course of time," he went on, "plants, and people, can be gradually hardened off, ready to be exposed to the outside world. The outside world is a cold place."

In the yoga class they had to imagine they were a rose, opening up to the rays of the sun. Elsie was very good at it, so good that when it came to the second part of the exercise, closing their petals up again as the sun goes down, Elsie told the teacher her petals were brown and withered and scattered on the ground, and therefore could not be closed up again. That had given the doctor something to analyse at their next session.

She watched Henry uncoil a hosepipe and lay it along the passageway. Water trickled from the nozzle, which he picked up and adjusted, till water came out in a fine spray over the seed trays they had been filling.

He turned slightly and some of the water splashed over Elsie. She stepped back.

"Watch what you're doing."

He put the hosepipe down, closing off the water. "Are you all wet?"

"Of course I'm wet. That was stupid."

He reached out his hand and plucked at her sleeve. "Best take it off. You'll get cold."

"No, it's all right," she said, trying to shake off his hand.

"Come on, take it off." He tightened his grip, and now his fingers were digging into her arm. He turned and began pulling her to the far end of the greenhouse.

"There's a stove up here. We'll soon have it dry." he said.

She looked back over her shoulder. The door was growing smaller and smaller in the distance, the perspective swinging round, blocking off her escape. She stumbled, her feet clumsy in their heavy shoes. Henry's hand was hurting her. "Let me go," she cried.

The stove stood in a corner of the greenhouse, surrounded by the paraphernalia of a man's howff, a dirty wooden chair, a stool which had once been a chair, muddy outdoor shoes tucked under the stove, drying. There was a cardboard box filled with gardening magazines. There was a tin box filled with coal and some logs beside it. There was a cupboard with double doors, the top piled with sprays and cartons and balls of twine. A blackened teapot steamed gently on top of the stove.

Elsie sat down in the chair, relieved that at least Henry had stopped touching her. She watched him as he opened the cupboard and pulled out a packet of tea. He scrabbled in it, drawing out a large handful of tea-leaves which he dropped into the teapot. He threw a piece of coal into the stove and kicked the door shut.

Elsie picked up a gardening magazine from the box beside her. This uncovered a naked woman smiling up at her from a copy of Playboy. Blushing, she dropped the gardening magazine. Henry was busying himself with mugs.

The tea was very strong, and without asking her he topped both mugs with condensed milk poured from a tin through furry brown holes.

"You can hang your cardigan over the line." He indicated a rope strung above the stove. "It'll dry in no time."

She took off the cardigan and handed it to him. He untied one end of the

rope and threaded it through, first one sleeve, then across the back and down the other sleeve, and hooked the rope up again.

The cardigan hung there, sleeves outstretched, like a pink feminine crucifixion, till Elsie could bear it no longer and rose and unhooked the line.

She slid the cardigan off and retied the rope and folded the cardigan over it neatly, looping up the sleeves close to the body so it no longer looked alive.

She sat down again, relieved, and sipped her tea. She pointed to the cupboard, the door of which Henry had left open. "You read a lot?"

He reached in, pulled out some of the books and handed them to her. She read the titles.

Psychology for Everyman.

An Introduction to Psychoanalysis.

The Role of the Psychiatrist in a Modern Industrial Society.

"You have to keep up to date in this business," said Henry. "Theories keep changing." He took the books from her and returned them to the cupboard beside the others.

"I'm going home in a few days," said Elsie. "I've got better."

She saw now that he wasn't as old as she'd first thought. There was very little grey in his thinning hair, and what she had mistaken for wrinkles round his eyes were merely whiter flecks of skin, as if he spent a lot of time outside screwing up his eyes against the sun. His hands were blackened. She glanced at her cardigan, making out the darker patches of dirt.

"Someone coming," he said.

Since Elsie had come into the greenhouse it had started to rain, a fine shower which distorted the glass without obscuring it. They could see a woman walking up the path which led from the side gate to the main block of the hospital. Despite the mild weather, she wore a fur coat, but no hat, and her hair was frizzed with a halo of moisture. Her progress was jerky, for the path was only compacted earth stepped with old railway sleepers, and the woman was wearing stiletto heels. She paused occasionally. Elsie had seen her before. She came regularly to visit her husband, who did not know her.

As they watched, there was a flurry of movement among the trees above the walker, and down the path there ran a woman in a summer dress, wearing bedroom slippers. She was crying. The woman in the fur coat spoke to her, but she shook her head, and plunged on down the path, disappearing from the view of the watchers in the greenhouse. The woman in the fur coat looked after her for a moment, then turned and walked on until she too was out of sight.

"Visitor," said Henry.

Elsie's cardigan swung gently in the rising heat.

"Know anything about flowers?"

She shook her head. "My grandfather had a greenhouse, but I was too young."

"I had a badge for wild flowers in the Guides," she said. "Only I didn't really." She was fluent in the telling, for this was one of the things she'd already told the doctor. "I was in the Guides. You got badges for all sorts of things. Cooking. Sewing. Map reading. Swimming. Anything you were good at. You sewed them onto your sleeve. One girl had them going up both sleeves. I just had the one you get for being in a year. One day the patrol leader gave me a book about wild flowers and told me to write about them. It was all laid out, a flower to a page, description, habitat, everything. I copied out about a dozen of them and put it into proper sentences, and handed it in. And they gave me a badge. I had to step out of the circle before Taps to collect it. I left the Guides after that."

"What for? You'd got your badge."

"They must have known. It was all in the same order as in the book. Nobody asked me any questions. They must have known."

She began to cry.

"Nerves," said Henry. He reached into the back of the cupboard and pulled out a shoe box. It was full to the brim with bottle of pills, bottles of capsules, foil sheets of tablets, ampoules of liquid. He rummaged through it.

"What are you on? I've got most of them here. Xanax, Mianserin, Mogadon, Oxazepam. Name your poison." He knelt down in front of the cupboard and reached into the bottom of it. "I've got some amphetamines here. Left over from the old days." He pulled out a tin which had once contained Quality Street and eased off the lid to reveal it half full of loose pills, multi-coloured. He selected a blue one and offered it to her. "Go on. Do you good."

"I'm nearly better," she said. "I'll be going home soon."

He shrugged. "Suit yourself." He dropped the pill back in the tin and returned it to the back of the cupboard.

She put down her mug on the floor and reached up for her cardigan. He was on his feet too, taking it from her, and then he was holding it open for her to put it on.

She turned her back on him and eased one arm into the sleeve. As she did so, his hand closed over her right breast and squeezed. She leapt away from him, banging her hip on the staging, one arm tangled in the cardigan, the other flailing at him.

"Aw come on," he said. He caught her hand and pulled her towards him.

"I'll tell them," she sobbed.

"Who'd believe you?" he laughed. "Tell me, who would believe you?"

The loose panes rattled gently as the nurse pushed open the door.

On the way back to the main building the nurse asked, "Are you going again on Thursday?"

Elsie shook her head.

"No," said the nurse. "Dirty kind of work, really. We'll try something different. Raffia maybe. Or embroidery. Embroidery's nice."

P. S. MURRAY

P. C. Graham Fraser

Crazy with pain he came down the hill and fell like a stricken tree across the village street. A cold wind raced past the houses to reach him first, pushed at his hair and clothes and moved on. The few who saw gathered slowly to stare, blank as sheep, and only the daft lad ran from them for the doctor. He arrived in time to hear the dying moans which shuddered the length of him as the blood flowed. There was nothing to cure.

And Graham Fraser, coming home for supper, found them there. Through the windscreen they formed a surreal tableau, like a hologram held by the street light, but as he began his walk down the empty road their quietness and distance grew almost loud. For an elongated moment he was the only moving one, but his arrival triggered their release and they all talked towards him at once, whilst he stared.

How could it be that the fierce one, the man of the wood, lay here? And what was he, policing the quiet patch, to do and to say?

He had to become an automaton so that form was observed, the feeling man at bay and afraid, watching himself through the ritual. Ambulance called and names taken, all in another key, always against an insistent pain in his head which spoke of the fierce one and the dark blood, the carcass and the dark blood. Late into the night its beating kept him upright, unable to rest for the re-living.

And who was she of the wild hair, shivering and marked with his blood, dumb where he'd put her in the police car and on her way to the cells?

Lord I wish I could pray, Lord — Lord I wish you would hear.

He snapped himself into the present, clenching his fists and jaw to get a grip. Shock is all that it was, and he let go, watching his hands tremble, until it passed and they stopped.

Craggy and cantankerous they read his face and nature in the village, a cracked vessel they could only keep trying to fill with guesses, who had lived beside them twenty years. His carvings found him fame elsewhere, but few friends among them, so in place of the facts grew the rumours: that the limp in his leg was a wound from the war when he'd worked as an agent, was taken and tortured; his eyes had seen bestial men, they said in the store and the bar. He put fear in them, walking between them with no words beyond the greetings.

"Rainer Tremayne, the fierce one, is dead." he told Catrine at home when the procedures were done, and in her face he'd seen the shock too. "Sit down, you must be tired," was all she'd said and brought in tea to revive him. Such men surely lived on for years. So were assumptions laid.

He had told her no more just then, preferring to be with her in the first shock, that he had not been allowed. He is dead. Not contorted in his own blood, scowling to the end. Not ripped apart by his own knife and blundering in pain. Spare her the details, now and forever, amen. He opened his eyes after a long while to see her gazing into the flames and moved nearer to the fire, nearer to her, to be held. In silence then they had gone to bed, lying close and curled together until she slept, leaving him alone and awake.

George, who'd taken over for the next shift, had recently transferred up from Glasgow. A man Graham hardly knew yet, but capable, unflustered, uninvolved. But the woman, her face came back, with her wild hair. And her silence. She too haunted his long night, white and regal nearly, half witch and Lady Macbeth, gliding across behind his closed eyes and waking each weary drift he made into sleep. By morning he felt and moved like lead.

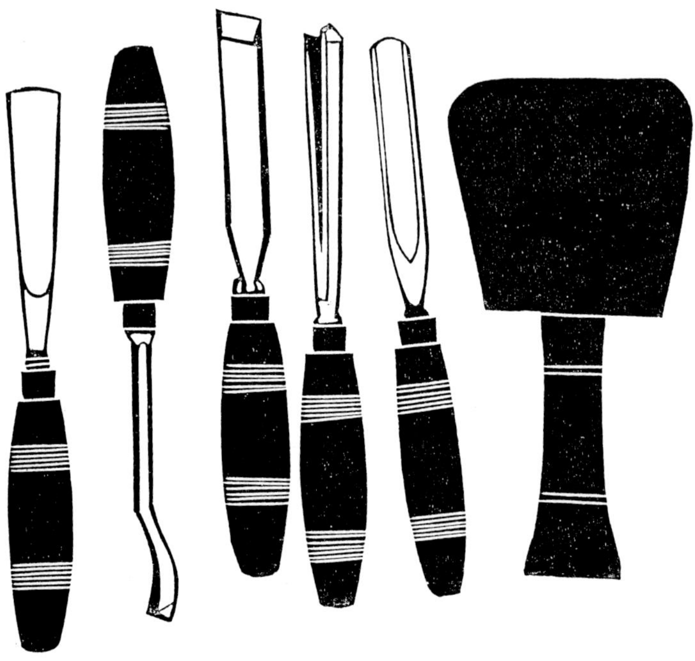

It was then that he told Catrine it had been murder, so that she knew the facts before the gossip — washed and shaved and went into work, in grey November daylight driving past the spot where he'd fallen, now washed clean by the rain.

The woman wasn't speaking today, either, not even her name. But they did know she had been before and that she modelled for him, sketches had been found, loads of them, and he was carving from them. But no name, clue, or a lead to one. She was clearly shocked, clearly guilty, and clever with it, George wouldn't wonder. Graham was to go back up the hill to look round again and keep people away. He certainly hadn't come from hereabouts, had he either, with a name like Tremayne . . .

Graham's father carved wood in his spare time, had done all his life and, since his retiral, all the time now. And he'd unashamedly begged, borrowed, and, when necessary, bought from Rainer, who had been generous to the kindred spirit. The fierce one because of his habitual scowl, his red beard and curling mass of hair, and because of his height. A fallen log.

Inside the car, behind the regular swish-click of the wipers, it felt like a morning confused by drink from the night before, where all light colours look new, and the familiar is estranged. When could I say I had last seen him alive? It seemed hard to tell, the memory of the living was bleared by the sight of him dead. Raising him from the street . . . then remembering the face alive with a nod from the Post Office door . . . that was just yesterday morning, there had been no time to say more — Maclean's dog had bitten his neighbour again — and the process of law . . . he saw the brief nod once more, trying to fix the live man in his mind.

He knew his dad was one of the few to visit, knew too that the old man would miss him, there had been grief behind that too-long shaking of the head when he'd heard. Did it make it easier to accept that death came, being old? He doubted it, behind the swish-click.

He would not walk up here again. He would not walk again. The grey morning unrolled. Mrs MacDonald's in her neat new bungalow had heard no unusual sound, slept undisturbed through the drama and now clicked her teeth between sighs, dear oh dear, behind the venetian blinds. Neither had Jeannie O'Reardon; made newly brave by his departure, she ventured to his door for the first time, peering behind Graham all the while she said nothing over again, hands twisting her apron, beady-eyed. The grain in the wood could be beautiful, brought to the light by his hands.

Still the woman in the cells said nothing and the mess in the kitchen less; had there been a struggle it was hard to see how he'd lost. Graham saw the chairs flying aside as he'd reeled back from the knife, but the murder team would find out, talking over like a machine. It rained all day. Collating information.

Nothing is touching me Rainer. Man in me, man to me,
gone from me, how? They stare and say things Rainer.
Turn to me, turn to me — smiling. Held I am — by you.
Turn me, turn to me smiling again. I could touch your
face — but nothing. What is this place? Nothing is
touching me Rainer. When that happens there is no warning.
I call you. The morning clouds. I sit here without you.
Who are they? They walk around and nothing is touching me.
Far and away my dear one. Come here and see. I found
there were three new kittens, damp and warm. In the dark
you came to me but I know your face in these times, there
was no need for light Rainer . . .

Her eyes were closed and left alone she held onto the tops of her arms and seemed to register nothing.

Once we swam under the waterfall and played in the pool
like children — that day was beautiful, rich in all we
sensed and talked, under the summer trees. I had never
been a woman before, feeling so sure. Your laughter warms me through.
The doors clang and the lights are bare.

Shock paralyses people — catatonia is a form of schizophrenia. Yes she was here, she would hear, but was held by a stupor.

They had found so much Graham had stared at the report in disbelief. The talk of the village of the mad woman stabbing him for his lust, and now the facts. 'The Murder of the Tall Cornish Man' : 'Who Killed Rainer the Woodcarver?' Headlines were followed by nothing save: 'A woman was being detained.' But for questioning read blank sheets. She still received without sign, 'the unknown woman', her eyes the deep blue that babies usually lose.

She was too tall. George thought she was acting, fooling them all, "She's canny, we're all too soft." The words sounded false as he spoke. Soft, thought Graham, that's what we are not.

There were signs of the presence of a third party in the room on that night. We will take fingerprints to eliminate and had found dark wool caught on the door-latch, clues and footprints, to go with what the post-mortem revealed. And James Fraser knew her name. Why hadn't Graham thought? His father'd been there often enough . . .

"No, it wouldn't be Ellen, hold her as long as you may. Never with the way they were to each other." The old man was shaking his head at his son, standing amidst his own carvings. Panels with intricate patterns. Graham did not understand the language between the two men, spoken by their hands. He had caught them once, the white head and the russet curls, bent together, sharing the shapes in what looked to him like a piece of old driftwood, so intent that they had not heard him enter, so he had withdrawn, unseen. Now he watched the old man polishing, moving with the grain. "I'd best be getting back, Catrine will be wondering, you'll lock the door tonight, Dad."

The woman, Ellen, was talking and weeping all the while, words with tears, telling all she had seen. Her hair was wild, her face white, and her eyes dark-ringed. The curls tumbled over her face at the end as her head sank in her hands.

He went out alone for the logs, leaving her curled by the fire. The first noise she'd thought was a log dropped, but then he hadn't appeared. The sounds, those sound still in her ears . . . Were? . . . Three of the kitchen chairs and the armful of logs — and a shout. When she had reached the door he'd already been up on his knees, blood all over his hands. But, standing he'd pushed her back and away — "Stay, I'll get him. Stay safely in." Desperation and strength, a man to believe not question. She had seen the blood, yet listened to him, always listened to him, stayed there with his knife and his blood, scared by what she didn't know, until they came . . . Had she seen anyone else? . . . No, only Rainer, covered in his blood.

There would be no need to detain her any longer, but would she be staying locally? No, she came from Edinburgh. She shouldn't travel back tonight alone. Was there someone to phone? (Was there anyone to care?) Catrine kept a bed made up in the small front room. She could travel back in the morning. The rain turned to sleet, ice darts in the skin. The wild-haired woman of the fierce one drinking their cocoa, and Catrine winding wool.

That night he'd needed her, seeking to sleep and leave the images . . . graven images they made . . . wooden idols for the grave . . . bury them deep and make them stay away . . . flaming-haired the fierce one in the sun . . . make them stay away . . . Catrine, my Catrine. And exhaustion he'd achieved.

We must all answer the questions. Account for your movements between the hours of 8 and 10 on the night in question.

Catrine saw Ellen onto the train, wishing her well, watching her shiver again and hold her head high. And they called him the fierce one, this would drive some people insane.

He had a brother, Tom Tremayne, living in England. "A murder most foul", said the minister, "a devil come into our midst". Knowing Rainer ignored the pulpit we still remember in Sunday service — and read what the papers say. The village tried to settle but watched itself on T.V., while the news was fresh: 'Mystery killer still at large — little for police to go on'. And the week wore in.

He rolled away from Catrine again, loathing the way she always gave. Once, when the light was on he'd seen resignation, the look of many women, written in faces which were tolerating, bearing with sufferance. Fate decreed and they obeyed, and set their faces. The dismay that had hit him then made sure that he always turned the light off now. In the dark he could imagine sometimes that she responded with joy, as she had done, his Catrine, of the smiles and laughter between. Wishing he could wish that look away, for all the world he'd wanted not to join them, the faces of resignation. He did not understand, for him their warmth had always been joy.

All that winter the murder of Rainer Tremayne remained a mystery. Evidence had been sifted, but the crime stayed unexplained. The woman, Ellen came back to the village for the funeral and Tom Tremayne took his brother's works away, save the ones he gave to Ellen and to James Fraser, allowing them to choose.

Now Graham was reminded of the wild hair of the fierce one's woman every time he visited his father. Held there in wood, carved in his way, by his hands. Hands that James admired, they had brought him a little fame in his life but gave him a greater one in death. Such men surely did live on.

The day had been warm but his thoughts made him as cold as clay. He had stopped the car, seeing before him the welcome that softened his mother's eyes, always there for those she loved, until the moment she died. And was hit again with dismay. Catrine — we decay.

A lump was sinking in his throat, making him sick. All that had been good was forming an unknown mass that now slowly rose to choke him. It stuck so that he breathed heavily, and swallowed.

Then he'd walked to leave it all behind. Confine her set face to the night. He'd thought if his father — knowing that love had given him strength — a faith in his life that had come from its fullness — not dismay and decay. He had walked to leave it all behind . . . But they had stopped him . . .

He had caught her face in the sunlight, with her wild hair, in his firm hands, turning to him in smiles, on that day. Rainer Tremayne.

JOHN GLENDAY

Incomplete Fixation

I think he looked like me
when he was young.
He said this self-portrait
was not his best, but the first
print he developed for himself.

You'll notice it was incompletely
fixed. Salts have remained
which, tarnished with the years,
have darkened the emulsion.
Permanence fell victim

to his youthful eagerness.
When he had struck his pose,
and squeezed the bulb, he trapped
an innocence which now endures
no better in the album

than the man. Nothing is truly
fixed. That which seems so,
is changing at the same rate
as ourselves. I wonder; when
he stooped to gauge the frame,

and peered out through the lens,
would he have seen
the bright inverted space
where he would stand, and from
the edges, darkness crowding in?

Woman With a Pale Hand

for my father

winter
has pale hands
she waits in shadows
where the year hinges

holding a letter for me
her pale lips brush
against my name
already I can hear

the birds of my lungs
sing anxiously in the branches
of the ruined tree
she will surely pull them down

winter has pale thin teeth
how silently
they grow towards me
as I sleep

they are like
pegs of hyacinth
lifting the scab of earth
beneath an old man's bed

In Praise of Wireless

The dark walls
step aside.
He sees valves
glow behind their
hardboard screen
like house lights
in a distant town.
He relishes
the bitterness
of old electrons
caged in dust.
A wind from the attic

riffles the stack
of long abandoned
magazines. He searches
the frequencies for static,
wondering if some day
this same wind

might move through Berlin,
Moscow, Hilversum.
In another room,
his sleeping wife
recites the names
of dead men

she once knew.
He watches the cursor's
finger touch
each city of dull
segmented light,
and pass clean through.

Flounder Fishing

*

Without the lid on, it reminded me
Of his flat-prowed rowing boat. You'd have thought

I'd come across him dozing in the bilge's
Buttoned silk. We once caught fish enough to swamp it.
A foul day. East wind. He held his face
Turned from the gusts; the taut line

Dug into a cigarette-stained hand.
I leaned across, tugging against his grip

To make him jump and laugh. Later we lost
Our anchor, rode the surf towards the shore.

The wind-blown spray drifted over us,
Settling on our lips like blood.

*

Like most keen fishers, he would not eat fish;
And those the neighbours didn't take

Flapped in an inch of water in the outhouse sink.
Later that evening, when I should have been asleep,

I crept back down to touch them ; to draw blood
Upon the hidden prickles of their fins,

Then slide a finger in between the gills. Looping
the frilly garter where the hook had dragged,

I thrilled as the dying muscle gagged and pumped.
Their small, flat deaths held on to me, like love.

*

I didn’t mind the waste; it added voltage to delight.
The next day, when I placed those tile-like fishes

In the bin, I turned them belly up.
There they remained, forever smooth and shiny

In my mind – I saw them gleaming
As he sailed towards the fire –

And when I found his boat split
Like a broom pod in the uncut grass,
I felt his fingers tugging,
Though they couldn’t draw me in.

Red Shift

Sunsets are spectacular
these days. Our skin burns painlessly
in the fly-sprung twilight.

When salmon flesh droops
crimson for the knife, we remember
the hanging poacher's blood,

slicker than asphalt.
Those small mountain poppies,
fragile as butterflies,

tremble in their cyanotic
beauty. Philosophers detachedly
remove the petals, saying,

"Beauty is enhanced by transience."
The physicists agree.
They have deduced

from blemishes on the skeleton
of light, that something is leaving
our world.

Honesty

Lunaria biennis

Pale oblongs
sink their roots
into the wall;

safe behind pictures once.
We must have generated shadows
where our two lives crossed,

like nimbus clouds,
or friction
wearing wallpaper to dust.

While you arranged
dried grasses in a vase
I laid my paintbrush down,

content to watch the north light
gradually decline.
Now that's all gone.

Somehow discarded honesty survived,
cushioned in mounting dirt
beneath our walnut chest.

Hidden from scouring hoovers
with the dusty pencil,
rubber bands,

dropped pennies.
How could I have known,
as the years went drifting,
that the small change would accumulate
and the cluttered room
fill up with silence
like the ballast in a wall?
And who was there to tell me I would feel
your fragile coins

grow warm against my palm;
their only weight
the dark seed they contain?

RUTH MCILROY

A Persian Painting of the 17th Century

In a gilt, faded field
on a stilted platform
a falconer with masterful air
sits poised to begin the delicate strip
of gauntlet from pointed fingers.
Central, an ancient ivory stick
symbolic of possession.
But the falcon, a wash of black on his thigh,
averts an intricate stare,
curving its neck to allow the pattern
and looking, for the minute, elsewhere.

Winter Solstice, Glencoe

at this pivot
the heavens lurch
lose all, go to nothing
we drive down the glen
blinded by dark, and the snow's light
one of us is calling up visitors
she is harvesting memories
other journeys, hogmanays
the one who matters
rides above her, an invisible stream
of bitterness in her ear
so she is distracted and cannot answer me

we are of an age for reaping
I conceal it better, my familiars are fainter
I want to tell her about how they fade
but she has company and cannot talk

two of us at the pass of Glencoe
and several more besides.

DONALD ADAMSON

Landscaping

A maker of gardens
who'd cleared rough places, raked and levelled
the soil for sowing
you were dying

in that high hospital block when I looked
outside to the cold air
streets, a river, fields beyond

and beyond
the wasteland of hills
and the sky of broken stones

places for landscaping.

Passing Barlae Hill

What was lost by a child
playing on that hillside lies
in the bracken.

                    I drive
past the spot and imagine
something eased from dank roots

that flakes in the hand, crumbles
like a nut or a pod.

BRENDA LECKIE

Letter From The Interior

Here paths are lost
among the trees. The rain
hammers all night. By day
the jungle exudes darkness. Vines
slither from tree to tree, a flower
consumes a moth. At home
magnolias fill their porcelain cups
with honey, and the butterflies
uncoil their tongues to sip.
Pa says
we camped in orchards where the plums
dripped sweetness on the tent. A crowd
cheered us with flags along
the Champs Elysees.
It was a clean war, Pa says.

I've smelt
corruption in the orchid, seen
the marsh-gas flare above my corpse,
fungus infect my brain.

This illness manifests itself
in various ways.
A lump in otherwise smooth flesh,
issue of blood, or pain
(– sunlight polishes the lecturer's bald head,
his chalky fingers emphasise a point –)
often the disease takes hold
a year or two before the patient knows.
We must
at all times reassure
that all goes well.

I feel
the jungle's virulent green
in every bone.
On Saturdays, our green Connecticut lawn

bristled with cacti. We clicked our plastic guns
at badmen in black hats, who died
without a fuss. The girls in summer camp
flirted their pony-tails
through the hot woods of Maine.
We weren't supposed to linger
in those woods, but did.

A water-buffalo dipped
its muzzle where the moon's reflection
smouldered in the dusk.
Along the river bank
a child strolled home, resting her bamboo pole
over slim shoulders. The hard-worked fields
relaxed, and frogs
burbled among the reeds. Fireflies
hung jewels on every twig.

I saw
how night as black as blood filled all
the tracks my boots had made
in the rich earth. I saw
thick weeds sprout through the polished floor,
strangling the rocking-chair, the clock,
the family bible and the baby's cot.

Thunder attacks
the hunched back of the forest. Wrapped
in glutinous air I try to patch
my brain, that spilled
its grey sludge on the table;
repair the blister of my skin.
The past is amputated, all
the girls, the football and the barbecues
dull to an ache, and something else
grows in their place
from the chopped half of the worm.

Today I saw a child beg rice.
I pulled the trigger of my Armalite.

The Visitor

This is a good land for growing
rye and millet, barley and peas;
our lord's domaine is a wide one,
our lady honours the saints,
sending us corn in the famine years,
prayers in the plague years.

Our river runs slow and deep.
At the height of summer
the water is sweet, refreshing the crops.
The valley is sheltered from storms.
On that ridge to the west, the trees
all bend one way, deformed
by the power of a wind
we scarcely feel. Beyond
the ridge, the country's unknown.
There is forest to the North and East;
somewhere to the South
there's a town.

It was a stranger who came
across the meadow, one calm
grey evening as mist rose up
out of the river. He wasn't
a jongleur or minstrel or wandering priest
nor a craftsman in stone or thatch.
He stood over there, on the patch
of grass beyond the house;
just by the wall of the byre. He placed
his wallet on the ground,
then flung the cloak back
from his shoulders and spoke;
to the air at first, but then
as people gathered round, he shot
his words at them. Such things
as we'd not heard from priests.

He spoke of war. There's some
among us who remember war;
but not like that. He spoke of peace
as if it were something more
than ripe fruit, ripe corn, and rest
after a day's toil.
But we listened; I think now
as cattle gathered round a gate
at milking time, patient, expectant,
wait.

Nothing much has occurred.
You are the third stranger,
counting him, who's come
this way since then.

We still plough the land,
sow seed, harvest the crop
that rain and blight has left;
gather the straw
for beast and man in Winter.

War-Wounded at Erskine

He left his wits on the Western Front
where others left their arms or legs
or burst their hearts. He's whole
of limb but lacking in the head.
He was a simple man, and all
was soon tipped out to mix with mud,
so he returned here, empty. For sixty years
he's gazed out of blank windows at the Clyde,
while breadlines, bombers and the death of shipyards
have left his face unscarred.
Only in November does he stir
as if to join the ranks that march
through the white fog that rises from the river,
and taps his foot on the polished floor
to an echo of 'Tipperary'.
It's an old song, but history's
the present day to him. Quite soon
the poppies fade and he is lost again
along the dark road to the Erskine ferry.

Grandfather's Attic

Grandfather goes upstairs and rummages
the lumber of his eighty-year-old attic.
He blows the sand from that seaside day
in nineteen-six — or was it eight?
when the donkey munched Aunt Dora's hat;
or polishes the faces of his brothers
who are poplar trees in Flanders.
When we speak to him, his puzzled eyes
gaze from the attic window as he tries
to find an answer that he's sure is hidden
among the lifetime's jumble, but he can't
quite lay a hand to. He sifts the piles
of jubilee mugs and wedding photographs,
then comes downstairs
clutching a faded album or a broken plate.
One day he'll decide
to stay there, and we'll never guess
what he has found, however much
we patch and glue the fragments of his years.

JANICE GALLOWAY

The Meat

The carcass hung in the shop for nine days till the edges congested and turned brown in the air.

People came and went. They bought wafers of beef, pale veal, ham from the slicer, joints, fillets, mutton chops. They took tomatoes and brown eggs, tins of fruit cocktail, cherries, handfuls of green parsley, bones. But no-one wanted the meat. It dropped overhead from a claw hook, flayed and split down the spinal column: familiar enough in its way. It was cheap. But they asked for shin and oxtail, potted head, trotters. The meat refused to sell. Folk seemed embarrassed even to be caught keeking in its direction. One or two made tentative enquires about a plate of sausages coiled to the left of the dangling shadow while the yellowing hulk hung restless, twisting on spike. These were never followed through. The sausages sat on, pink and greasy, never shrinking by so much as a link. He moved the sausages to another part of the shop where they sold within the hour. Something about the meat was infecting.

By the tenth day, the fat on its surface turned leathery and translucent like the rind of an old cheese. Flies landed in the curves of the neck and he did not brush them away. The deepest ball of bone sunk in the shoulder turned pale blue. There was no denying the fact: it had to be moved. The ribs were sticky and the smell had begun to repulse him, clogging the air of the already clammy interior of the shop and he could detect its unmistakable seep under the door to his living-room when he was alone in the evening. So he fetched a stool and reached out to the lard hook, seized the meat and with one accurate slice of the cleaver, cut it down. It languished on the sawdust floor till nightfall when he threw it into the back close parallel to the street. As he closed the shutter on the back door, he could hear the scuffling of small animals and strays.

In the morning, all that remained was the hair and a strip of tartan ribbon. These he salvaged and sealed in a plain wooden box beneath the marital bed. A wee minding.

JACKIE WHITTET

Prior To The Weigh In

I remember her smile, though if I saw her in the street today I probably wouldn't recognise her.

She was the first person there when I awoke.

Everything seemed so peaceful and I felt more relaxed at that moment than I had for months. But that particular feeling was totally alien to me, and soon passed.

I was trying hard to get my bearings, wondering where I was; how I got there; but my mind was a blank.

"How are you? Just relax, don't worry, you'll be alright. Would you like a cup of tea?"

"Aye, okay."

"Milk and sugar?"

"Milk and two sugars."

I tried to sit up but was a bit confused. Slowly, I began to paint a picture of my surroundings. I was still confused; didn't seem to have any bumps or bruises — just a hangover of some kind.

There were other people in the room, four or five of them; some looked bruised, others had broken limbs. And here was me just broken, or maybe I was only just damaged. Yes, that would be nearer the mark. Damaged, almost beyond repair.

"Here's a nice cup of the real home brew," said Bright Eyes. "Drink it up. If you want some more, just ask."

"How's it goin', china?" came the remark from the next bed. "What happened to you then?"

She came to my rescue. "Now, now, nosey; curiosity killed the cat."

"I wonder if it was the same curiosity that hit me with a bottle last night."

"No, that was your wife! Now, give the man peace."

The pangs of despair were slowly returning and the thought of what I was going to do now was beginning to gnaw.

"Hey, you haven't touched your tea; it's getting cold."

I looked at the clock. It had left lunchtime. "How long have I been here?"

"Since just after midnight."

Christ, that's over twelve hours, and I couldn't remember a thing.

"The doctor will be along to see you in a couple of minutes. Come on, try a smile . . . you smiled a lot in your sleep."

"Aye, that's because I thought I was in heaven."

"You'll never be as close as you were this morning," she replied.

The doctor came in, gave me the once-over, and a lecture on the evils of drink. I wasn't really listening. My mind was slowly building a picture of last night, and the tranquil feeling was beginning to be replaced by anger. The bastards! The fucken stinking bastards!

It had been like the end of a love affair. I had trusted them, given them everything I could, loved them even. I should have known better. I should have done them when I had the chance. Thieving lying bastards!

"We'd like you to stay here for a few days; get a bit of a rest."

"It's okay, I feel fine now." I was telling lies; my stomach was churning.

"You're lucky to be alive," said Bright Eyes. At that particular time I honestly didn't agree with her.

"Alright, you can go, if you promise to take things easy. And lay off the bevy and the pills."

"But the pills are prescribed!"

"But not in handfuls!"

I got my gear on. Bright Eyes took me to the door leading to the corridor.

"Cheerio, look after yourself," she called. "And, by the way, I remember you when you used to sing."

"God, I wasn't that bad, was I?"

She blushed and wished me good luck.

When I used to sing I wouldn't see those bastards in my road. But now, I was on the ropes and didn't care if I went down for the count and never got up.

It was like a nightmare, only this was real. I wasn't able to handle the situation. At this point I couldn't deal with the liars, the backstabbers, the set-ups. My mind was in a turmoil; maybe I should have taken the doctor's advice and stayed on. But the last time I had to stay in hospital, it gave the Philistines the time they needed to cover their tracks.

I looked back to give Bright Eyes a final wave.

Reaching the reception I made my way to the telephone to get a taxi home. Standing there, by herself, was an old grey-haired lady. At her feet was an equally old suitcase which had seen better days. She had obviously been crying, but there was something about her that was dignified. "Here, missus, I'll take your case to the spare seat over there . . . Would you like tea or something till your taxi comes? It's a great thing — tea — isn't it, cures everything."

At first I thought she'd been taking things into somebody.

"He was all I had, son, all I ever needed; ever wanted. Now he's gone."

Christ, the old yin wasn't taking things in, the poor soul was bringing them out. And I thought I had troubles!

We shared a taxi, silently, both with different thoughts, different destinations but, somehow, with something in common.

The house was warm, silent, and a bit strenuous. Outside, the rain drizzled lazily on the pavements; people hurried by as I leaned against the window frame. I was still there when darkness fell and the street lights danced with the rain reflecting all around.

I sensed someone within the room watching me. Without turning, I could see her reflection on the window. She never spoke, but the look of concern and pity in her eyes said everything. At that moment I felt a shiver and an overwhelming feeling of sickness in the pit of my stomach. And I felt Hatred!

My mind flashed back to the hospital and the old soul with the suitcase. That could have been my clothes, my suitcase somebody was taking home. My clothes coming out the front door in a suitcase. And me coming out the back door in a box. Bastards!

I turned away from the window. By this time the concerned face was hidden behind a pop magazine. I felt rough, but decided there and then I was going to get better and fitter than I had been for years.

For months their names and faces never left my mind, and sometimes I thought I'd never make it. Every press-up, every secret mile I ran and every sleepless night, their faces were with me, and the thought of them kept me going. Every glass of juice I swallowed had their faces at the bottom of the glass. There was also another face and another reason.

It was laughable, in a way, them helping me. By then, it was getting very obvious that the scales of Justice weren't operating properly, for reasons better known to the operators, but I had my suspicions; the scales were rigged.

It was then I decided to use my own scales. Or to be exact — weigh the bastards — physically, financially and mentally. Put it this way — their cards were marked!

HENRY LONGMORE

Archie

It was a long haul climbing the stairs to the top of the four storey building. The staircase was spiral with a banister of cast iron, the uprights of the handrail looking like the sinewy legs of a horse. I had first met him a few months previously while installing a socket for his television.

"Thanks son," he had said. "That's great, save me a lot of bother, I'll be able to switch that off easy. It's my emphysema you know, the old lungs are not so good now, those winters in France, but that socket's great. Mind now if you're ever passing come up and see me, maybe I'll have some beer in the next time."

Now I was back in the street, hoping he would be glad to see me; if not, then maybe the cans in the carrier bag would please him.

"Remember me."

"Aye son I never forget a face, come in."

"Thought you might like a beer Archie."

He dusted off a chair with a newspaper which had been stuffed down the side of it. I sat while he poured a couple of the cans.

"Nice of you to come and see me, son."

"Well I was passing and thought you could do with a bit of company."

"Never see anyone nowadays. Mrs. Corrigan across the landing knocks now and again to see if I need anything, But that's about all I see of anybody. Wife left me you know, son, aye about twenty years now."

"Do you know where she went?" I enquired.

"No never heard a word, Och! I don't blame her, nothing for her here." His arm caressed the room.

"Were you in the army?"

"Aye." He opened another couple of cans. "Things were a lot different then, infantry it was; H.L.I. Look son if you look in that press over there, bring me down a box I'll show you."

"Which one Archie."

"The San Domingo sherry one."

I brought the box over and laid it at his feet. He undid the flaps and lifted out an old biscuit tin. He thumbed through the photographs before passing them to me. I looked at them. Archie was in most of them; in uniform, there was a drab sameness about them that you often see in bundles of old photographs.

I stopped at the one which caught my attention: because of the woman. She was beautiful, even in the faded picture she had an elegance of poise which doesn't always show in a snapshot.

"Who's this Archie?"

He took the picture from me and looked; his eyes brightened.

"That's the wife, Aye, that's her, nice looking woman son eh!"

"She's beautiful Archie. It must have been terrible after she left."

"Aye. Nothing for her here. There's more in those other boxes you know, they are all different years; you might say my life's in that press, medals; revolver; everything."

"I would like to see the revolver."

"Go ahead son; the Creamola Foam box."

I went back to the press and got the box down.

The pistol was lying underneath some magazines, it was in a holster made of webbing.

"Will it be alright to take it out, Archie?"

"Sure son, it's not loaded never brought back any ammo."

I held the pistol, balancing it in my hand, I hadn't seen one before; well, only in the movies. It was bigger than I imagined, and heavier.

"This is great, Archie, did you kill any Germans with it?"

"No. Well, I fired it a lot. Maybe I did; who knows. They are not good things anyway. Should have thrown it away years ago."

"It must have been rough in France during the war."

"You bet it was. When the S.S. appeared it was send in the H.L.I. You know, those S.S. bastards never knew when to give up."

"Do you think it was worth it, Archie?"

"What do you mean was it worth it?" he growled.

"Well, I mean people seem to have forgotten. They drive about in Volkswagens and Datsuns, Germany's doing well; look at Japan: HiFi's, cameras, motorbikes, anything you care to mention. Look at yourself, I'll bet you can't even manage on the pension they give you."

"You a commie or something?"

"No, but you've got to admit it's true."

"Aye, you're right." He started to cough.

"You O.K., Archie?"

"I'm fine. I'm fine. Aye, you're right son, we always learn when it's too late. I suppose at the time it was great, the flag wagging and all the rest of it. You know what I'm going to tell you, as far as I'm concerned, they could go and fight it themselves." He coughed violently. "I wouldn't lift a wee finger to help them again." I could see he was getting tired and needed a rest. I told him I had to get home. He tried to rise, but slumped back in the chair and coughed.

"You'll need to show yourself out, son." His face was white.

"I'll come up again and see you, Archie." I shouted as I left.

The visit hadn't turned out the way I had expected, I should have realised no one can bring much pleasure to a man living his life in a chronology of cardboard boxes.

When I returned from a spell of working out of town, I decided to go and see the old man again, this time taking a bag of groceries along with the beer.

I was waiting for him to answer, when a door opened across the landing. A woman appeared, followed by a cloud of steam and the smell of boiling cabbage.

I looked at her and asked if Archie was at home.

"Oh! Archie died a fortnight ago. Took a stroke, you know. Died the same day.

"What about his things?"

"Oh! his daughter came up from England, cleared the house."

"I didn't know he had a daughter."

"Aye. She never came up much after her mother left."

Turning to leave, I remembered the groceries, handed them to the woman and made my way down the stair.

NAN SPROTT

One Of The Crowd

The sign said 'Department of Health and Social Security'.

I climbed a flight of grey stairs to a landing with a dirty window. I met no one. Was 9.30 early?

The next landing had a door with a twelve-inch square pane of glass. I looked through that large lens at people, with their backs to me, in groups. Some on orange chairs, others on yellow ones facing brown doors. The rest, further over, were on benches. They faced ENQUIRIES. Under this notice a woman stood, her three children like a set of jugs behind her. The air was blue-tinged. A lasting picture. Click! Click!

I pushed the door. Nobody looked when I sat beside the bloke half-way along the front bench. Aftershave overpowered the smoke in the atmosphere.

A clerk stood in front of the woman with the children. She went berserk at whatever he told her.

"I'm not leaving here till I get help," she shouted. "I can't send my kids to school without shoes. I'll wait here all day!"

The clerk goldfished. She paid no heed. He leaned forward, touched her arm and pointed to the end of the counter where he appeared a moment later and led her and her children, in their holey trainers, through a brown door.

Everyone watched and listened.

He was back, the weary-looking clerk: "Next."

We all slid along. It was the rule. After the woman's raised voice it was very quiet.

The aftershave emanated from the man next to me. He must have bathed in it! His hair shone like black patent leather, so heavily was it 'fixed'. His shirt lay open almost to his navel, a gold-plated medallion, hanging by a chain, on his bare, hairless chest.

It did not lie well because of his jutting collar-bones and protruding ribs. He whistled softly, nonchalantly, through his teeth.

We slid, again and again, even though the benches behind were empty. Aftershave was but a moment at the counter and back before I could fill his place.

The clerk was gone a full ten minutes.

"Having his bliddy tea!" the woman after me reckoned.

Then he was back with his "Next."

I looked at Aftershave questioningly. "You're next, missus. I've to wait", he said. His voice was kind, his smile gentle, reaching his eyes. "Thanks," I said, meaning, for thawing some of the ice in me.

"Widows on the top floor!" the clerk barked. Widow, first time I'd been called that. Aftershave gave me a sympathetic smile.

Up, up more grey stairs and through the door to the topmost landing. Little groups, as on the first floor, but no coloured chairs. A large placard at the far end said WIDOWS. I made for it like a homing pigeon. The only person there, a frail-looking old lady, was dull of hearing which made conversation between us difficult. I had to nudge her when a clerkess, in the open doorway on our left, said "Come this way!" I had the Widows section to myself.

I thought of downstairs: the angry woman, her children, Aftershave. When I get home I must tell . . . I caught myself thinking. I couldn't anymore, never again. Wasn't that why I was here? Don't think of it, not now anyway.

Look at the two toddlers happily chasing each other round the seats over there, watched by their unsmiling mothers. They too have problems. "Can I help you?" said the clerkess who'd led the old lady off, now seated behind the counter. She indicated the chair on my side, but I stood. Having rehearsed it, I fired at her.

"The amount on my book is two-thirds of what I expected."

Book in hand, she checked in a file directly behind her. Then I sat, still tense. It took her a minute or two.

"Clerical error," she said and laughed, "You'll hear from us tomorrow or the day after."

I floated out, relieved it was over.

On the lift door a paper said 'Out of Order'. Who cared? I gladly hurried down the stairs.

Coming out of the first floor office was Aftershave.

"Hello there," he said with a warm smile. "You O.K.?"

"Yes, I'm fine!"

He was off, clutching his medallion and whistling.

On the landing below, reading a letter close to the dirty window, was the woman with the children. The three who'd stood silently behind their mother and followed her obediently through the brown door, were now creating a racket while pummelling each other. The mother, letter still in hand, landed the eldest such a wallop he bounced off the wall.

"You lot'll drive me round the bend!" she said as I passed.

JOHN McMURRAY

Episode Seventy-Three

Just a quick recap of what happened last week — Sir Edmund and The Archbishop were seen by Felicity playing tennis in the nude under the full moon. Cynthia's headache cleared up quickly and she decided to attend the fancy-dress party after all, where she was seduced by someone wearing a gorilla costume. She had assumed it was Ronald, Earl of Millport, but became hysterical when it turned out to be Luigi, a waiter from the local wine bar, who couldn't believe his luck.

Irresistible Madeleine Richter, ex-mistress of playboy millionaire Richard 'Kinky' Freemantle, announced that she will marry Count Otto Smirnoff, as soon as he gets a divorce from his sixth wife Harriet.

At their long awaited reunion, Andrew, running to embrace Penelope, slipped on a dog turd, and broke his leg.

Is Derek, Flora's husband, only pretending to be infatuated by Gertrude? And who stole her bra from the washing line? Sarah isn't speaking to Harold, who in turn isn't speaking to Reggie; Joyce is talking to Peter, incessantly, and he wishes she'd shut up. Jeff realises that Ronnie has only taken up stamp collecting so that no one will suspect he is sleeping with Gwendoline, the ski instructress, whose husband is abroad, leading an expedition to discover the source of something. Exactly what, only he knows. Wherever it is, he hasn't succeeded in finding it; only in getting lost. Gwendoline, who doesn't want to see him again, is discreetly discouraging all attempts to organise a rescue party.

Meanwhile Fiona had promised to spend the weekend with Bertram, at his cottage. But when Susan tells her that he asked her first, she attempts suicide. Then, while having her stomach pumped out in the local hospital, her eyes meet those of the nurse holding the basin into which she is vomitting, and in that instant she realises she is a lesbian. She is working up the courage to tell her husband George, when he announces that he is gay.

Cedric is inconsolable after discovering that the exquisite creature he glimpsed in the garden was really Herbert in drag. And why is Cyril so upset? Will Arthur agree to share his wig with Frederick? Can Amanda ever trust Jennifer again? What is the significance of the sporran? Who poisoned George's kipper? Is Lady Fletcher Roderick's mother? Will the vicar discover that the nunnery is just a front for a brothel? Is the cat having a nervous breakdown?

JANE WEBSTER

Juliet

She didn't look any different. They were walking down the Sunday-empty street now, and she could just see herself in the shop windows as they went past. Just the same as yesterday, only a bit paler. Deep purple circles under her eyes; her lips almost white, varnished with muck. Small red spots were breaking out round her nose and mouth. But she was always like that after the glue, anyway.

She would have liked to stop and look at her face more closely, see if her eyes were different. But she could hardly do that with Spikes there; he'd think she really fancied herself. And she'd already embarrassed him enough, that was plain.

He did look different. He looked wrong in sunlight, and in an empty street. Smaller and younger than he looked last night, up in the graveyard. He was walking stooped over, as if he knew he was out of place, and was trying to muffle the clank of the chains round his neck and waist, trying to hide the mud and stains on his denims.

His hair made him look different, too, his mohican sticking to the middle of his head like a piece of fake fur, instead of pointing up into its usual cockscomb. She'd asked him this morning why he wasn't doing his hair and he'd given her a funny look and muttered that he'd no setting gel. He must have thought it was really daft, a lassie asking a question like that. So it was. She should have known better.

Besides, she supposed he wouldn't want to do things like that in front of her. Any more than she'd want to put make-up on in front of him. Not that she could have done, anyway. She'd lost all that last night; must have scattered her eye-pencils and mascara all over the graveyard. Well, she just hoped the ghosts appreciated them.

There was another difference; a difference she hadn't wanted to notice but had known all along. He wasn't looking at her. He was looking everywhere else; at his feet, safely buried in their Docs, the other side of the street, every parked car they passed. Everywhere but her.

All last night he'd watched her like a hawk. She'd been frightened of it, before the glue. Just the feel of his eyes in her back, and the way he'd smiled when he'd made her turn round. And he'd watched her this morning; made her clumsy as she struggled to zip her denims, fumbled with the laces of her kicks. And now she was frightened because he wasn't watching her.

She decided to try talking.

"Spikes?"

"Aah?"

But he didn't stop walking, didn't look up from the pavement.

"Forget it."

He did. She might as well not have spoken, might as well not be there walking beside him. Even if she kicked him he wouldn't look up.

She must have been really bad, then. If only she could have explained to him, got him to tell her how to do it properly. But no. Not her. As usual she hadn't known what to do, and just made things worse by doing nothing. And now he knew just what an idiot she was, and you could bet your life that by tea-time tonight he'd have told everybody. Everything. Every single last detail.

Maybe he wouldn't remember everything, because of the glue. She couldn't. She couldn't remember Spuds or Oddball leaving, or them smashing into the hut.

But she could remember it this morning; the damp, clinging coldness, the rough feel of the tarpaulin under her face, and the reek of glue filling the place. There were cracks of light splintering through the broken door. One of them caught on the edge of a spade, showed up the mud crusted on to it.

It was then that she clicked. This must be the gravediggers hut. That spade must have been used to dig graves. That mud was from somebody's grave.

Then she'd felt as if it had been her that had been buried. She'd lain there like a stiff, frightened even to shiver in case she woke him, wondering what to do next.

She should have done what she felt like and got up and gone, there and then. Then she'd have been saved all this. But no. Daft Juliet hadn't known what to do again. And now here she was, being led round the streets like an unwanted pup.

Maybe if he found some convenient railings he'd tie her up to them with his dog-collar and chain. That was probably why he wore them.

As they turned the corner she noticed two figures bobbing around at the end of the street. One tall and thin, the other short and fat. Both with skinheads and green pilot jackets, zipped up even though it was warm. They didn't move up the street, but spun round each other like clockwork toys winding down. Spuds and Oddball. Juliet's heart plummeted, and she prayed that by some miracle Spikes would keep up his study of the pavement and not notice them.

Too late. He had. She didn't know how she knew, because he wasn't staring at them, hadn't started running or anything obvious like that. But again he was different. Relieved.

They drew level with the two figures on the other side of the street. And again she didn't know what to do. She would have liked to split; just say, "Cheerio, I'll need to run for that bus." But then they'd all know she was running away. And when Spikes didn't try to stop her the other two would know how terrible she'd been. So she did nothing.

The two couples stopped, opposite each other, all waiting for somebody else to make the first move. And just for a second Juliet thought that Spikes didn't know what to do either. There they were, the four of them, as if somebody had clicked a video on to pause. Then Spikes lifted his hand and the film ran on again.

Spuds and Oddball ware crossing over now, daft grins right across their faces. They looked just like her dog slinking up to her Da, trying to work out whether it was going to get fussed over or thrashed.

"Hiya Spikes, Jools. Good night, eh?" That was Spuds, leering at her neck, counting the bruises. She looked away from him, wishing she'd kept her hair long so she could have hidden behind it.

"Ah'm jist walking Jools down to get her bus. Coming?" said Spikes.

"Going home then Jools? What're ye wanting to do that fur?" said Spuds, from between his grin.

Because she wanted a bath. Because she wanted to wash away every sign and smell of him, the dead sweat and the dead blood, scrub his bruises out of her neck and breasts, the memory of him heaving in and out of her out of her mind. Because she wanted to stop remembering what she'd hoped for. Because she wanted to stop even trying to fit in with them.

But she couldn't say that.

"Me maw'll be worried," was what she came out with, like a wee lassie.

Spikes laughed, and the other two joined in.

"Bit late fur that, eh?" said Spuds.

But at least they were moving now, she and Spikes in front, with the other two treading on their heels like over eager bridesmaids.

They were too close. She could smell herself now, a thick ugly smell of rot that clung to her under the last remaining fumes of glue. And they were so close they must be able to smell her too. She felt like sprinting away from them, had to clench her whole body stiff as death to keep her legs to a walk.

And there at last was the bus-stop, empty in the Sunday-struck street. Juliet stopped, and the three boys stopped too, in a cluster, a little away from her.

Ten minutes till her bus came. And it was always late. Ten minutes, and there wasn't anything she could say to him with them there. Not that she'd managed to say anything to him before they came along. But she couldn't stand them gawking at her like an animal in the zoo.

"Youz three get on; Ah can easy enough get the bus mysel'."

She'd said the wrong thing, as usual. She knew it was wrong the minute she'd finished saying it, though for the life of her she couldn't think why. But the three of them had drawn even closer together, straightened up as if she'd called them a load of wanks.

Spuds spoke for them all, like he always did.

"Ach no, Jools. We couldnae do a thing like that. Leave a puir wee innocent lassie like yoursel' standing alone in the middle of a busy street like that? Anything might happen. And your Maw wouldn't like that, would she now?"

Spuds was repulsive. There should be a law against fat people becoming skinheads. With his hair sprouting back in like that he looked exactly like a hedgehog that had been run over by a lawnmower. She should have told him that but instead she smiled; a small silly smile for nobody in particular.

Oddball sniggered. Juliet shrank in to the bus shelter wall, staring down the road, willing the bus to come, willing it all to be over.

That was all her life was, wishing that things were over. She could remember last night, willing the other two to go away so she could be alone with him. And then when she was alone with him and it was actually happening, praying that soon he'd finish and it would be over and done with. Lying beside him, pretending to be asleep, and all the time wishing it was morning and she could get up and go. And soon she'd be standing between her Ma and Da, crying while they screamed at her and at each other, wishing it was all over.

The bus was never going to come. She edged away from the other three, squashed herself even more into the bus-shelter wall.

"Sore back, eh, Jools?" said Spuds.

"Comes of too much lying on it." sniggered Oddball.

Spikes just smiled. He was leaning against the street wall, arms spread along the top of it, facing her. She and he were like two wrestlers, resting in their opposite corners before the next bout. Only there wasn't going to be a next bout. He caught her looking at him and smiled. She looked away, down at her hands, started trying to pick some of the blackening glue off them. Then she realised they were all staring at her, and she shoved her hands in her pockets, staring down the empty street again.

The bus was coming, lumbering its way up the road like an old blind horse. She moved out from the shelter, ignoring the three boys. If Spikes so much as laid a finger on her in front of these two she'd lynch him, so she would.

But he didn't even try, just stood leaning against the wall as if it was too much effort even to wave. Or as if he, too, didn't know what to do. And it was Spuds who shouted after her:

"Cheerio, Jools. Come and see us anytime, eh?"

Spikes did swipe him one for that, but he was laughing.

The bus driver didn't even question her half. So much for turning into a woman.

A. D. FOOTE

Rooms

With
Or without a view, they accept
With equanimity all that goes on in them:
The noisy party, the beer bottle thrown,
And even fornication.

Some owners are not happy with them,
Writing endless letters to the Town Council,
But I never heard
Of a room that complained of its owner.

Only Red Indians
And Hottentots in general dislike them,
Relics of our nomadic past;
But without them
History would have no location
And mankind no refuge
From the elemental flux.

We repay their fidelity
By adorning them gaily
With potted plants
And photographs of children.

For all their imperturbability,
Are they not perhaps the teeniest
Bit lonelier when we die?

Mrs Benning

Mrs. Benning was our landlady
Before we found a place of our own:
'Riverside Mansions' — her signboard read.
All the curtains were ash brown,
Colour of dead leaves on an autumn bonfire –
And the hangings on the furniture
Were somber too.

There was an autumn smell about Mrs. Benning:
Smell of hands worn by years of scrubbing,
Smell of loins worn out by childbearing:
Three sons, one dead, two living in England.

Sometimes she knitted or watched T.V. –
'Nothing but murder' she would say
As she tucked the rent money into her faded apron.

Till the day when she took ill, incurably –
But went down smiling, sure of the next life.
In his address the minister remarked,
'She always kept the house ship-shape'.

Achaemenid

When I ask him a technical question
About Persian linguistics,
He doesn't know.
Or mention the weather in Teheran:
He was born and brought up there,
But never noticed what the weather was like.
No Muslim, he worships Karl Marx,
And next to Marx, his cutie girlfriend.
Six days a week
Dressed in greasy overalls, tightening nuts
To the greater glory of Toyota.
A smile as enigmatic as Stalin's:
Unlikely descendant of a King of Kings.

Homework

'Which things being so, it seemed good to Caesar
To attack on the third day' — a jungle
Of oblique cases and subordinate clauses
Boggles and befuddles the mind.

The exercises get longer and more intricate:
'Repeat the above in the past conditional':
Teacher's approval is also conditional on getting this
Finished by Friday night.

After an hour, his brain is an ocean
Cluttered with icebergs, lethal with reefs
From which no communication with the outside world
Is practicable, no S.O.S.
Ever likely to be intercepted.

Exhausted, he straightens out the sheets of paper
Covered with boyish scrawl,
Till the T.V. reminds him of the twentieth century
Where Caesar is a dead letter, better abandoned
His conquest of Gaul.

Eventide

Since the State considers her low priority,
And she doesn't belong to an elite minority,
She must wash each hoarded tea-bag out three times.
To her lone apartment, up four flights, she climbs
And shares her bed with cockchafer and flea.
Passing her door in the morning, I used to see
Her timid, peering, mouse-like face
As she greedily downed a jammy-piece.
Why are we so compassionate towards the old?
Because they are so childlike, and we are bold
To deny we may finish like this carline wife,
Who had been an arrent hussy all her life.

Six Bad Things

Not to know English
And to hear of a good English detective story
Not yet translated into German.

To see a full glass of beer
During a heat-wave
Without the money to buy it.

To have a new idea,
And not be able to turn it into perfect hexameters,
As the schoolmasters do.

At night, to hear the waves under the bridge splashing,
And to say to oneself: That is what they always do.

Very bad: to be invited out,
When at home there is a cosier fire,
Stronger coffee,
And no need to make conversation.

Worst of all:
Not to die in summer,
When all is sunlight
And the soil lies lightly on the spade.

BARRY FOWLER

Stolen Thunder

There was no real need to ask. The group
of people scattered here and there
along the platform meant that soon
another train was due. A pair
of teenagers waltzed up and down
the platform wearing roller-skates
and headphones. As I watched I saw
them making signs across the space

between their separate, spinning worlds
where silent music, blaring in
their ears, made speech impossible.
Just then the tube arrived and I
slipped quietly in between the doors
and took a seat some distance from
the others as it fled into
the tunnels like escaping thunder.

Across from me an old man sat.
I watched him as his hands caressed
an open bottle which, from time
to time, he put up to his lips
to drink its contents down in hot,
wet kisses. As his heavy breaths
took shape as vapour (only to
be shrivelled by the cold) I wondered
how many thoughts could have been voiced
as words on every breath instead
of being dispersed as cloud, lost to
the evening air. I thought of how
unlike the anonymity
and intimacy of the rush

hour journey home two hours before
this trip back in to meet you was.
At night, the passengers may not
acknowledge one another. All
alone, their gazes never meet.
Each sits in silence staring at
his own reflection in the black
square of the window opposite:
their features caught there by the light,
so distant, yet so well defined.

Like them, I had to sit until
at last the tunnels opened and
we pulled into the station. As
I stood beside the doors to leave
that sightless company, your face
appeared beyond the glass. You waved
at me across the platform. Then
the doors slid open and I stepped

into your arms. Yet even as
I held you, close enough to see
my own reflection in your eyes,
or whisper words of love to you,
how quickly, skillfully you put
your lips to mine and skipped your tongue
into my open mouth to steal
the thunder from between my lips.

Lasting Images

For hours just sitting, reading aloud.
Repeating every line, each phrase.
Attempting to induce a flood
of ideas, lasting images
in this hotel room. The T.V.
pours forth a withered landscape, drained
of all but skeletons: a tree,
a fish (both suffocated, drowned
in air) beside a dried up river.
A dying woman, while, up high
above, black crosses, vultures hover
to offer their kind of purgatory.

The camera follows. As she wades
through tides of drifting desert sands,
past carcasses of plough-share blades.
Her breasts like leather pouches. Hands
cupped, begging. Chanting out loud cries
for jagged mountain tops to gore
the underside of barren skies
and wash the hinterland's dry pores
with rain. As land devoid of crops
where blades of quite a different kind
now bring the harvest: parcel drops
from aircraft, sown amongst the wind.

I turn the television off.
Go downstairs to the poolside bar,
deciding I'd had my fill of
such pictures. Ordering a beer
I look around. A cool-legged, fair-
skinned girl sun-bathing soaks in oil,
to stop her body's surface layer
from flaking off like dry top-soil.
(Her stay judged in amounts of dead

skin). Manicured toes dangle in
the water from the edge, her head
gorged full on diets — to stay thin.
The barman, winking at me, says
'a pretty mouthful, eh? No waste.'
Each cupped hand held out in a way
suggestive of the young girl's breasts.
Meanwhile beneath the circled shade
of parasols, some fat men, pal
consuming liquid lunches paid
for out of bulging leather wallets,
indulge themselves in mental rape
it seems. Their sweaty fingers fold
around the wine glasses' full shape
which now the barman has refilled.

I tilt my head back as I drain
my tumbler's contents. Up above
me fan blades circle with a drone
like that of insects as I move
towards the stairwell. Having reached
my room once more, I close the blind.
Develop images still etched
by sunlight deep upon my mind;
in semi-darkness soak up sounds.
The halyards in the harbour rattle
against the slim masts. Like bells around
the scrawny necks of desert cattle.

Full Circle

You would often pull
small flowers to pieces, then declare
each petal to be beautiful.
I like things left they way they were,
no need to spoil such beauty to
discover what you felt for me,
nor break that circled strength gained through
its perfect, geometrically

unflawed design. You always liked
doing puzzles to stretch your mind, compelled
to find solutions. But I looked
in your accomplished eyes that held
all that I felt I had to know.
My head was governed by my heart,
yours by the search for knowledge. So
you tore our love's full bloom apart.

With one last 'loves me not' you'd gone.
One more relationship had ended:
a puzzle which, once it is done,
now lies discarded, unattended.
We've come full circle. Now I sit
for hours writing of you, pose
myself such problems. Try to fit
each word, a sort of jigsaw piece,
into the right place on the page.
Whenever I pick up the phone
and dial your number, it's engaged
(no answer, just that certain tone.)
I call you at work, to be told
that you are otherwise involved

or asked if I would like to hold.
That's it exactly: problem solved.

Outside my window office blocks
at night, an angled concrete cancer,
some windows lit up, others black,
are like giant crosswords, without answers.
This quest for knowledge does not bring
me satisfaction, since with him
tonight you lie, content with things
the way they are. Your tangled limbs

a twisted metal puzzle. Front-
to-back you fit together sound
asleep perhaps. Yet still I don't
know how to put my feelings down
on paper. When I try to cram
them in a letter to you words
become a jumbled anagram,
a cryptic clue that sounds absurd.
Such games are all I have left.
Cut from your encircling arms, my shattered
heart, once strong, feels so delicate
as when a rose, no longer watered,
will lose its completeness, shed its petals.
Each time I try to phone, repeat
that numbered puzzle on the dial
my finger never quite completes

the circle.

MAUD DEVINE

Moonscape

I painted a picture of my home at night.
I put the smart, grey houses, neat lawns and roses
on the pock-marked surface of a bombed-out planet.
Inside the rooms glowed warmly with light.
Outside white ghosts with tapering fingers
touched the doors and breathed ice patterns
on the window panes. I outlined my terrace
with an eerie, silver beam from a Goya moon
whose distorted features laughed and cried
at the centre of my canvas.

Rigor Vitae

Explorer,
you have found
the land of ice
surrendered to sleep
in the bitter might
wakened a statue.
A century later
discovered in a state
of perfect preservation,
fragile as parchment,
you have become an exhibit
refrigerated
to prevent decay.
Hundreds file past
then walk into sunshine.
They say that you
look almost alive.

JAMES P. SPENCE

Shooo

Radio Three pours relentlessly from the kitchen
with the clang of mixing bowl,
the opening of drawers, containers and
a wrapper or two unrustled amidst
the sound of filling water.

And running through all this,
imitation bursts of machine gun fire,
that move upstairs, issued by the boy,
which changes to the gentler
shooo of an aeroplane drifting down
into the living room to be drowned
by the oxygenated water in the cistern.

Further out the birds scree and chirrup;
an occasional car abrupts and shifts the air
but not for long; it too is swallowed
in the cacophony and I delicately
scratch the white page endeavoring
to transcribe these soundings.
On this day of rest the world weaves
and interlinks, creatively building
but less crudely than this. Listen to the motion.
It's like the water that sparks
and engines every molecule of life.

The Open Window

By the open patio door
you coax the shirt from my back
to let my scars breathe for once
to let the sun cleanse my body.
You hold my wary hand and face
to reassure this unthought step.
Shading my timid back with net drape,
I then face you with a nervous smile
appreciative of the love you show
and of what you reveal about me;
and my opened wounds heal before you.

BRENDA SHAW

The Immigrant

I used to think I'd go back;
that this new role
wasn't permanent.
But the new role's old now —
and so am I.
In my own country friends have scattered
into villages and graves.
The home I knew lies under concrete
and auto salerooms,
while here, my new home
grows old with me;
new friends become old friends.
A network of love and regard
tightens.
I'm at peace now —
except sometimes, off-guard,
in dreams.

Possible Consequences

I don't fear death for myself,
but for him
as the surgeons pummel and tear soft flesh,
rend bone from bone.
The serums of sleep course his veins,
enter his brain,
where three minutes' anoxia is final.
So fine a line between life and death —
as wide as human error.
Routine procedure, the surgeon says.
For him, perhaps.

TOM HUBBARD

European Capital

You were so innocent, loving the incongruous;
So thrawnly eager to reach some ill-known corner,
Some destination left unvisited
By all, it seemed, except your younger self . . .

The tram rattled, its bell ting'd
Its solo in the city's orchestra;
You were fifteen, exhilarated, foolish.
Did you remark, however fleetingly,
Looming before the bridge on the canal,
Those sculptural figures bearing the name of 'Labour'?
Your head rattled with darting images
Of silent nineteenth century legacy:
Avenue after avenue of mansions,
And the murky green of unlit lamps in file
That followed the high fencing of a park
Dour as the night;
The tram lurched, and from another angle
The city spread its serendipitous riches
That shimmered in the April afternoon.

You were so innocent, loving the incongruous,
So thrawnly eager to reach that ill-known corner
Where most rushed by on the way to somewhere else.
There were the objects of your pilgrimage:
Chinese pavilion, Japanese pagoda,
You'd quite ignore in China and Japan,
Bordering the suburbs and the palace grounds.
You were fifteen, exhilarated, foolish,
Unmindful of that larger Royal Domain

South of the alps, the sea, the desert, jungle,
From where the king and his go-getting minions
Extracted growth of ivory and rubber
And blood . . . so here, he makes his due return,
His tribute to all folk without white skins,
In raising up such droll exotica.

And yet, today they're fousty and forgotten.
No longer here, at the dragons and lanterns,
No longer here, nor king nor belle epoque.
Now, most rush by on the way to somewhere else,
And you . . . you followed them down a tentacle
Back to the swill and rumble of our time,
The towering blocks that snatch the very sky:
Cacophonous centre of one continent
That sucks and spews the centre of another.

Not that you saw that then, and barely now –
Through streets where everything and everyone
Seem fabricated just a minute ago –
Could you connect such serendipitous riches
With muffled protestations near at hand
Or flies and skeletons in a darker land.

You remain innocent, faced with the incongruous.

A. L. KENNEDY

The Moving House

Grace drinks and feels the water from the tap and finds it sweet. That means her mouth is sour. She feels sick.

She can remember dreaming, although she doesn't think she slept. She wouldn't have slept. But the dream is sharp in her mind, as if it had happened again in sleep and she had seen what she always did see — a door, opened smoothly on a room with the curtains drawn. The familiar dream.

Think of something else to keep it away. The first thing you remember: think of that. Cold of the cold tap, laid along your cheek and think of that.

Your father.

Grace's father went away when she was small and didn't write letters, or a postcard, or come back. There is only one memory of him; the first she has of anything, full stop. The first thing she knows that happened to her.

The sitting room was dark and the curtains were drawn — night-time dogs and cars outside them. Everything she looked at was changed and dim and being there was like a secret: a private thing, between the two of them.

Her father had carried her, up out of bed in his arms, her feet in his jacket pockets, his shoulder under her head. She remembers the bitter smell of his short, warm breath and his hands beneath and behind her, holding her up. He sat with her on his lap, in the deep arm chair and the skin of his face was rough, but not rough. She pressed against it a little, to be sure. Her hand in his was good, surrounded, and Grace fell asleep by the rise and fall of his chest. When she woke, it was finished; she didn't have any more of him after that.

A few years on from when he left them and Grace was gone, too. Maybe at the time, they didn't tell her, but it seemed they hadn't meant it like that. She just went away to Aunt Ivy's, took a wee case, and slowly, other things of hers arrived. The day they bought a bed for her, she knew she would stay.

She slept in the front room, first on the folding down sofa and then on her own, bought bed. Her aunt would have moved away the china: her good things and her glass, but she never did, because Grace was a careful child.

I'll put them away, Grace. You'll break them.

I promised, I won't. They're better out. You like them like that.

If you break one, just one thing, then all of them go.

Clear eyes, looking up.

Uh hu.

So Grace's room had vases and white linen and dark wood.

Together they emptied drawers for her own stuff and, in the day, she had a coverlet and cushions to put on the bed. It was prettier than the couch; they both thought that. In the late afternoons, Grace would stand in her wide, bay window and watch the light in the ruby crystal bowl, its rim hung with clear, glass drops. She liked to see the colours on the tablecloth: the curves of red and white, and it wasn't hers, it was hers to look after which was different and made it special; something to do with love.

More. You want more of that. Brush you hair and brush your teeth. Quiet, and the pain won't come. You should sit.

Grace saying Aunt Ivy wasn't right: Ivy was her mother's mother's sister, which made her a Great Aunt. And Ivy would have been a great aunt, anyway; that was their joke. If Grace ever wanted something, she only had to say

Please, Great Aunt and the skin across Ivy's nose would redden and, most times, the answer would be yes. It was too easy, so Grace didn't say it a lot.

Difficult parts; there were difficult parts as well. Her aunt worked in the hospital, cleaning, and the hours for that were queer. Halfway through the afternoon, she started and then she wasn't home until the night. This was good in the mornings, because nobody was hurrying but Grace and going to school could be slow and quite nice. The problem was coming home to an empty house.

Letting herself in was lonely.

No, don't remember that. Not waking too late in the morning with no breakfast smell and no radio and everything too late. Something had been altered while she slept and now it was wrong. So she went to her auntie's room and let herself in and it smelt of talcum and camphor and hand cream which wasn't a change, but she felt there was something missing, or something replaced. There was a new smell there now, a smell you could almost see. She'd been expecting it, because you shouldn't trust old people, they always die, and as soon as she opened the door, she knew.

Back at the start: the beginning: remember that.

At the start, Mrs. Cruikshank from down the stair had wanted to take her in; just for those hours in the evening when Grace was alone. Mrs.

Cruikshank's own children could be seen in ranks on her mantelpiece; smiling progressively older smiles, and she had a piano that played itself from a cardboard roll. That was nice. But Grace said, very nicely, that she wanted to learn how to cook and she asked for a key of her own to Aunt Ivy's flat.

Letting herself in was lonely, in the winter it was dark, and it seemed as if no one else lived there — as if she could wait and no one else would come. She would turn on the television set in the kitchen and go and do her homework in her room, with the sound of other voices at her back. Then she would change and go to stay in the kitchen with the talking and the fire, make a cup of tea and have a snack, nothing too much. The meal would always wait until her aunt was back and, unless the bus was late, Grace would have it ready, just right.

Both of them would have stories from where they had been. They would eat and speak and listen a while and eat.

This is very good, Grace.

Of course.

You weren't too hot on Monday.

Monday was a new thing, maybe it should be like that.

Well, the recipe should have said so; I'd have put in an old pair of teeth.

He was smiling, you saw him, how he smiles. The eyes were closed and the lips were back from the teeth. A smile looks like that.

Why did you come here, back to your mother? They said you were going home, but it never was home and you grew up into you somewhere else. If you'd been older, if you could have left the school. With a job, they would have let you stay away, but nobody gets jobs now, not straight out of school, not proper jobs. You'll be out on the street, or stuck here for life. Whichever way, you'll be nothing. You won't be anything.

It was lonely, letting herself in, but that black, lonely feeling: it turned itself inside out. Not sure when. It began to be waiting whenever you left the flat. People out there, you could tell, there was something about them, making them hard. You were only safe with old folk, the ones with other lessons learned. That, or sitting in the blocks of sun, through the kitchen window and being just quiet and by yourself.

Not that she'd really wanted to be by herself, but Ivy had started shrinking away, long before she was ill. There came a lightness in her movements that frightened Grace. She came into a room and her body apologized: her eyes would say she was sorry for being old. Aunt Ivy now finished everyday tasks as if she was saying goodbye and it hurt to share a room with her, watching her tire.

Grace sits on the toilet and the pain seems suddenly fresh. She sees the blood, is sick, cold after.

Don't stay here. Get out. You mustn't be late. They'll ask why, if you're late.

She goes to put on her uniform. It has stayed the same, a children's thing, it should be that it no longer fits.

She presses her hands against her head.

Something good. Something good.

The day they saw the rainbow, that was good. Because of the times Auntie Ivy worked, Sunday was their day. They made it important and kept it to themselves: a proper Sunday Lunch and then the park, to walk it off. When they went out that day, the sun shone, it was hot, but there was thunder in it, you could tell. Then it rained and they were caught out — the rain so fast and so wet that it was funny. Fresh.

Will you look at that. A rainbow. A whole one, Gracie, there.

They took the path on the rise, until they could see it all: hazy arching over, then thick and shining colour near the ground. Grace said they were daft, but she was smiling, and Ivy told her not to be so old. They couldn't get any wetter — not now.

At home, Grace lit the summer fire she had laid in the kitchen and they sat in their dressing gowns with tea.

She doesn't want to pass the room. The door will be closed: he closed it, but she doesn't want to pass the room. If she carries her shoes, doesn't wear them, he won't hear. She passes and down the stairs in stocking feet, don't slip, don't stop. At the bottom, her head is spinning and she bends forward, holding her ache. From the room above her, no sound.

Grace had been in charge of the fires. She knew how to make them — fetched coal up in the bucket and chopped wood. Her aunt had a joiner friend who came round, once a fortnight, with offcuts in a sack. Sometimes there was hardboard — hard to break up.

The joiner, Mr Taylor, has been a friend of Ivy's since the war. She always said he should stay for his tea and he always said that next time he would. He came to Aunt Ivy's funeral, right inside the crematorium, and Grace's mother laughed.

Christ, is that old bugger still alive?

Grace had wanted to speak to him afterwards, but Charlie and her mother took her away. She had wanted to turn round and smile at him, but she couldn't get her mouth to work and, anyway, she couldn't smile — not there.

Charlie was her mother's friend, but her mother called him Chick. He was the one who came with a van to take Grace's things from the flat. He was the one who moved her in.

The first night, all three of them had sat and watched TV. Chick went out and bought them fish suppers. His treat. Grace had tomato ketchup; burnt her tongue.

I'll have to go to bed now. School.

Well, you know where it is. You're home now.

Chick shouted up from the living room door.

Night, night.

Then she realised: he lived here, too. Later, their voices woke her through the wall. They made her feel far away from herself and sad.

This isn't the first time she's thought it, making the walk for the bus. She doesn't have to catch the one to school. There are buses to take her anywhere. Away: Dumbarton, Balloch, Oban, just away. Even on the right bus, she could stay in her seat and roll on past the stop.

But today, she wants to be there, where she knows things and it's warm. It's the bus that takes her home she wouldn't catch.

Hiya, Gracie.

Hello.

Been out tonight, Gracie. Had a nice time. Is your mother back?

No, she's not.

So mummy's out on the town as well, uh hu?

I'm sorry, it's late, I was just going up.

Oh, don't do that, Gracie. I came home to see you.

He dropped his head to one side and looked at her; frowned. As she went upstairs, he took her arm.

Grace was glad it happened in their room; not her own. Not her bed.

She looks at the bus ahead of hers and, across the back window, four boys. Their head and backs are swaying all together. As if they were hearing a music that she can't. One of them turns and sees her, jerks up the finger, gives it a twist.

Please, Grace, don't. You're a good girl; don't tell her. If you tell her, she'll be angry; she'll be sad. Nobody has to know, Grace, please.

She could hear that he was crying. As if he had taken everything now: even the sounds she would make.

Please , Grace. Grace. Fuckun say it. You won tell. You don even think about it.

Stupid cunt. Nobody's gonny believe you. Who are you? You're fuckun nothun. See if they do believe you; they'll say it was your fault. You. Pretty, Gracie, fuckun you. Just you fuckun sleep on that. You do not tell. Think I couldn make it worse? You do not fuckun tell.

He almost carried her out on to the landing; she didn't know if she could walk. The smell of him close again made her wretch.

And in the morning, she could smell him on her and on her bed and in her sheets with the repeated rosebuds and the matching pillow case. The sheets that Aunty Ivy bought her in the summer. He had spoiled them, the way that he had spoiled her skin. She couldn't wash enough; he was in the bone and he came back like another dream.

You'll get to like it, Gracie, all of us do.

She had felt his hands across her cheeks and his fingers in her hair.

It's something you do with a friend, Grace, and I'm your friend. I'll be good to you. Don't worry, honey, the next time, it won't hurt.

He told her to go to bed now, and before he closed the door, sleep tight.

J. C. FARRELL

The Myth

Bryce was pleading with her. His voice was soft and gentle as he grimaced ever so plausibly to win her over. He knew he could just as easily have told her she was doing it and that would've been that, but he felt reasonably good with himself and this encouraged him to act a little contrite after the slapping around he'd given her the other evening. Women, he grinned smugly, like to be martyred. It was just a question of entertaining their moods until they came round, and if that failed or they pushed their luck . . . well.

The whining noise from her hair dryer irritated him, but he kept his cool and humoured her sulkiness. He knew this one well and all the sulky acts that went with it. Maybe half a dozen times she'd tried to threaten him by saying she was leaving, and when he'd called her bluff by tossing her bodily out the front she was always back two minutes later with all the usual tears and excuses of no where to go and all the other poor me's that went with it. Still, he had to do a bit of coaxing here if he was going to get her to come out shoplifting with him . . . she was just stupid enough to be a good decoy for him.

From his seat on the edge of the bed he leaned over and ran a testing fingertip across her bare shoulder and down her arm. She reacted just as he expected and he laughed at her exaggerated disapproval as she shrugged her shoulder away from his touch. "Come on doll." He humoured her with another smile. "Do this little favour for me and me and you will go out for a Chinky the night . . . huh, what do you say?"

Lena gave no sign of interest, only a dismissive toss of her head as she swept the hair dryer across it. Her thoughts were that this time she was making a stand for herself. It was just a question of not being afraid to go through with it. This was a new low for Bryce, asking her to go shoplifting with him, what next for God's sake? Maybe she was one of those women who were supposed to like being abused and beaten by her man. She didn't know anymore.

"Come on." He persisted with his goading smile. "It's no big deal, honest. Just this one time and I won't ask you again. We'll be in and out the store in five minutes, no sweat I promise."

"Forget it." She answered him dryly. "That's all I need on top of everything else, to end up in jail on a shoplifting charge . . . God!"

"Hey." He stood up with a patronizing grin on his face. "Who said anything about going to jail? Jesus Lena you've got some imagination, as if I'd let something like that happen to you. But just as a point of interest, you being a first offender, nothing more than a fine. I guarantee it."

"That's a big comfort." She sneered sarcastically at him and switched off the hair dryer."Just forget it, eh?" She snubbed him with cold finality and went back to the rest of her toiletry on the vanity table.

Bryce suffered a smile to calm his mounting anger with her. She was taking advantage of him and he didn't like it too well. There was only so much a man could take, but he was willing to give it one more try.

"You're still mad at me, eh? Okay Lena I'll say it again, I'm sorry, alright? Just say the word and I'll do it but for Christ's sakes don't make a life's devotion out of it, 'cause it was as much your fault as anybody's, right?"

Lena studied him a second, her smile feint and derisive. She should have been used to it by now, nothing was ever his fault. He couldn't even apologise without adding the postscript of its grudge. But she felt a little reckless today and as she leaned forward towards the vanity mirror with her lipstick poised for application she couldn't keep the contempt out of her voice. "Sure Nick, it's always somebody else's fault." She rolled her lips together. "But I'm getting fed up being used as a punchbag everytime you get those wild ideas into your head. Why don't you pick on a man for a change."

She might as well have poked a mad dog with a stick. Bryce's eyes turned wild with rage. His face was a mask of hate and viciousness as he swept everything off of the vanity table, and then turning on Lena he whacked the back of her head with his open palm. The sudden violence of the attack startled her back on her stool where she automatically curled up with her hands protecting her head from the next expected blow. Bryce went for her hair though, and grabbing a handful he yanked her head back with all the savagery at his command where he twisted at the roots till the tears were squeezed out of her eyes.

"What do you say now?" He yelled into her pain contorted face. "Eh, what do you say now bitch? Is there something else you want to say?" There was a demonic look about his face as he twisted her hair further when she tried to plead with him.

"Please Nick." She gasped in pain. "Please . . . "

"I'll please you alright." He twisted a bit more and shook her head. "You try talking smart to me girl, eh?"

Her voice was desperate as the tears blinded her. "Oh please Nick I'm sorry, you're hurting me. Oh God stop it Nick, I'm sorry, I'm sorry."

"You better be." He warned her with the threat of more unmistakable violence in his voice. "You damned better be, and you give me any more of your daft lip and you'll get what you got the other night . . . remember what you got the other night?" He shoved her head away from him and went over to the drinks cabinet. "God I need a drink." He sighed heavily and ran his fingers through his dark hair. "My fuckin nerves with you woman." He shot her a victimised look.

She watched as his hands trembled as he poured himself a large whisky and then paused to control himself with some hard breathing as he spread his hands on either side of the cabinet. "Go on you bastard," she said to her self. "Drink it and have another one. Let's see the big man when he has his mouth dressed." But he didn't, instead he brought the glass over and set it down on her vanity table while he took up his former seat on the edge of the bed.

He was calm again and he even felt a little pity for her, but it was a guiltless pity, more like one of those concessions where he would be nice to her if she would be nice to him. He'd no time for those women who didn't know their place, or started getting ideas above themselves just because they were a woman. A skelp on the ear every now and then did them no harm at all.

He leaned back on the bed with his hands behind him for support and studied her with cruel and silent scrutiny as though to rub the salt in further, or even to see if she would dare to challenge his superiority by making any kind of accusation. Naturally she didn't and naturally he was smiling again.

"Okay." He clicked his tongue and tossed up his head with benevolent resignation. "I was out of order there, but there you are Lena, that's the kind of guy I am and you will noise me up something terrible with that nippy tongue of yours. I mean, why are you giving me such a hard time? I'm only asking you to come out as a cover for me, I'm not asking you to lift the gear, I'll do that, you just keep the saleswoman busy and I'll do the rest. It's a cantor, honest."

She wondered how all of this could have happened to her, for she wasn't a bad person and neither was she so ugly in appearance that all she'd become fit for was as a doormat. She was still a young woman and it was hard to imagine how in their eight years together she'd become a Dickensian type drudge without even noticing that it was fear and not love that had blinded her. Plenty of well meaning friends had told her to pack up and leave on many an occasion, but it wasn't quite that simple, at least not for her it wasn't. The fear of Nick Bryce catching up with her when she thought of such a thing was so fraught with trauma that it immobilised her completely. The only way she ever saw herself being rid of this man was whenever she was dead or he was dead. There was no longer any middle road.

"Hey there." He waved his hand in front of her blank face. "You're away in another world there, thinking about it were you? Don't worry I'll look after you. It's just that I've promised this customer a couple of cashmeres and I don't like letting him down. You'll get a couple of bob out of the deal too, don't worry about that doll."

She turned to him and smiled. He'd become so despicable that she was actually gaining in confidence from her detestation of him.

"Aren't you going to drink that whisky?" She nodded with a grimace at its close proximity on her vanity table. "You know I hate the smell of that stuff."

This change of heart for his manly comforts and her observations of them had him feeling slightly more conducive towards her where at that point he was quite willing to admit that she wasn't the worst in the world. It also proved the other point to all of those henpecked wimps who had to ask the wife whether they could breathe or not that a good clout round the ears was what the little woman really loved. As for the whisky he was going to have a good couple of belts before they went out, but first things first.

She'd only a slip on over her underclothes and suddenly he was standing behind her, running his hands with unmistakable intentions over her bare shoulders and down the silky material of her ribs. She closed her eyes and tried to concentrate in space and all the millions of stars out there. She'd read somewhere a long time ago to try and concentrate on one star when sleeplessness or stress was making you anxious. She was trying to effect a self hypnotic catharsis for the next event.

His preparations were nonexistent, he didn't even bother to remove either his jacket or shoes, just a hurried exercise of lust.

It didn't matter though as she kept her eyes closed and focussed all of her energy on that one star out in space. It was good to have so much room in her mind, no predators were there, just the bright star in the distance with its promise of freedom. Never once did she need to respond or associate with the animal gruntings in her ear, she was just wondering why it had taken her so long to think of putting that weed killer into the whisky bottle.

JIM GLEN

Relics

He found it lying in a corner of the attic, a ragged lump of grey metal. In his search for more obvious treasure he would have passed on had he not noticed the markings. The paintwork was dirty and faded with time but the numbers were still legible. There was also a white strip radiating from the centre and ending abruptly where the metal seemed to have been torn away from something larger. He picked it up and rubbed at the dust and grime with the arm of his jersey but it made little difference. Also, it was heavier than he had anticipated.

He turned round to look at his grandfather who was at his bench as usual, engrossed in fitting the rigging to a model ship. Normally he would have been at his side ready to supply him with various tools and equipment, but the rigging was a fiddly, time-consuming job and Colin had quickly become bored at being merely a spectator to the old man's skills. He had gone off to explore dark corners of the attic, careful to step only on the wooden beams for fear of putting a foot through the floor.

The attic was crammed with the junk of ages, most of it his grandfather's. When Colin's gran had died, his father decided that the old man couldn't be left on his own so the house was cleared and sold. He was given the room opposite Colin, but had insisted on taking all of his junk with him. His 'relics' he called them. There had been a terrible row over this which his grandfather had won but at a cost; a life-sentence to the attic for him and his 'relics'. He didn't seem to mind. In fact, he was happiest up there working at his bench from morning to night on his various schemes and projects.

His first creations had been works of his own invention — cigarette dispensers and other mechanical gadgets — but they rarely worked, so he had turned instead to model-making. Not the easy kind which Colin enjoyed, sticking cut-out plastic parts together, but building them from scratch — finding the materials, selecting and cutting the wood, assembling the parts and finally painting the finished work, all of which could take six or seven weeks. Although his sight was poor, he worked by touch and a degree of patience which Colin had seen in no-one else, (certainly not his father) producing works that made his Airfix kits pale into insignificance. For over a month now he had been working on a replica of the Mayflower which he had spotted in one of Colin's schoolbooks. It was almost finished and would be a masterpiece like the others.

Colin carried the lump of metal over to the bench. He noticed the old man's half-smoked cigarette had fallen onto the floor and was lying smouldering, a tiny red glow in the gloom. He picked it up and placed it securely in the ash-tray. It felt warm and spongy between his thumb and forefinger. His grandfather stopped working and looked at him. Colin offered up his discovery for an explanation.

He thought the old man had said something like 'ankle' but that didn't make sense so he asked again. This time he said 'Heinkel'. Colin knew what a Heinkel was — a German bomber used by the Luftwaffe in the Second World War. He had a model of one hanging from his bedroom ceiling, a Heinkel 111. It was being attacked by a Spitfire. The Heinkel had been a birthday present from his father and the Spitfire he'd bought with his own pocket money. But although he knew what a Heinkel was, he did not fully understand what his grandfather meant. He looked at the dirty grey lump before him and frowned. Something did not connect.

"Part of a Heinkel," the old man explained. "Shot down trying to bomb the Forth Bridge. One of our guns caught his tail. Lost his steering. Managed to get clear of the water but crashed into a field. That was our first hit, so we all raced out to have a look. Must have exploded on impact, bits scattered all over the place. I took that home as a souvenir." He picked it up and held it close to his face. "Shouldn't have taken it though. Could have got into trouble but, well . . . everyone took something. Plenty to go round." He was quiet for a moment, then placed it carefully on the side of the bench and went back to the Mayflower. Colin asked about the crew. "Dead," he answered, dabbing a spot of glue onto one of the masts. "All dead."

That night Colin dreamed he was the pilot of the stricken Heinkel. His grandfather had delivered the fatal blow from his ack-ack gun, and now the plane was careering wildly above the dark waters of the Forth. The cockpit was filling with black smoke. He looked back. The tail section was in flames. His navigator lay dead in his seat and the others, panic-stricken, were screaming in their incomprehensible German. He turned back to the controls. The stick was heavy and the plane failed to respond. He managed to clear the water but now the earth was rushing towards him. It was becoming impossible to see anything, only dense oily smoke that burned his lungs with each breath. Knowing he was about to die, he was determined to face it bravely, not like the rest of them, not like the cowardly Germans who died every week in the pages of his Air Ace picture library.

He took one last gulp of the choking air and closed his eyes.

But hands reached out and plucked him from the blazing wreckage and were madly rushing him downstairs and outside where all was noise and confusion. His mother was standing in the front garden in her nightdress and she ran to him and hugged him till he nearly passed out. Bells were ringing in his head and his bare feet were cold on the pavement. Someone wrapped a blanket round his shoulders and led him inside where he was given warm milky tea to drink. A man came inside and checked his pulse and temperature, then he was tucked up on a couch and the bells in his head began to fade at last.

His grandfather went away and did not come back. It was as simple as that, and not the way he had imagined it would be. Not like his gran, where he had known for weeks and the house had seemed full of strangers and whispers. Even after the thing happened he had seen her, that time he kissed her in the box. That had been strange. It still looked like gran, but her face had been cold and hard as if she was cross at being dead. But at least Colin had known she was going away. Grandfather's sudden exit seemed deceitful and a bit of a cheat.

He lived with an aunt for six months while the house was being repaired. When he returned every room was fresh with the smell of new wood and plaster, particularly the attic. His father had paid extra to have pine-flooring laid down and a large window replaced the old skylight, flooding the room with light. The walls were painted.

ALEX McLAUGHLIN

Charles

Charles stopped mid-sentence. The last person left the common room, and the laughter drained from his face. In the corridor outside he could hear people continue conversations. He thought about his problem. Charles had ten minutes to wonder why no-one liked him: a long time to be alone in a building full of people. By the next class he had found a solution, using his computer to pinpoint his faults.

The computer was kept under lock and key — well away from his sister — in the bedroom, a thing apart from the rest of the house. It was a two-up, two-down, one toilet, a kitchen and a cupboard where the dog lived along with the brushes. The decor was bland at best. Basically an ordinary place, until you came to his bedroom. Black was the predominant colour: Charles thought it chic. The venetian blinds remained permanently closed, to prevent glare on the monitor. A hardly used bed sat in the corner, alongside his desk. On top sat a graphic printer, while the next shelf held a desk light and dozens of printouts. The bottom held a twin disk-drive, joystick, a computer monitor and the computer itself. A green light shrouded the room when Charles switched on to begin work.

The program took two hours to complete, and he was disappointed when the simple answers appeared on screen;

THE PROBLEM AREAS ARE:-
1. CLOTHING
2. CONVERSATIONAL OUTPUT
3. LACK OF COMMON INTEREST(S) WITH COMPANIONS
4. LACK OF FEMALE COMPANIONSHIP
5. LACK OF STYLE
6. ACNE

Charles flinched — where were the spots?

When the weekend arrived, Charles began to work, asking his father for money to buy new clothes and some records. His current collection consisted entirely of one single by the Eurovision Song Contest winner of the previous year, which was not a great topic at school. When he'd persuaded his sister Pat, who did not suffer from problem number five, to go with him, Charles set out. Right after watching Children's Saturday Television for the first time.

Since early childhood his mother had bought his clothes, so she could be given some of the blame when Pat had to drag him away from the 'Gentleman's Tailors'

"Charlie, why don't we go into a young man's shop and you can try something on," said Pat. "Just try something!"

He did and didn't like it.

After another three tailors, Pat broke the monotony and took Charles into a Virgin record store. Starting under 'A' they worked through a catalogue. When he reached 'B', she held her breath and let it out again when he picked a Baron Knights album. She persuaded him they weren't in vogue and when Charles said The Who, Pat asked the same. When she screamed, he relented, taking a couple of the top fifty long players.

"Suppose I'll get used to it," Charles mumbled.

Pat prayed he would and, after round one, she needed a breather.

"You're buying," she told Charles, once inside the cafe.

Not ashamed of her brother, well not exactly, Pat sat at a table right at the back where it was darkest, so nobody could see her clearly. Nobody she knew would come in — she hoped — but there was no sense in taking risks. With her back to the wall, she had a perfect view of the door and anyone who came through it. And Charles wouldn't notice if she occasionally glanced behind him.

"But what about leaving?" she said aloud.

"Did you say something?" asked Charles.

"Yes. Are you going to take my advice, or can I leave you to it?"

Pat knew who wore what, where and when. There was to be no argument over what he would buy. Charles needed to have complete faith. She would not let him down and, above all, he would look very good. He agreed to keep quiet and take what was offered.

They talked some more about what colour he suited, while the coffee grew cold and the cafe filled. From behind a line of people came the voice of the school gossip. Pat shrank behind her hand, casually sliding under the table to tie the lace on her slip-on shoes, hoping Charles wouldn't notice the difference. She prayed his unpopularity would keep the gossip away.

"Hi Charles. Out chasing girls?" asked the gossip.

"No. Patricia and I are out shopping, actually."

"Actually, I'm doing the same with Sandra Bates. You know her, don't you Pat?"

Pat sat up and smiled, casually kicking Charles in the groin. He doubled over, knocking coffee all over the uninvited guest.

"Charles! Are you okay?" asked Pat, as she helped him outside.

Once there, Pat demanded to know how he could embarrass her like that. Only he was more unpopular than the girl they'd just left.

"If anyone finds out that I spoke to her, I'll never live it down," she said. "No one — no one — ever tells her anything. In fact no one even speaks to her, except Bates!"

"I know how she feels," said Charles.

Pat threw up her arms, exasperated with her older brother.

Following a further three hours of abuse and insults, the silence of his room was a welcome relief for Charles. He could hear her continued tirade of complaints downstairs, as he hung the white trousers and lemon slipover neatly onto a hanger. One of the albums turned slowly on its player, the instantly forgotten sound drifting quietly around the room. He turned down the volume and switched on the computer.

In bright green letters, the remaining problems stared steadily back at him. He deleted problem number two (deciding it was a state of mind), and numbers one and three were on the way out. Number six, felt Charles, wasn't really a problem. Just the same, a bottle of cream took pride of place on the desk. Charles considered number four in the dark.

The acne was still there next morning, even after a good wash. Charles wondered why it was so easy to come by and so difficult to get rid of. He dressed, then checked again; still there.

The local Sunday disco was something Charles avoided, although most of the sixth year went along faithfully week after week, never missing the sacred pilgrimage. This was to be the day he attended, dressed in his new robes, to either get drunk or make new friends. Perhaps both.

Dull was the only word for it. Despite the neons and strobes, it was almost as dull as his bedroom. Charles felt right at home.

"Could I have a double vodka please?" asked Charles quietly.

"Come again?" shouted the barman.

"A double vodka!" he said, determined that his teetotal days were over.

"No need to shout."

Charles looked around. Behind a bank of lights, the middle-aged disc jockey bopped to the rhythm of the beat and blew the barman a kiss. The seats were tightly packed around the dance floor and sofas lined the wall. A couple of televisions sat precariously on shelves, waiting for somebody to try and turn them off by hand. The vodka arrived. Charles downed it in one, ordered another and sat down near the toilet.

When the sixth year arrived, Charles was slowly sinking into his own wonderfully warm little world. From the corner of his eye he saw them come in groups of two and four. A group of girls strolled in, trying to look mature and sat down across from him on the other side of the room. He looked them over, catching the eye of one from physics, who pointed him out and went to spread the news.

For a long time Charles simply sat with the vodka, keeping it warm between his legs, watching the ice melt. Occasionally he watched them dance, pairing off until there was only one left. He smiled and waved her over.

"It's Charles, isn't it?

"Hope so. An' you're," he drifted.

"That's right: Jenny," she said with a shy smile.

"Looks like it's just you and me."

Charles smiled.

"Is anyone sitting here?"

Charles smiled.

"I'll just sit down then shall I?"

He bought her a drink, taking too much care walking to and from the bar. She asked him if he went to the disco often and of course he did. He grinned and kissed her. She kissed him back. He tried again and she touched his leg. They kissed some more and then it was closing time.

"Do you live near here?" Charles asked outside.

"Just round the corner," Jenny said, her long black hair catching the light of the street.

He walked her home. She supported him under one arm. Charles said he loved her. Outside the house, he said that her complexion did not do justice to her perfect bone structure. He compared her body to Venus, goddess of love and threw-up on the lawn. Charles apologized. Jenny told him not to worry and sent him home in a taxi.

Quietly closing the door, Jenny called to her mother, who sat in the living room in front of a blank screen. Jenny sighed; Charles wasn't much, but he would have to do. She entered the bedroom and turned on the computer; now for the acne.

J. N. REILLY

The Artist

Morning of a postcard melting. A cerulean sky in impasto. A blue and white gingham table-cloth and a knife illumined by sunlight. The holes in the sheets on my bed inviting and facilitating the infiltration of summer scents and airs, their patterns and scenes: little boys soaked in the amazing grin, tractable women on the border of the field, a harvester spurting yellow and red, flowers growing from my wardrobe, my cupboards and drawers. All my windows thrown open: the laburnum pendants of exquisite barbs, her pink languid thrashing music of cotton, birds and engines: I am trailing my fingers in impossible colours, blouses and hairs, avenues and the girl smiling and waving at me from the shore, and cuneiforms in the walls and geomantic paths.

I am sick of being poor. I shall soon have been receiving supplementary benefit for seven years. It would not be so frustrating if I were not married with two sons and were not an artist. We receive barely enough money to buy food and clothes and pay for other necessities let alone buy paint. For the last few years I have been saying, this is it, this year, this spring, this autumn, but unfortunately my finances have not been sufficient to allow me to present you with optical delights. Now that I am satisfied with my written work, I say to my wife, "let's hope we shall make some money from my books, if we do, we shall have a little security and I will resume painting." However, can you believe that I, probably the most magnificent and profound artist creating in Britain, sent poems to literary magazines: not desiring remuneration but merely publication; which were rejected. I must admit that I was shocked, for having read the magazine I had sent my poems to, I was certain they would have been published, would have been gratefully published, for as you know, literary magazines are simply packed with the flatulently fatuous whimpering noxious emanations of the bourgeois. When I received the first rejection; a scribble on the letter which had accompanied my poems; I was so angry I beat the arm of my chair with my manuscript and was about to rip up the only copy in my possession of this particular magazine which I had hoped my poems would have graced and inspirited, when I decided to re-read the magazine. Might I have been erroneous in my appraisal of the magazine's contents? Definitely not, crap would be too indulgent an epithet to bestow on what assails those who unfortunately read that magazine. The audacity, the upstart, I shouted; my three year old son turning and gazing as if to say, 'Is he at it again'; and instantly began writing a rejoinder to the editor of this London based magazine. I then expected rejections from the three other magazines I had sent poems to. I subsequently received them. Nevertheless, although displeased by the rejections, I was saddened when thinking of the consequences of the fallacious culture dissembled as art which is being disseminated by philistines such as editors of so-called literary magazines, numerous critics, writers, painters and their acolyte amongst others.

So here I am, the glorious combination of threnody and epithalamium, which pervades Easterhouse and the marketplace, surging through me as I listen to the old woman and her friends next door, singing along with the christian hymns blasting from the radio — enough eschatological drivel, enough lies — in suburbia where they wait for death, I advance naked, from the wailing woeful streets of Glasgow, from its plaintive, joyous and unknown places, its mysteries and madness, its music kissing, caressing, cutting and cursing me, its perversity calling me, hoop-la hoop-la, Honey's in her bedroom, pulling on her knickers, laughing in her mirror in a view to bleed a demon, I am attending to phenomena and reality, as fantastic as a stone, for our pleasure, freedom and enlightenment, by art revealing expounding art as art and my humble moments passing with cars and jets, hashish and kings, the roses in my garden, why the chairmen believe life is a western, depraved to be sure, pushing you towards the gulf and into pipes, machines and paramount propaganda presenting dreams of penthouse scenes, and jars of coffee, without disclosing the cost in misery, broken hearts and broken bodies. Hoop-la hoop-la, storms, all winds blowing, palm-striped sand-monkeys swinging from the light, stamps and rainbow-tissues converging as showers of confetti, spanners, clockworks and dioramic conches. I laughed at the sights and more inventions in the wild night, a ship's horn distantly blasting through me and computer-music sweeping out of amusement arcades, pink and scarlet onanistic reveries seeping from the skin and eyes of the boy on the prowl, living on neon flesh wheels spinning fortune. She lay back and opened her legs — get your libido into this, sweetheart — my sanctum embodied in her leaning on her sill — the light soft on her — gazing from her window, the oriflamme of my days orphean prayers I am bestowing the country road, the universal church of skies and all spilling over like a fountain, her hirsute oasis, the raindrops trickling down the window-pane like pearls of molten glass, death-films appearing with poor ragged children sitting on the steps of a bar, an icy wind whipping them, a brilliant moon suspended low over the rooftops, we waltzed, slowly at first, to the murmur of a piano revealing vast rooms with chandeliers draped with intestines, other vital organs and flesh, then violins joined by cellos then French horns, sprinkling silver, ribbons and a host of symmetrical shapes. I was smiling, 123, 123, around and around, amongst live calligraphy, I saw them, laughing and grinning at us, still grotesque in their joy engendered by our gaiety, our glorious indefatigability which you are now partaking of, my darling. So around and around — curtains, calendulas, camisoles and campions — hoop-la hoop-la, hoopoe, hippo, hep, hip hip hippeastrum. Yes, that is right, I was a dictionary at one point, also dandy and drudge of wicked streets, femme fatale for diffident boys, hermaphrodite confusing selfsatisfied folks and ensnaring the bold up west, right up west, where I turned into a three-piece suite, handmade of course, handmade you feel, thinking about the price of one or the other, while they are signing for more misery for you, yenning for a dollar or a pound of arse, a bottle of whisky, a meal and a watch, a chain of office to choke you with. Around and around. Bassoons and oboes satirizing pantisocrats, exposing hairy protuberances, For Sale signs and the obsequious gaze of a dog shitting. What time is it? That doesn't matter. I love all of myself. Do you love yourself? Sparks. What age am I? Twenty? Twenty-three? A million and eight?

I am the one. I am my own. I am life, death and resurrection. How could I not be?

Where was I? To whom am I talking? Oh yes, you. Then every second Thursday I make my way along the Great Western Road to Anniesland and the social security office where I sign for supplementary benefit — the usual faces and shabbiness — tokens of diabolic schemes, then off to some shopping at Anniesland Cross: only a flicker of living here, sometimes embellished by carefree ebullience without age, which I meet with grateful approbation.

Pardon? What about the people waiting at the bus-stop? the passers-by, shoppers and shop-assistants? Indeed, I appreciate your concern. However, when I look at these people around me, I perceive dying. I see automatons, somnambulists, and I hear a terrible silence proceeding from their cluttered spaces, though when I enter Gillespie's; the butcher's; I am in the presence of an alacrity which pleases me. The assistants in this shop treat one with courtesy, no matter who one is, which is indeed rare. It is also rare to find not only a good butcher's shop but an excellent one, which Gillespie's certainly is. Mr Hope, the proprietor; a stout man whose face expresses determination and what I perceive as an uncompromisingly scrupulous attitude in regard his trade as butcher; purveys the best of meats which I would purchase a great deal more of if I could afford to. I must also tell you that he sells scrumptious sausage rolls and sausages, especially square sliced sausages, a favourite of mine, which are fit to be eaten by gods, gorillas and gamblers. My goodness, I am hungry, which reminds me of Hamsun's Hunger. Nevertheless I discern a murderous thoughtlessness and denial in the streets and go about my business. Into the newsagent's for tobacco, sometimes a newspaper though I find the tabloids tedious and infuriating; the young woman assistant wearing glasses always gives me a look which I will not guess at the meaning of. Sometimes I go into the chemist, sometimes the supermarket. I like shops. I would enjoy spending money. Money does not talk, it whispers — Spend me, spend me — looks good, feels good and smells good, and if I do not lay my hands on some soon, I think I shall turn to a life of crime so that my family will not want for what they need and what they should have. I shall probably start stealing paint soon. If I do, the shop's loss will be nothing compared to the optical treasures I will present to you. Let's hope I shall not need to steal. Mind you, I stole a good few books when I was younger. Being involved in stealing, especially the moments preceeding the act, is exciting, akin to the lingering thrill in the belly which one experiences before fucking, and the white fluttering of solitude in sanguine strolls. As it is, I will get as much money as possible from my father.

Check his wallet, Igor.

Sure, boss, right away, boss.

I will paint in the summertime, definitely this summer.

No. You take it. No. No more of this.

Do you know the war has started? said a little girl.

I was ascending a stairway at the time.

We're at war, said a local boy.

I heard planes, but saw only one.

So I talked about the little things, TV talkies of how you do and where you have been, popcorn fantasies and felicific fancies. When they departed I scattered my stones and beads before me — distant masts swaying paradise, virescent scents enticing me — and then night again, I passed through doleful bed-sitters.

Where is your hi-fi?

The flat was broke into. It's been stolen.

Are you insured for burglary?

Yes.

That's not so bad then. You should be awarded a few pounds.

To tell the truth, I robbed myself — if you see what I mean — for the insurance money.

What did you tell the insurance investigator? How did you go about it?

I took my camera and hi-fi next door, to my neighbour's, then I went out and told this cop who was standing at the bottom of the street that my flat had been broke into. He took particulars. Then I phoned the insurance company. It was so easy I'm pissed off I didn't claim for more than my camera and hi-fi. I should get some money in a couple of weeks.

You look rather tired.

I'm bloody done in. I was at a party last night. I was wasted. Everybody seemed to have dope. I'm shattered. I was into everything. Booze and acid and smoke. I didn't get back home until five this morning, and I thought the flat had really been broke into because the window was wide open. But a girl I used to go around with had been round to see me. Because I wasn't in she climbed through the window. The girl next door told me she saw her walking around in the nude. It's not the first time she's come here acting crazy. I don't know what to do with her. She's only eighteen. She's been in the loony bin. Now she's seeing a psychiatrist. I've been talking to her in an attempt to help her, but I was wasting my time. I hate this country. Are you still writing, John?

Yes.

I looked at the threadbare carpet, the rumpled bed, and the paperback novels by authors favoured by youths of tertian rebelliousness. Melancholic, I stepped onto the rain-swept street, tired, yearning for the blacker spaces of this night I started walking:

We remember the day as if it were yesterday.

Aye. It was a warm day. A bank holiday, said her husband, not without difficulty as his lungs were practically useless.

When we got home we heard from the television that there had been an accident, but that there was no need for public concern. That's what they said. The wee ones were in their beds and we were having some tea before getting off to bed ourselves.

It's a bloody crime. They're criminals.

Take it easy now. You know you've not to get excited.

They should be hung. They don't give a damn. He turned away, partly to catch his breath and partly to conceal the tears welling up in his eyes. Why them. It should have been us. He paused and, It's got a hold of me, I'm done for. I'll be lucky if I last till the end of the year.

Malcolm was our youngest. He passed away when he was twenty-three.

Simon, our eldest, passed away a year later. Both of them had leukemia. Father has lung cancer and he's never smoked a cigarette in his life. They say the radioactivity has nothing to do with our sons passing away or father's illness.

The bastards don't give a damn. They're mad . . . bloody . . . mad.

I passed the Quarter Gill bar and shady characters. I was on my way to check out a bar only a block away, which I shortly entered.

Though preferring a glass of dry white wine; I had long since abstained from imbibing beers and spirits such as whisky and brandy; I nonetheless ordered a half pint of lager, so as not to look out of place and because it would be something to sip now and then while scrutinizing this hole in the wall bar; a dismal place with a dozen or so dreary customers, a handful of those being a group of men in their thirties whom I had been informed about. Local thieves and drug dealers, they were clustered around a scarred, circular wooden table below a television on a wooden shelf. As they played cards, their voices loud, raucous and persistent, I knew they could not be trusted, that they were probably so venal they would betray one another at the drop of a hat if the going got rough, not to mention an outsider, a stranger such as myself; not that it was necessary for me to cultivate an acquaintanceship with them, knowing as I do other thieves and drug dealers whom I can avail myself of if I require goods cheaply or hashish. Nevertheless, I must emphasize that I do not avail myself of thieves, that hashish is outwith my means and I only indulge in that pleasure every three months or so, if I can extract the money necessary from my father; ostensibly to purchase a book — my father will always give me money to purchase a book if he can, bless his nylon socks. If those men had emanated seemingly trustworthy characters; for certain thieves are relatively trustworthy; I would have approached them and ingratiated myself to have more hashish dealing contacts, for on those few occasions when I desire some hashish it can be difficult to obtain. However, hashish should be a legal substance, available from newsagents and tobacconists. It would engender jobs, boost economies and keep most folk who partake of hashish; especially young people; out of the immoral company of those drug dealers who purvey heroin, who given half the chance will introduce naive hashish smokers to that nightmarish drug which subjugates its user. Be warned, there is not anything enjoyable about experiencing heroin. It simply makes you feel lethargic and ill and works like an emetic; every time you vomit, you do not feel so ill.

Suddenly the door to the street was violently pushed open by a local character forcing a young woman into the bar. I had seen her previously.

She had been coming along the street with two women as I had been heading for the bar. Although one of her companions had been wearing a mini-skirt which barely covered her buttocks, exposing fleshy legs with ample thighs clad in black nylon, my gaze had been particularly drawn to this woman who was now half-heartedly struggling and shouting in protest in the arms of her captor, because with the equally short length of her bright red mini-skirt and the thin, white nylon sweater stretched over what I described inwardly as Tits the size of melons — which in no way describes her breasts as concealed — she imparted a specific type of fuck which can only be found and experienced amidst penury, desperate amidst desuetude, the decay of tenements — graffiti, the scream of fighting, a baby crying, the paint on the window-frame peeling. The customers howled in delight, guffawed, coughed, laughed, and the woman was allowed to run out, smiling, not in the least upset.

I discreetly looked around before departing.

The rain was pouring and, as usually happens while I am out walking, I began creating, the words harmoniously inundated me, I composed eloquent meandering sentences giving praise, delineating the cracked and crumbling pavements, the shoddy window-displays such as one finds along Dumbarton Road and similar areas — the torn and grimy purple crepe paper and outdated advertisements — and I resolved a swarm of words with fairy-wings to flutter around expensive window-displays illuminated by colourful spotlights and the yearning gaze of a destitute boy, teasing, satirizing. So much for so little, and, I must remember, it must be written — laminated lines impressing the brickwork of tenements and the night sky and I, as I optically fancied, with holograms of anger and disgust, the mysteries of streets, recalling the demi-vierge we have all known, the deterioration of all that I have loved, dreams mingling with the evil and ignorant, moral cowards and moral criminals, and other lines as lambrequins, other lines as hyacinths complimenting the eternal beauty, I mused on painting — what mediums to utilize, what brushes, what colours and curves — and partying drunks and vomit in the gutter newspaper headlines of murder and poverty, and:

What's daddy doing, mummy?

He's recording.

Laughing boys sharing a cigarette and the rain pouring, all winds blowing, my fibrositis paining me, and other lines heliconian and demulcent largess placed on white sheets for you now, whenever I reach out and find girls and boys of the wasted night ablaze with dreams, sitting in bedrooms, listening to pop music, biting finger-nails and watching television, wanking in bright bathrooms and cosy mornings of indigence, afternoons of streets and Do you fancy him? Yes. She said she had done it. Football results.

Coming out to play?

Beep.

Give me more.

Let's lallygag.

But they've still got bombs.

Holy shit, what are you doing here. Give me peace.

Are you going dancing tonight?

Fish'n'chips, whiskey, buses, amber, neon signs reflected from the boy's eyes exploding into rubious rhombohedronal crystals drifting over parks, garages, Quick-Tan, Esso, Wrangler, and merging with starlight, each facet manifesting a distinctive dream, fantasy or nightmare: a dazzling field with a kite in the sky engendering sighs of languorous contentment, her lips and cunt glistening in sunlight, a mutilated body as found on a night stroll in a sinister area of the city.

I did warn you.

You're not going out, are you, Josie?

All my fuckin' days, work, work, work.

Is it a bird . . .

Do you know what is beneath your wallpaper?

Rip it off, Rip it off.

. . . and I want to hear you Dirty swine eviscerated you are my Evaporating lotion shoulders, 45:27mpg, strike from witnessed carnage, spark plugs, Chanel, Fisher Toys, Asda Price, muppets, moppets, Kit-Kats, videos . . .

It was cold, the rain had ceased. I was sitting on the top deck of a bus, chagrined because I had forgotten my pen and notebook, weary of poverty, oppressed by the thought of the operations my eldest son, John, will have to undergo, and the possibility of my youngest son, Henry, dying due to the weak cartilages and narrowness of his windpipe. The poor boy did not have a happy start to life for he was also born with a blocked ureter and inflamed kidneys which thankfully were successfully operated on when he was a week old. When Ann and I were first informed of Henry's troubles, we were not surprised. Without being aware of it, I think we expected him to have something physiologically amiss. And what a horrible place the Queen Mother Maternity Hospital is, not only drab and grimy looking but extremely draughty, so draughty that Henry caught cold when he was only three days old. I was shocked when during an afternoon visit there, while talking to Ann, I happened to lower my gaze and catch sight of an insect of some sort scurrying from beneath the skirting board behind Ann's bed.

Obviously I moved quickly from my seat and crushed it. I was to learn that at night these insects would appear in groups of ten or more. They're silver-fish, I was told, they're harmless. Whether or not silver-fish, also known as bristletails, are harmless, I do not know, but I believe their freedom of the hospital should be a matter of urgent concern, that action for the sake of hygiene should have been taken, but as I was about to say, when Henry was allowed home from hospital, Ann and I could not help but feel that something was wrong with him, because of the sound we could clearly hear with every breath he took; a disconcerting sound similar to the type one hears from those suffering bronchitis. At first we thought that because of the cold he had had there was still.mucus to be cleared, that it would pass. It did not. Over the following three months we grew more and more discomforted that this alarming sound could still be heard, and whenever relatives visited they would call attention to it by saying something like He's got a bad chest, you had better take him to the doctor. We would inform whomever that we had called the attentions of the hospital doctors; who had examined him in regards his kidney; to this sound, that they had repeatedly told us they could not find anything wrong with him, that indeed there was nothing wrong with him.

I still say there's something wrong with him. He sounds like some old man who smokes eighty cigarettes a day.

I know, I know. I keep telling the doctors there's something wrong, but they say there isn't. What the hell can I do. I do not have the money to get a private doctor to look at him, who would give him a thorough examination.

So it was a beautiful summer's evening. Ann was in the kitchen; which adjoins the living-room; and I was in the living-room with John and Henry. The film Sinbad was on the television. The sun was pouring through the window. I had just finished giving Henry his milk and was about to help him bring up some wind, when he began crying. I tried to console him but to no avail. As he was now letting out what was a painfully violent cry, I lifted him from my lap and held him up, noticing his face had turned extremely white. What's wrong with him? I said to Ann who had been brought to the kitchen door by his cry. As soon as she caught sight of him she called out, He can't breathe, rushed over, took him from me, began hitting his back, though now with him lying across her knees — bear in mind that what took place happened in the space of seconds — and I could see that he was turning blue.

I'll phone for an ambulance.

So saying I ran to our upstairs neighbours' door and frantically rang their bell. Valerie, the McLeans' daughter, opened the door.

I've got to phone for an ambulance. Henry can't breathe.

Right. I'll see if I can help.

I bounded up the stairs to the McLeans' telephone.

Valerie hurried to my house. After what seemed like a wait of ages, my 999 call was answered. I was so excited I simply called out, Send an ambulance to . . .

What service please?

Ambulance. I need an ambulance.

As I was being connected with the ambulance service I heard Ann screaming out, and the next thing, Valerie appeared on the stairway with Henry, calling for her mother and father. Henry was rigid, his arms and legs sticking straight out from his body. She rushed past me into the living-room. I saw her parents rising from their chairs, her father taking Henry, instantly holding him upside-down and hurrying into the kitchen. Valerie came and took the telephone receiver from me, saying, I'll do this. I went into the kitchen. Donald McLean was holding Henry over the sink. The cold water was running. I do not know whether he had been trickling the water into Henry's mouth, splashing his face with it or what. I cannot distinctly recall what Donald and his wife Helen were saying to one another, but Donald was slapping Henry's back. There was not a sign of life to be detected from him. His eyes were closed. Such a beautiful baby. He's dead, is he dead, I said inwardly, the balmy old sun illuminating the kitchen, and then he belched, bringing up a small amount of vomit which I cleared from his mouth with my fingers, to aid the passage of air. He inhaled sharply, then again — He's alive — began moving slightly and opened his eyes. Although I knew that deep down I was overjoyed, I did not experience any distinctive emotion forby a barely perceptible abstraction of relief. However, the ambulance shortly arrived and I went downstairs to collect my jacket.

Pull yourself together, I said to Ann, sitting on the settee with John on her lap and Valerie by her side. She had obviously been crying. Henry is all right. The ambulance is here. I will stay at the hospital with him tonight. I will phone the McLeans and let you know what's happening.

On reaching the hospital, Henry was taken to an examination room and I gave particulars such as name, address and occupation to the receptionist before joining him. The nurse who was with him left the room when I entered. Darling Henry, lying on the examination table, was his usual happy little self, smiling, without a care as to what he had undergone. A plump lady doctor soon entered and began examining him, reassuring me that he had not suffered brain damage by not being able to breathe, but that he should stay in hospital for observation and tests. Unexpectedly, Ann entered, she could not stay at home, she said, that Mrs McLean had driven her to the hospital, that John was with Donald and Valerie. He's all right.

Then the wait began.

I stayed in the hospital overnight — Ann would take over from me the following day for the remaining period of Henry's hospitalization.

Although Henry was only four months old, I was surprised by how much I had grown to love him, how much I cared about him; he had just been a lovely little baby who happened to be my son, whom I indubitably loved, but whom I had not had the opportunity to spend a great deal of time in loving, for he had been in hospital for the first five weeks of his life, and slept a lot when home, while I was always writing; which were manifested, if only to myself, in my distress the following day at lunch-time, when I went to the University Cafe on Byres Road for a cup of tea and a snack, before going to the Western Infirmary where my mother is a nurse; to inform her about Henry; for it was there, when I had finished my tea and asked three women sitting at the same table as me; I had overheard them talking about working in the Western; if they knew my mother; in the hope of ascertaining which hospital building she was working in, to save me the possible bother of going to the wrong building; that the tears welled up in my eyes. The women told me they did not know my mother. I excused myself for my obvious distress by giving a brief explanation of what had happened to Henry, then went and paid my bill and left, in case I should burst out crying. As I made my way to the Western, I was barely able to refrain from crying, though when I arrived at the recovery room where my mother was on duty and began telling her what had happened, the terrible events of Henry's encounter with death overwhelmed me and I wept as I have never wept, I could not control myself, which caused me some annoyance, for if compelled to weep I would prefer to do so in private or in the company of Ann. I knew my mother was shocked by my tears, paradoxically by the real emotion naked before her, probably by the fact that I am a human being after all, that I bleed, that I am not merely the prodigious being she has refrained from truthfully gazing at and holding absolute faith in, and even loathed? for reasons I know well, which I am virtually indifferent to. Nevertheless, I have an affection for her even if it is only issuing from sympathy and filial loyalty. However, I have written about consanguineous matters in Maybe A Boy, maybe you have read that book, maybe not, maybe you never will, maybe my glorious beacons of refuge, hope and faith will be seen by only those few friends I cherish, which does concern me, for if it did not concern me, I should not be caring about you, your actions and scarcity of actions, their consequences and possible consequences, which would mean I do not care about my family and myself and may as well throw away my pen and the few tubes of paint I possess.

When I regained some composure I told my mother the cardinal reason for my grief — cardinal reason? because undoubtedly my grief was being abetted and exacerbated by years of misfortune.

But the waiting, the interminable waiting congested with anguish. I gazed into the night, the horizons all atwinkle, and I prayed to my guardian angels, the saints of afflatus and fruition, and I came across the boy, crouched by a fuliginous wall by the docks. When he saw me, he smiled, held up a small polythene bag, which I knew contained glue, then threw it to the ground with a disdainful gesture employed for my benefit, as befitted his tragically humourous disposition. I sat down beside him.

It's a fine night, John, he said, good for us all.

It is indeed, I rejoined.

Do you see the rockets? He nodded across the river to the black sky above the rooftops of factories and tenements.

They are beautiful, said I. They are consolation — our passing moments. And more, much more.

Aye, but how those moments die. Wonderful. I'm happy, John. This might well be paradise. If I didn't know any better I'd believe I'm in paradise. Are you happy?

No. But I have given my sorrows to the rockets. They will keep them for a while.

I'm never sad, John. If I'm not happy, I don't give a damn. I like Clark Gable. Don't you?

Yes.

A fine shape, good eyes, and the kind of moustache I like. I might grow one like that. You should paint a series of paintings where everyone sports a Clark Gable moustache, women and children included. Are you going to paint my poly-bag of pictures?

I decided to do so a while ago, but you know how things have been lately.

I tried to write poetry like you've been doing for that book, what's it called? Raining fuckin' Blossoms?

No. Raining Joy Blossoms.

That's it.I like that. I enjoyed scribbling down a few poems the other night. It felt like living. You know what I mean. Like sitting here, hanging around watching the insanity. But what does it matter, I'll be dead soon.

You are dead.

Don't be like that. Talk to me. Tell me a story. Tell me anything.

I don't know why I should.

You love living, John. Like me. That's why.

Ultimately I love living, but definitely not like you. And what has that got to do with telling you a story as you say?

Who cares. You're here, that's reason enough, for me, and for you.

Partly true, though if I interpret what you previously said as what I believe you meant to mean, then you are correct — even if you only understand in abstraction what my loving living means. Anyway, I will talk to you for a little while. Let's becalm ourselves with this, I was fifteen years old, I was with Andy Alexander and Bob Smith and we were in the woods that enclose Gartloch Mental Hospital. I distinctly remember sitting below an electricity pylon, listening to and watching Andy and Bob arguing over which of them should stand on the little weather beaten tree stump beside us. It was a desperate, malicious and at times hilarious argument which I am sure they learned a great deal from. That we were experiencing the effects of L.S.D. — as was our want now and then in those wild days — is neither here nor there, for it had no bearing on our reality as individuals. So, the sun was dipping beyond the treetops and we decided to take the longest route home through the hospital grounds. When we passed the main hospital building, night was upon us and, as I have always done when passing that building, I turned and looked at its left hand tower, and sure enough, appearing from the door at the top of the tower as she always has — whether in the sober light of an afternoon or the calm of an evening — was the crazy woman in tattered skirt, blouse and shawl, letting out her despairing silent scream before vanishing back through the door. Refreshed by that apparition I attended to my walk home with Andy and Bob. We were happy simply being together, blessed by a cool, still evening and the trees on either side of us forming a solemn corridor to Gardener's Lodge — the house in which my sister Jennifer and her husband Eddie had once lived — and our passing two men whom I discerned were patients of the hospital, not only by their extremely circumspect gazes, as if in awe, but by the heavy material and cut of the suits they were wearing, which were hospital suits that are easily identifiable because they do not retain the creases one would wish — no matter how often one irons them — and are always ill-fitting, as was so with the suits the men were wearing — trouser-legs at half-mast and jackets that were too small. With a few remarks of wondering from Andy and Bob regarding the psychological state of the men, we turned left onto the dirt road curving further left. It was here on this road that I experienced the beautiful revealing sight of the grassy field to our right, covered as it was by a thick layer of eddying mist enhanced by the delicate sounds of what I believe were insects and foliage trembling in breezes. Indeed I believe that Andy and Bob were also gladdened by this sight and the sounds. But what joy, what revelation when we left the road and crossed the concrete bridge over the burn and began slowly making our way across another field, towards the burn in the woods before the tenements of Easterhouse, for without the close proximity of trees the sky was revealed, illumined by a relucent moon which I saw as brilliant blue and white neon Pan-Am globes encompassed by luminous longitudinal and latitudinal lines created by the movements of ultrasonic aircrafts. When I turned my gaze from this, I thought of William Blake's poem Eternity, that I have always kissed the joy as it flies, just as I was doing, grateful for such ecstasy. My goodness, so grateful. However, do not assume that I am an admirer of Blake's work. Of the poems of his which I have read there are only a few I like, the others are tedious. In fact the English are rarely poetic and are a generally unartistic even plebeian race. I do not want to ruin the story for you, so I will not digress further.

Digress all you want, John, you couldn't ruin your story. I love your digressions.

Be that as it may. On a night like this my digressions would be essentially generalizations which would fail to communicate my meaning.

That doesn't matter.

It does. I do not have time to squander. Now where was I. Yes. Andy, Bob and myself left the field and crossed the burn in the woods. Oh what breezes wafting between the trunks and branches of the trees, carrying down from the streets and tenements the odours of evening meals, the curses, laughter and muffled conversations of children, older words of contention, love, wishes and foredoomed plans nibbled by mice and sparrows. Oh yes, the real and the fancied intermingled as they always are, such reality, mantic. And buoyed up by the scents of earth and foliage were droplets of semen, pictures of living-rooms and kitchens, previously unseen subtly colourful wallpaper designs blending with television and radio sounds and that universal language that communicates in abstraction with all souls, even if unfortunately only for a moment or once in a lifetime. As we drew closer to the tenements we could feel the heat, the heat of bodies, all that living. Our eyes gleaming . . .

Go on, John, continue.

I can't. Other things are forcing their way into me.

Thinking about your oldest son are you?

Yes. His operation did not work out as planned. He has been going through agony, and I mean agony, the severest of pain.

Bad enough to make you pray to God, eh John?

I pray, but never to a god as you mean. Certainly not. Henry Miller said that if there were a god, he would meet him calmly and spit in his face, whereas I say if there were a god I would meet him calmly and kill him.

Too true, John, too true. I'm with you there.

You do not mean that. You would ask him for a loan of a fiver.

You're probably right. Fancy a smoke?

From his jacket pocket he produced a crumpled though smokeable joint.

It's good Pakistani black, John, your favourite.

No. Not tonight. I am going home. I have talked more than enough with the dead.

I rose and headed for a bus home via the city stretched out like a great black beast splashed with the pus-yellow of streetlamps, with revealing positions to be filled, with lies, jealousy and perfidy, dribbling and licking its lips in anticipation of you . . . What . . . Wrap me in furs and feathers, videos and vermeil, for I am cold, I am anguish — the rain and voices of the dead . . . What in the name of fuck am I doing? I said inwardly. You are taking your fill of all you can, John, I replied to myself, being it without relinquishing yourself, on this occasion to save yourself from the despair creeping up on you, to soothe your grief. You are doing as you always do one way or another, whether happy, saddened or eating your dinner. You are simply exhausted. No wonder with all you are undergoing. Circumstances are making you question what you do not need to question. Go on, renew your strength. Even you need to do that once in a while. You have been enduring a hell of a lot lately. Do not worry about wee John, he will be fine. Things will work out. You know they will.

I know, I know.

At first the . . .

And I want to hear all your sinners. I want to hear you.

Does your little boy get his football shorts as dirty as this?

The police now have the right to enter your premises without a warrant.

Toots, radial, radium, J.V.C. Honda, Harry's bedroom, Honey in a Rolls Royce singing for me.

I don't feel very well.

A Whole Nut, a Fruit and Nut, a Cream Egg and a bottle of lemonade, please.

John and Henry fast asleep in their beds, Ann and I sat down to cups of tea.

It is nice to be home together, eh Kid.

Yes, said Ann, finishing her bar of chocolate, and:

What about your books? In what order do you want to send them to the publishers?

We will send Triptych first. I only have a couple of pages to write for the second panel to complete it. It won't take you as long to type that as it will to type Maybe A Boy. And anyway, Maybe A Boy is a couple of hundred thousand words long. Publishers are rarely interested in publishing a book of that length by a new author, no matter how good it is. Most of the time they do not know what good literature is and what bad literature is. Mind you, I am only talking about so-called reputable publishers, not the publishers of what are termed romantic novels — what misuse of the word romantic — they do not give a damn about literature, they are only interested in money. Sure, publishing companies have to make profits, as does any business, or fall into bankruptcy, but they do not need to publish crap to make profits. Publishers who moan about losing money on so-called good literature have only themselves to blame, for the simple reason that they are hopeless business people, they do not market books the way they should. You would think advertising does not exist the way they go on. As for bookshops, well, I suppose the book trade will remain in its pathetic state until someone with imagination, who cares about good literature, arrives and changes things, someone not afraid of putting his money where his beliefs are, namely myself. As I have said, all I need is to get my foot in the door. Triptych is really short, which is in my favour, but the content might frighten them. If we get it published, I shall be on my way. As soon as it is typed we will send it to Calder's. If they do not accept it then we shall try Faber and Faber, Canongate, just work our way through the publishers it stands a chance of being published by. Then you can type The Pink Book. I should finish The Fall Of Joseph Smith by next spring at the latest, and . . .

What about Maybe A Boy? You could send that after The Pink Book.

No. I want to keep a hold of that. Remember, of all my books — that is if Triptych is published, and being prudently pessimistic — The Fall Of

Joseph Smith will establish me. It is sure to engender a little scandal, most certainly in Glasgow. We shall just have to wait and see. Maybe Triptych will sell well. It really all depends on whoever publishes it, and reviewers. Jesus fuck, whoever publishes it should get some good publicity for me out of the facts that I lived for twenty-two of my twenty-six years in a housing-scheme in the east-end of Glasgow, left school at the age of fifteen and for the last seven years have been receiving supplementary benefit, and that the odds were against me ever writing a book, let alone brilliant books, not to mention painting. Indubitably I shall — within five to ten years of the publication of Triptych — be recognized as one of the most prodigious artists not only of the twentieth century but of all time — which is neither here nor there, for what really matters is that we can afford to feed ourselves and our children and keep a warm home. By fuck, I will succeed. Think of Raining Joy Blossoms. Magnificent prose. What do you think of the two poems I wrote for it the other day?

What can I say, they are beautiful.

By the way, I had a look at the calendar in my notebook and tallied the bills we have to pay. We are well and truly financially buggered for the next six months.

We're buggered financially until your work makes some money.

I know, but it's getting worse. We shall be a month late in paying the gas bill, and by that time the electricity bill will be due.

We'll take it as it comes.

That's all we can do.

Will you be staying up to write tonight?

Yes. I'll finish Triptych.

I'm off to bed now, all right?

Fine.

Night night.

Night night.

Coming, from tenements and plazas, I see her on a street without fear, the sails of destiny fluttering in the blue, my shirt of white foaming in impasto sundrenched sailing, shitting gold and jewels in the dust dancing her mellifluous motions, darling notions, so high in the blue cities shitting tenements and plazas, my destiny shirt fluttering in the glory fear, foaming jewels in impasto, street gold, mellifluous sails of white sundrenched dancing, coming in my shirt motions, sailing her glory, destiny notions — get the picture swelling — and you too can be engorged and hirsute and aching exquisitely.

JOHN MacCOLL

Dying For It

The salmon, when he ejaculates, sends
A stream of hot sperm through the water.
Open-mouthed they spawn together,
Male and female. No shyness there —
He doesn't feel she smirks at his desire.
He quivers; his tail flicks,
And in that spurt his power's all expended
(After so many roaring battles
With cliffs of water).

At fifteen I stood almost stock still
(Just a little tremble) in a cruel school passageway,
While she passed by, oblivious.
One with chestnut hair and fondant skin,
Who left a spice of scent behind to tickle in my heart.
My body all one gulp
I cast my eyes round desperately
And tried to hide my unappealingness:
Her breasts and moister parts
Stood fierce in my imagination
With all the shocking force
Of a plunge into wild water.

She wouldn't feel my heated stream
(Talking of bigger boys)
Nor know that all last night I'd been
Johnny Weismuller,
Thrashing through tropical torrents —
One virile squib of muscles;
Tossing crocodiles aside
To rescue her, my languid and
Extraordinarily grateful island queen.

In St Mary's, Haddington

Miracles were said to happen in these parts.
I wondered at the chapel within the church,
One tradition guarding another, a sermon in stone and wood.

The wind flourished in the ancient town, later in the year
Than when a Pope walked barefoot through the frost to seek a cure
Where a crucifix maimed a thief, and a woman was made well again.

Plain, leaded glass filled a huge window, in which
Trees shimmered and strained, becoming shadows, changing, becoming,
While the prayers rose, waterfalls of leaves of light.

Carefully we began the hymn, rinsing the stone-ribbed vaults
With our voices. I hoped for little,
Certainly not miracles, but the gestures of a priest arrested me,

His hands falling like leaves, touched his heart, flamed briefly
In his fingers. Transfixed they followed him, the deaf and dumb
Singing with their arms like sea anemones.

Jan De Cock: Adoration Of The Shepherds

This detail from a Dutch nativity
(Sixteenth century) just does not inspire in me
A holy Christmas peace.
I'm quite disappointed.

It's full of frustrating detail.
One shepherd shows amazement, yes
(The other's hat brim cancels out his eyes),
But you can see he's most amazed about
That stagey angel, garlanded and peach,
With those improbable wings;
Or the two unwelcome cherubs, floating
With a length of inexplicable gauze.

An ox and ass hunch at the back
Like pantomime dependables
Filling in the bit between the Virgin
And a soaring marble pillar
(Behind there is this grand recessive building,
Inner archways showing off perspective
And the use of light).
The Virgin looks unhappy
And seems to ask the woman bent above the child
To take away her awful face.
Jesus, like an unbaked loaf
Is horizontal, waving fat white legs.

Perhaps the artist's age expected
Themes, motifs, and evidence
Of traditions understood:
The whole a sort of reference work —
No effort made to get emotion over
(And after all, there could be no assurance
Of success in that).

The awe we feel at Christmas
Does not come from being thus reminded of
Those luminous archetypes, representing
The heaven-to-earthly chain,

But from the fact
That those first shepherds also are reborn
Year after year, in us;
Standing in stupidity
With all our recognition quite unmade,
And desperate for only this: that we be reconciled
Before the Word which speaks into the dark,
This tiny child.

Autumn Through

Last year and the year before taunt me
Walking through the park. The trees have made that show again
Of shape and colour so powerfully combined
I wonder it should shock so much each time.

I have failed before to describe
This briefest of relationships. She's gone
Before I've grown accustomed to a ticklish tenderness.
Her bedroom now bare-boarded, all bills paid.

Of course there is a moral in it.
I recognise the feeling not of losing the chance
But of having lost it.

And yet this helplessness is true, and will be
No less true for recognition. We know how things will end
And can't adjust, but coming into money simply spend.

KEN CAMPBELL

Growing Up

Some kids came to my door
Offering a starling with a broken wing:
"Can you fix it?" they asked.

I said, "They die of fright,
But leave it with me;
I'll see it doesn't suffer."

They chose to put it in a box
with some straw and to feed it,
so I lent them an eye-dropper.

Later on they told me
The starling had escaped under a hedge.
They don't bring their lame ducks here any more.

ELIZABETH BURNS

Chagall's Angel

Chagall's angel
has a violin painted
inside it.

Ally learned
to play poker, won
a hundred pounds
and with her winnings
bought a miniature
violin
for when Charlie
was older.
But Charlie lives
with his father
and once every
three weeks is not enough
to be with her child
or to teach him to play
the violin.

Inside Ally there is a violin
shaped hollow.

KATHERINE WHITE

Nightmares

Nightmares are different now.
How blissful, once, to turn
Into the striped back, warm and strong,
And drift into sheltered sleep,
Gently rocked by gentle breathing,
As a boat leans against the harbour wall,
Home from the terrifying sea
And lulled by the lapping tide.

Nightmares are different now.
Nightmares are nightmares now.

JOHN BREWSTER

Nuggets

To Arthur Rimbaud

Ask him. He's old enough to remember.

Pearl butterflies? O they would haunt
her towelled up hair and clasps or clips
or was it clinging pins spining her neck
to make a tongue play bagatelle?

You remember the old ground?

Quilted satin and the fragrance of her
hands.
The grass would green my elbows
but not her shoulder blades.

The old mine?

Now all mine. Seams are dreams
that men seam no more.

Or seem no more?

I've seen them all
in the seamlands of her stockings.
After the goldrush her partings
spat black rubies.

I've asked him. And?
He's old enough to remember.

Venus Flytrap

A hairy chap
in open flap

the silent lap
of rising sap

a dunce's cap
in folds unwrap

the hidden map
of single clap

a moment's nap
in throaty gap

the hairy bob of talcumed arse
initiates the fragrant farce

tap tap tap
snap snap snap

to Apollinaire.

ROBERT JOHNSTONE

Unititled

I would gladly throw the sea off the edge of the world for you,
or send the sun to the other end of the universe
at your tiny command,
or bring the sky down to kiss your brow
or banish the wind from here forever.
Yes, and I would petrify running water
and turn comets into chasing their tails,
just to see you once again.

If you asked the mountains politely,
then they'd surely move aside,
or you could send all the rivers back from whence they came
or charm the night into day.
And I'd carry a cupful of stars
and diamonds that couldn't live with you;
and birds would be struck dumb
and angels would quit heaven.

Leaves would fall passionately from trees
whenever they see you approach
and my blood would retreat.
Don't you know your smile could melt the very poles.
And that I would laugh like Daniel, if left in a den of lions.

(And if things turn out alright, I'll meet you on the moon tonight).

JANE STRUTH

Whooping Cough

It's a virus he said
as they doubled up
coughing and choked
phlegm dribbling darkly
on to his white antiseptic floor

He handed her a prescription
a blank panacea to make
the well feel better
but his indifferent eyes
held no hope

For days and endless nights
their small bodies
wracked and heaved
jerking on an invisible string
clinging for comfort

As they slid into an uneasy sleep
she did not think of the
swollen bellied children
staring hungrily at an empty camera
or the battered babies
shut in drawers

JOHN MORRISON

Woodhall

It was day of summer —
In early April.
Yellow coltsfoot and celandine
Were fully out;
A shepherd called to his ewes,
And rooks tumbled in the sky.
Were these the same serious birds
That stumped the fields?

Suddenly, as if by signal,
They all flew up, black flecks on blue,
Calling, swooping, playing —
A mass courtship,
Curtain raiser to summer.

The Landlady

The landlady sits
In her ladder back chair,
Orange headscarf glowing;
She is mistress
Of cupboard and stair,
Queen of the teapot
And the pouring.

O pearl white cups
And blue-black pot
And rainbow jug gleaming,
O quiet old face
Rough modelled by age,
Stained by the years
And sorrowing.

How grey is that face
In a dull day light
With cool shadows falling;
How bright in the sun
Are its mellow tints —
Youth's colours broken
Yet still glowing.

ISHBEL GRAY

Ordinary Miracles

You could have
peeled away
all that I am
layer by layer
flesh over flesh
crushed me from within
shaken every cell loose
and tossed them out
like yesterday's garbage
yet you held on and waited
for an ordinary miracle —
like me loving you.

Black & White

Wait
let me turn out
the light and rest
for a while
in the dark.
I'll stay inside
my anger and you
can lick your lips
all you like
but don't ask

for more.
because I'm tired of
evenings like this.
My head aches with
your crossword puzzle
conversations and draughty
kisses and anyway
who needs a rule
book to play
solitaire?

GAIL McGARVA

Night Out

You can come and sit beside me,
I'm really not so shy,
I've been staring at you all night,
Admiring your tie.

Would I like a drink? Oh, thank you,
A lager'll do just fine;
Oh, wait a minute, Rodney,
With just a drop of lime.

Would I like to dance? Oh, thank you,
The music suits me fine.
You seem to have good rhythm,
For your beat's as good as mine.

You'll walk me home; oh, thank you,
I've had a real good night.
I'll go and get my coat, dear.
I liked his tie all right.

PHILIP McGRADE

First Impressions

His father decided to go back home for the all Ireland final and Paul was delighted to be told that he was to go with him. He was almost four.

They took the night boat over and he asked if the black children he saw on the same crossing were black babies. His brother was always asking for black baby money at lunch time before he went back to school. As he was later to learn, the black baby scheme worked in such a way that when you contributed enough money you were given a sheet with a photo of a grinning black child on the one side and a space on the other in which you got to choose a name for a black baby. He took a perverse pleasure in giving them names which he thought were immensely funny, like Horace or Wilhemina. He began to have his doubts about the whole operation when he later noticed that other people were getting to re-name his black babies. He worried that one day they might band together, trace him and come seeking bloody revenge for their ridiculous names, like in 'A Boy Named Sue'.

They hitched all the way to Dublin and at one stage even got a lift in the back of a Land Rover. He noisily sucked on the dregs of his Coca Cola bottle through the narrow, flattened end of a paper straw as they bumped along the road. This was the life.

Everyone in Ireland gave him two bob. His father insisted that they shouldn't, then when they did he took the money off him, telling him that he would keep it for him, as he would need money when he was getting married.

His father took him to the post office in O'Connel street where the Easter rising had begun. At that time, a corner of it had been left intact as a sort of shrine to the nationalist martyrs. There were rosary beads lying on a window sill and there was a big painting on one wall. His father had him put his four year old fingers into one of the bullet holes in the walls, like Jesus made Thomas do, as if to prove that they had indeed risen. He doubted no more.

This was one part of who he was, like the rowdy records whose covers had wooden boxes, their lids slightly open, revealing rows of long gleaming bullets. On top of the tricolour which was draped across them lay a luger pistol. They had names like 'Irish Songs of Freedom Volume 9'.

One of the records had a dark haired man with a thick drooping moustache and a white shirt on. He was strapped to an old fashioned wooden chair by two or three heavy leather belts, because he could not sit up on his own. Standing opposite him was a firing squad poised to shoot. There were two songs about him, 'His Name Was Connolly' and 'They Murdered James Connolly'.

They were the English. He had once tried unsuccessfully to memorise a poem called 'Who is Ireland's Enemy?'. It was a full list of the names of the countries who weren't 'Ireland's Enemies', and blamed England for poisoned kings and priests who had their heads spiked on fences.

His favorite of all the records was one entitled 'Up went Nelson!' This was a celebration in song of the dynamiting of Nelson's Column in O'Connel Street.

At the start the singers shouted "Up Went Nelson!" and then there was this massive explosion followed by an introductory flourish on the accordion. He was not allowed to have it on at full blast and when the troubles started the records disappeared.

When the queen came on the telly, his father would say "Look out, shit the bed!" On occasion he would qualify this by stating "She should be summonsed for being bad looking." The queen was herself English and it was an almost pavlovian reaction for them to rush towards the telly to switch it off when it started to blare out the short drum roll which was a preamble to the national anthem. At the football, the Celtic fans would sing the Irish national anthem, or at least that part of the first verse that they were confident of. It began 'Soldiers are we' and they all added the afterthought 'some are big!'

His father's family's farm was in the North and at midday they arrived at a long, winding path with several cattle fences which they had to stop and open and close behind them.

His Uncle Paddy was there to meet them off the bus from Dublin and he was a slim dark giant who spoke like Paul's father and winked at him. Paul wondered why they all did that and sensed that he might give him some money. He hoped that it would be when his father was not there.

His granny had not been feeling well, nothing serious but she was in bed. There were hens clucking about all over the place, all walking that funny way they do, and an old black and white dog who looked like Lassie's uncle. The dog loved being clapped and seemed to smile when Paul smoothed his hand along his muzzle.

The house was a low white-washed building with half doors so you could watch the cows stomping past at milking time, shitting everywhere, without any real danger of them biting you.

It was a house which was full of wonders. Giants with flat caps who chuckled every time he spoke whether it was meant to be funny or not.

There was a big turf fire in the room where they all sat. The flames crackled and licked at the charred backside of a big black witches' cauldron where they boiled the sour potatoes he pretended to eat but slipped to the dog.

They put their coats in the ornaments room which was reserved for entertaining visiting dignitaries such as Yankee cousins or the parish priest.

The whole house had a funny home-made feel about it, the stairs were wonky and so high that he had to goose step up them.

The beds his uncles slept in were like hospital beds. Under one of them a light blue plastic potty was visible through the slightly open door as they passed.

The woman he had been told was his granny lay on her back with her head turned towards them. Her dark curly hair stood out against the washed out yellow of the long thin bolster.

He offered her some jelly beans after being introduced. As he held them out to her nestled in a wrinkled white paper poke, they looked beautiful, all different colours, bright red and orange and green and blue and yellow, and all the same shape.

Whenever he had a quarter of them, he would eat the first few one at a time varying the colours in an attempt to work out if they all just tasted the same. He would soon tire of this and try to see how many he could cram into his mouth at one go, almost choking on the rich, syrupy saliva that filled his mouth.

He was relieved when she said no to his sweets and delighted when she offered him a drink of Lucozade. The bottle stood on the chest of drawers next to her bed. The midday sun poured in through the window lightening the yellow hue of the drink and illuminating the motes of dust which danced in this old people's room in a home-made house in another country. He was only given it at home when he was sick and the yellow sellophane crinkled and the liquid fizzed and foamed as his dad poured it into a white cup from a flask.

They went back downstairs and his attention was drawn away from the two flies who were dive bombing one another around the gas lamp to the hypnotic effect of the dancing flames of the turf fire. His father switched on the all too familiar sound of Radio Athlone. He always had it on at home.

They would be sitting in their damp tenement flat in Glasgow, when this broad shrill Dublin accent would proclaim excitedly 'Whether your sheep have worms or your corn is being attacked by slugs, Kilemrite has the solution'. To the tune of 'Oh, When the Saints' an army of gleeful Irish baritones would belt out,

'Oh when the slugs, make your corn slim,
Or when the worms make your sheep thin,
Kilemrite has all the answers,
So buy it now — it's in a tin!'

Uncle Paddy took a tray up to granny then came back down with it.

It was strange, all these big men with their caps and their pipes and their radio accents, tip-toeing round each other for the small woman who lay upstairs in bed.

She had died while he was downstairs looking at the flies and the flames. She had prayed to Our Lady that she would see Paul's father before she died and she said that the Virgin had never let her down.

There was a funeral and more people gave him money.

Afterwards they were driven back to the farm and he was sent into the ornament room with the coats. Above the empty fireplace hung the familiar painting of the Sacred Heart. The lack of definition in the eyes meant that it always seemed to be watching you, following you round the room, checking you were keeping the commandments, like God himself.

There was a plastic dome with the houses of parliament inside, the whole thing was full of water and it said on it 'A souvenir of London'. The sky behind parliament was a permanent and unconvincing blue and when you shook it the whole thing would suddenly become drenched in a cloud of silver snow.

He shook it up and down vigorously and watched the speckles drift in slow motion to the ground.

The water didn't go right up to the top and he noticed it was leaking a bit. He put it down and came out of the room in case he got the blame for breaking it.

SUSAN GOODSHIP

The Swing In The Park

The park is deserted although the sun is shining and a few cotton wool clouds flirt with the blue sky. Someone has dropped a bright plastic toy truck; swings hang forlornly from the crossbar; green painted seats wait for customers. The park is — not quite deserted after all. There is a figure. Just one.

Crouching on the grass. A young child in a print dress. A white nub of activity in the surrounding green. Fingers pluck daisies, white and as easy to touch as stars in the sky for Maisy the dreamer. Four-leafed clovers are harder to find. Finger tips touch mossy cushions, weave through grass stalks, tough and tall. She smells the earth, the rising sap; she is watching ants climbing through jungles, forests, untouched places.

'Down the garden where nobody knows, where the grass is so long that it tickles your toes'. She is singing, seeing the green spreading fairy rings, the dancing till day break. She is running, then stops to stoop, looking for the tell tale tracks, the flat imprint of fairy feet. Long flaxen hair streams down onto the grass. She is thinking small — ant small — sees the world that lives on in dance-song while she and giants sleep. Moist clover leaf umbrellas struggle with weighted dew-drops.

'Where they go to nobody knows', but she can guess. Gone to drive the clouds — to paint the rainbows — to ride those chariots around the class room walls. Some of the fairy folk are in the woods. She can see the mists of the dance, the retreating flags and banners. She can hear the music there, still echoing in the cathedral of trees. But, there are also bad things; faces and claws that live in the dark. She knows there are wolves in the wood. Better stay here on the grass, better not go too near the trees, just in case. She tries not to think of the wolves but of a dancing fairy in the sun. Red sandled feet pirouetting. A swirl of white. Translucent vortex as pale and delicate as a butterfly.

Trees hide wolves and men on the run.

"I think we're safe here". He lies horizontal on a branch of the giant oak; peers through leaf-sprayed spaces, watching the little girl far away on the open stretch of grass. A slow smile as the child comes closer, disappointment as she twirls away again. Alex is hot. His shirt sticks to his back; his collar hanging heavy around his neck; streaks of grime smear his forehead. Breathing is fast and shallow. "We can easily see when someone comes", his voice is gruff and stilted. A face peers through the leaves on the opposite branch.

"If the worst comes to the worst we can always . . . " Tom pats his hip pocket, smiles grimly. He looks across to the other branch, to the prone form among the sprouting twigs. Alex's eyes narrow, he turns his head suddenly, alive to every crackle, every whisper in the wood. He is satisfied. He shifts his position, is trying to ignore his cut elbow, the gnaw in his stomach. "If there's anything left I can see a place in the bushes where we can eat". Tom looks anxiously at Alex. Alex is two years older, the natural leader. Responsibility for Tom is easy, Tom is fleet of foot, never failing in his support. Tom springs from the branch, his shirt loose and flapping into the thick carpet of soggy leaves with the ease and grace of a flying squirrel. Earth-encrusted finger nails pick at the knotted plastic bag at the base of the tree. Thin plastic splits. Bread, apples, chocolate are thrust back again.

A furtive check. His brown eyes take in the silences, the empty places. "Come on Alex, no one about". Alex climbs down the massive trunk slowly, trying not to nurse his arm. He is running. Attacking the plastic bag. Devouring the food. Apples are eaten more slowly. The crunch as their teeth incise the firm apple flesh is loud, too loud. They are looking round in between bites. Tom spits out the apple stalk and turns over on his stomach, resting on his elbows. He is picking up a snail from among the leaves, is attracted by the ringed, glossy shell, he is watching the slimy snail foot slowly slipping back inside. He is wondering how hungry he would have to be to eat it. "How long do you think it will be?" He looks sideways at Alex for the answer, for the next part of the plan.

"We'll lay low today, move on tonight". The reply is slow, decisive. "We'll have to catch something to eat — combat the cold — keep our minds active". Tom looks into the blue eyes admiring the clear thinking yet he is wondering at the doubt that flickers there. But Alex springs to his feet. The look has gone. A rabbit meanders around the bushes. It hops, is stopping to nibble the young green blades spiking through the leaves like green tentative enquiries in case the season is wrong. "Quick". Alex snatches his knife but the rabbit is off, curving round the oaks, while the knife flies — out of the trees — across the grass.

Meggan opens the garden gate and steps into the park. A spaniel pulls at the lead that knots her fingers and winds around her. She is closing the gate, is disentangling the dog, is walking across the grass. It is early in the year, in the spring of her life. Flaxen hair, a bounce in her stride. Reeds bristle around the pond in the sudden breeze, rustle like taffeta. She is turning her face to the thin sun; to spider threads floating in the air, shining gossamer, falling to the grass. A flowering cherry blossoms over a garden fence, petals are breaking on the rough brown wood; but she is stopping to pick a daisy, to feel the fleshy stem, to marvel at the pink tipped perfection of the petals — delicate as skin. The swing in the distance creaks and begins to move, the green seat grating and grating backwards and forwards, backwards and . . . a chill catches her. She is shaking her head trying to toss away the unease that is falling around her shoulders, soft as a sigh. The spaniel is sniffing the air, is tugging at the lead. Guard hairs are rising on his back. Meggan is caught off balance, is pulled along. She must be walking too slowly, she knows the pulse of life is quick and fast. Away with her butterfly dreams, her morbid fancies. She regains control of the dog. She is stopping to pull the dog away from a torn, stained scrap of cotton print no longer recognisable. The spaniel does not want to come but she must find her daughter. She will be able to see her once past the next huddle of trees. Meggan picks up Maisy's plastic toy truck, she is hurrying. Maisy must be on one of the swings. Meggan thinks of the golden headed innocence riding through arcs of spring sunshine. The dog whines. Meggan begins to run.

MORELLE SMITH

Butterfly

I had no idea where it came from or how long it had been there. All the other butterflies that had settled into hibernation in mid-August had woken up and flown away after I got back and the autumn got warmer and I lit fires in the living-room and opened the windows and watched them flying out, one by one into the September sunshine.

There were about a dozen of them, all clustered together in the corners where the walls join the ceiling. They disturbed me in their stillness and the way they had grouped together and the fact that they were there at all in my house. They reminded me that since I had not shut them in when I left, there had been other people there while I was away, and I did not like the motionless butterflies with their dark folded wings, I did not like what they had left behind and even though the butterflies were not dead they looked as good as dead, and if they did not wake up soon, they would be there the whole winter — six or seven months until the spring.

When I was changing the sheets and pillowcases on my bed, I found a tangle of long fair hairs under one of the pillows as if someone had stuck them there after brushing their hair. They had not been there when I left and Tim's hair was short and dark. I cleared them away and pretended to forget about them, pretended not to care that he had come to my house while I was away, which I had expected , because I had told him that he could, but I had not expected him to come with a girl. It was like him thumbing his nose at me; anything you can do, I can do too, it seemed to say.

After changing the sheets, I cleaned up the whole house, trying to exorcise their presence, determined not to bother, not to care, he was free to do as he wanted, just as I was. Then there was the message written on the kitchen window:

'I love the rain when it falls on your hair'.

Don't bother, don't bother, I told myself. But I did. For what did that make of all the things he had said to me? Lies? What hurt most was the poetic tenderness of the message. It was not so much that I was jealous of this unknown girl, but of her ability to arouse in him a sense of poetry I had not been capable of touching, I was jealous of the feelings that they must have felt, I was jealous of the intimate tenderness of all lovers, because I was not one of them. I seemed to have forgotten that I had been, just a few months ago. Or perhaps I had not forgotten completely enough. I washed the kitchen windows.

Then it got warmer. At first, I had resigned myself to an early winter. It did not really seem odd that I should have come so quickly from ninety degree temperatures into autumn weather with that unmistakable chill in the air, even when the sun can still be warm on your face while the wind blows the cold air through your clothes. The wind ferrets out your areas of vulnerability, so recently exposed to summer sun. Cold is never so felt it seems, as in autumn. By the time winter comes you accept it and are prepared for it, but autumn winds come when you are still refusing to accept the possibility that summer is slipping downwards, into its evening.

Just before I left Baltimore I had taken a shower and washed my hair and the warm air had dried it by the time we got to the bus stop where I would catch the bus to take me to the airport. For the first time since I had come there I put on the clothes I wore when I arrived, which had been far too hot to wear since then — a long-sleeved shirt, my jeans and desert boots. I could feel my old familiar persona coming back to me. I was impatient to leave. Impatient to be me again. But if I had not been myself then who had I been? The thought caused an eddy of darkness to circle in me, like the smooth surface of a weir glinting in sunshine. Nothing, it seemed, could be as dark as sunshine. Nothing but sunshine could hide so much. My thoughts were confusing me. If I had not been myself in Baltimore, then who had I been?

I remembered a dream I had had, shortly before I went there. I was putting on a play, along with four other people, all women. One of them was lost, she had disappeared and some people were concerned for her safety. I was not worried because I felt sure she would be safe, and would return. The play could not be performed until the lost one had returned. When she did come back, we embraced and there was great warmth and love among us all.

The play was simply a display of the cross formation, the four of them around me, the four arms of the cross, and me in the middle. I, the one in the middle, was the one who wept, and had to return to hell. The director said we would do that next time. This time, we had all come together to form a whole. Next time, we would enact my return to hell.

I arrived in Baltimore in the evening and the next day we went to a second-hand clothes shop to get me some new clothes, for none of mine were suitable for these temperatures. Guido insisted I get shorts and a sleeveless shirt or vest. While we were in the shop someone recognized me.

I don't mean me, Martha Blair, because I did not know anyone in Baltimore apart from Guido. But she recognized something in me, or someone. And this could be an important clue, because I was still wearing my own clothes then — I know that I started to become someone else when I started wearing different clothes and started to become myself again when I put my old clothes back on.

The woman in the shop must have been watching me as I looked through the clothes.

"Have you been to India?" she asked.

At first, I did not realise she was addressing me. When I did, and replied that I had, I asked her how she knew.

"Is it because . . . "

I gestured to my clothes, because I happened to be wearing an Indian cotton shirt, but she did not give me time to finish the sentence.

"Oh no", she said, "lots of people wear Indian clothes, it's just something in your vibe".

And she smiled one of those special smiles, inscrutable I think they're called, that imply a wealth of secret inner knowledge which cannot be imparted in words. Still, she had told me quite a lot. What she recognized was something that went deeper than my clothes. Something underlying the facade of personal identity.

I wore my shorts and sleeveless shirt, adjusted to the humid temperatures, took three cold showers a day, morning, evening and in the middle of the night when I invariably woke up because of the heat, sweated profusely, and felt an indefinable anxiety build up inside me.

It came to a head one night, with police sirens in my dream and still sounding outside when I woke up. This person who I had become, or who I was masquerading as, came to an untimely end. She was brutally murdered in her bed by an escaped criminal whom the police were chasing. The next morning I felt more like myself again. Whose terror was it I felt, whose death did I feel approaching? Was this a memory of soul, from some previous existence? Was it something that had still to happen, in the future? Who in hell had I been in those weeks in Baltimore? Which reminds me of something. Hell, and my fated return. Was that what it had been — my promised return to hell?

I left a few days later and came back here to my house, to dirty sheets on the bed, a scrawled message on the window and a host of dark butterflies. I washed the sheets and window and tried not to harbour dark thoughts. When the weather got warmer, I let out the butterflies. They flew out into the sunlight like dreams made conscious or feelings released from imprisonment.

That was four months ago. It is December now, the heart of winter, just past the solstice. And I see that one butterfly did not leave in the summer, because it is moving, very slowly, up the wall. One of its wings is damaged, there is a piece of it missing. It must have been tempted out by the warmth of the fire. I find its damaged wing so repellent, its pain and effort so manifest, that I want to kill it, to end it now. But I cannot.

As the butterfly heads along the mantelpiece I know what is going to happen. And at the same time I know I cannot stop it happening. I have to sit and watch it carefully, inch by inch as it drags its way along the mantelpiece then falls off into the fireplace. I have some logs propped up against the fire grate. It is heading for the warmth.

It crawls slowly up one of the logs stacked against the fire grate. One wing whole, the other missing a bit, the red and black pattern spoiled. Mouse-nibbled, cat-chewed, who knows? It's just a body, just a form, this butterfly identity. Lame insect, heading for the warmth. Crawled out from some dark corner I had overlooked. Wings in pieces. Cannot fly.

Just a body, just an identity, but it's me, this butterfly. And just the slightest noise as it launches itself from the top of the log into the flames. Perhaps there was no noise at all, I only thought I heard something. Or maybe it was drowned by what I felt. The kind of shock you get when you touch something hot and draw your fingers back at lightning speed.

So what price identity? Not in this pain, this shock, this absence of blisters. Not in this memory, because it is hardly mine. Not in Guido, beginning to make claims, which was not how it started. It never is. Not in Tim, who brings some new lover to my house while I'm away. Perhaps only the burning tells us who we are. Hell tries to tempt us to believe in death, but I had a ticket that took me both ways, aller et retour. We did not form the cross for that, to make the trip to hell. That was just one of the by-products, you might say. A necessary condition. Perhaps we need the burning to tell us who we are. To engender faith, not in the transience of tattered wings and unfaithful lovers, but in what the cross of five-in-one represents.

The last trace of Tim's visit with his new lover has been burnt. But my thoughts are confusing me again. It has something to do with memory. Not of particular places or events, but of who we were before we started to remember things and who we still are and will always be.

Like the butterfly I have no memory of being a caterpillar and I too, am drawn to the fire. To others it might look like death, but how else can I remember except by shedding these personae, these disposable forms, old shells, old prisons, layers of forms peeled off like skins until the heart of the matter is revealed, the source of memory and its content too.

But of course! When you really know, then you become what it is you know; known and knower become one. Butterfly and I are passing through the flames in the process of becoming fire.

The hardest one to love is your enemy. Hardest to see yourself in him, know him to be a part of you. And enemies have a way of masquerading as lovers. But when you can love even the one who hurts you, who does you violence — perhaps then the cross has served its purpose and neither butterfly nor identity has died in vain.

Tim appeared the next day, with his usual uncanny sense of timing. His new girl had gone back to Oklahoma or Ohio or wherever it was she came from. It turned out it wasn't him who wrote the message on my window, but her. Whoever it was, it hardly matters now.

"How was your trip to Baltimore?" he asked.

"Oh." I grimaced. "Something tried to eat me, but I got away."

"How did you do that?"

"I left it my clothes, then ran away before it found out I'd tricked it."

"It's fairly taken the skin off you there."

"What?" I said.

He pointed to my arm which was rubbed raw by a piece of wood I had been sawing earlier that day.

"Oh that," I said. "I thought you meant the beast."

"What beast?"

"The one I was talking about. Don't you ever listen to me?"

"Come here," he said.

Tim's sense of timing had to do with the fact that I had to forget about him almost completely, before he appeared again. I had to give up hope, belief, even memory of him. And this was perhaps no bad thing, since my memories were invariably tinged with something unpleasant, something best forgotten anyway. But in the process of burying the unwelcome feelings, I tended to push everything underground. So it was always a surprise to see him, like seeing someone come back from the dead. It takes time to realise that however many images get broken, the real person is still living and in fact emerges more clearly with each successive broken image. And an even longer time maybe, to know that what gets buried has got to be uncovered sometime, someday. You could even say that hell is what we carry round with us because we cannot face it or uncover it, it is too unpleasant, too upsetting, too distant from our ideal. So instead, we form smooth surfaces, bounce images off each other, and call it relating. The beginning of the end of hell is the process of uncovering the lid, releasing these demons and these fallen angels. Which is what they want. That's what I think anyway. Some of them don't look so pretty though. They can give you quite a turn.

The winter sky is a threadbare veil, with points of light showing through all the holes and darns in the thinning fabric.

"I wonder which one you came from," I said to Tim as we sat in the firelight, looking out on the stars.

"Whichever one is closest to yours," he said.

SHEILA LEWIS

Mulgrew's View

Elizabeth hadn't given much thought to the practical aspect of day-to-day living in Peter's house when she moved in with him, but she did find it difficult coming to terms with the square, squat bungalow. She hated it and Peter didn't seem to like it much but he told her they weren't going to move, listing all sorts of boring reasons like mortgages, sound financial assets and legal moving fees.

He told her she was free to make any interior alterations that she fancied. Unspoken was the acknowledgement that the existing decorations were all the choice of his wife who'd walked out on him a few years ago.

Elizabeth had no intention of competing with anyone and so had never asked him about her. It wasn't difficult to form her own opinions about her personality, if that term could be applied to a person who appeared to be obsessed with angles and squares and rectangles.

The unrelieved straight walled boxes which passed for rooms in the house were uniformly furnished with oblong sofas, square boxy chairs and hexagonal coffee tables. The carpets had diamond patterns, the curtains hung in conformity with their striped designs and many a good evening could have been spent playing noughts and crosses on the checked cushion covers.

Elizabeth ripped out the lot. Nothing could be done about the rectangular structure of the rooms but a curved sofa and club armchairs with the odd misshapen bean bag did eradicate some of the mathematical precision from the rooms.

The garden was her next challenge, though this began more as a need for penetration and discovery than any radical new design. It was a wilderness.

Some tired fruit trees staggered up beyond the garage, anonymous bushes spread and suckered in all directions, a few flowers nodded choking heads.

Peter told her to get some help for the heavy labouring, as he was pretty useless out of doors. A spot of digging now and then, the odd Sunday waltz with a flymo had always been his stretch.

When the worst of the tangle had been removed Elizabeth wasn't in the least surprised to find the remains of rectangular flower beds. How on earth had Peter lived with this woman for eight years?

A more pleasant discovery was a seven-foot high brick wall which bounded the rear of the garden. Since this had a south-facing aspect, she romantically visualized it adorned with wistaria, clematis and magnolia. This garden was going to be a testament to her warm, loving, creative personality. Next summer would see its flowering, now in late autumn she planted some evergreens to give colour over the winter.

There was a large house behind the bungalow, an ugly Victorian villa, its red brick stained with the very industrialisation soot which provided the money to build it. The lower half was obscured by the garden's brick wall, but the upper windows were clearly visible and someone sat at one of those every day, watching Elizabeth. Someone old, someone housebound, surmised Elizabeth, who would probably find great interest in the new garden as the year progressed.

While winter kept them all in hibernation, she planned. Soon every square room in the squat house was littered with drawings. The garden was taking shape, on paper at least. Peter had given her a free hand in all but one aspect. Outside the kitchen door a flagged path ran straight as a Roman road to the rear wall. He was very proud of the fact that he'd laid this path himself and wanted it left as evidence of his personal contribution to the garden.

It didn't fit in with Elizabeth's plans at all. She wanted to be totally rid of anything regimented, anything that bore even an echo of his wife's personality. Her ideal was clumps of flowers, no straight borders of lobelia and alyssium, but drifts of daffodils, hillocks of hydrangea and riots of roses. For days she walked up and down the flagged path trying to figure a way to incorporate it into her free-form plan. Her concentration was affected by the ever-present watcher in the Victorian villa.

She complained to Peter: "That person is always there, I'm beginning to find it a bit creepy. Why watch all the time, especially when there's nothing to see yet?"

"It's only old Mulgrew. Active chap in his time, services or something, can't quite remember. He's been sitting at the window for years now, nothing else to do. You're probably livening things up for him," he said.

She still found the watching presence an irritation though. One day she ventured a wave; there was no response. Not until the day the flagged path was lifted.

She organised it when Peter was on a business trip to Brussels, omitting to tell him beforehand. She was quite prepared to sustain his anger when he found out. What had been intended as a manifestation of her personality now had become something of an obsession. The garden had to be perfect, a necessary antidote to the bungalow from which she felt she'd never quite eradicated his wife's influence. Not that she pointed this out to Peter. He still never spoke of his wife, or the reasons for their split. And she never asked, but somehow the house would not let her forget.

She also wanted to show Mulgrew that she was capable of creating something wonderful.

She blurted out her confession as soon as Peter stepped in the door.

"I've put the flags alongside the garage temporarily and if you're terribly upset I'll have them laid again, but meantime look at all the shrubs and bulbs I've planted over the whole area. And guess what," she rushed on. "Mulgrew actually waved to me today!"

Peter went to the kitchen window and for a moment she thought he was going to lose his temper, but then he shrugged and commented that if both she and Mulgrew were happy without the path, he would let it rest.

From then on Elizabeth daily encouraged her tentative shoots, not quite keeping a lone vigil, because Mulgrew was always at his window, watching and waiting. At least Elizabeth assumed he was waiting for spring too; why else would he watch every day?

Soon the garden began to take on colour with the appearance of primroses, crocus, the promised daphne and an early revived rhododendron. The garden looked good from ground level but she was curious to see it from another angle — for example, from Mulgrew's elevated view. On impulse she gathered some of her daffodils and trudged round the block to his house. The door was opened by a woman in blue overalls.

"I'm just the home help, dear, I'll take the flowers but I doubt if he'll see you; sees nobody."

"Tell him I'm the lady with the garden and I'd like to know what he thinks of it now," Elizabeth said.

The home help returned a few moments later, giving an apologetic shrug.

"He says thanks for the flowers and it's too early to give an opinion," she said.

For a day or two Elizabeth ignored Mulgrew such was her disappointment not only at his comment but also at being denied an aerial view of her garden.

But that irritation was soon superseded by a nagging worry. Although the greater part of the garden was now alive with flowering bulbs and shrubs, there was an irregular area, dead centre of the garden in fact, which was resisting all her attempts at cultivation. None of her autumn plantings had survived and replacements were still bare of shoots. She dug everything out, sowed fertilizer and re-planted. Nothing happened. Surveying the bare patch one morning from her kitchen window, she realised it had previously been part of the straight flagged path. Perhaps some chemical substance from the flags had permeated the earth. She didn't know if this kind of thing was possible, but what other explanation could there be?

She felt the failure keenly, even though she was surrounded by a bounty of fertility. Peter was sympathetic. He suggested that she let the area lie fallow for a year, but she couldn't bear that. The patch haunted her; there seemed no earthly reason for it. She felt, a little irrationally, that she ought to apologise to Mulgrew. She cut some of her best roses and signalled to the watcher that she was coming to visit him.

This time the home help was impressed.

"You're to go right up today," she said.

So eager was she to stand at Mulgrew's window, that Elizabeth paid little attention to the house as she sped through a square, gloomy hall and up a wide staircase, carpeted only with a Turkey red runner. She did notice though that the house was chilly, lacking any warmth, even though it was now early June.

The winged armchair couldn't disguise the fact that Mulgrew was a big man. Or had been. His shoulders were broad and heavy and his lambswool pullover couldn't hide the muscular arms. A rug covered his legs which she surmised from their immobility was the reason for his imprisonment in the house. He was wearing a tie which she presumed was a regimental one. His face would seem to confirm this. He had a good head, but his expression was severe and cold. A man whose creed was authority and discipline.

He didn't reply to her greeting so she quickly moved to the window. The garden looked magnificent from the elevation. Her careful planning of graduated shrubs, balanced for height and colour and spread, was perfect. The round pond glistened in the sunlight, the quick orange flash of a fish momentarily illuminated in the rays. Birds darted from bush to bush, butterflies had found an Eden. Her garden was alive! She new a moment of pure, but brief, content.

She turned to him in triumph: "I'm so glad that it's turned out well. You must enjoy it much more than before."

Mulgrew looked at her, neither confirming nor denying her claim. Instead, he gestured to the centre of the garden. The bare patch! Elizabeth was furious, he would single that out. Why couldn't he have admired something first? Typical of a man.

She tried to sound casual: "Ah yes, the bare patch. I'm having a little trouble there. Any tips for a stubborn growth area?"

He hadn't taken his eyes off it. "Odd, isn't it?" he spoke at last.

"Odd? No, just irritating," Elizabeth said, trying to see if the view from this angle afforded an answer. It did in fact look different from above. It seemed at first to have a rectangular shape — about five feet long, and a foot and a half wide. But then it . . . tapered at both ends. It wasn't quite a pure rectangle, more a small coffin shape.

"Odd, isn't it?" Mulgrew repeated, and the words were round and smooth and cold, like pebbles; pebbles dropped into a fathomless pond, causing ripple after ripple after ripple. The image transposed itself into echoes in her brain and the three words repeated themselves in her aural consciousness over and over and over until they faded away like the spreading ripples on a pond.

"There's something," said Mulgrew in his cold, humourless voice, "in the ground, that's stopping growth. You may have to dig very deeply to find what it is. You may have to dig up the whole garden."

Dig it all up? Destroy everything? The flame-coloured azalea uprooted, the precious clump of canterbury bells decimated, her magnolia cut down in infancy?

Why should this manifestation of her personality be killed of?

She turned and faced him squarely: "Don't worry, I'll find something to cover that area."

"It seems that concrete has been the only successful means of concealing it so far," his voice now had a sly quality.

Elizabeth said nothing more to Peter about the bare patch. He hadn't wanted her to remove the flagged path in the first place. Perhaps he too had got tired of rectangles, first in the house and then in the garden. But she had never asked and wasn't going to begin to speculate.

It occurred to her that possibly Mulgrew had watched everything that had happened in the garden over the years and that was why he was always waiting.

But to Elizabeth the greater glory of the garden outweighed the claims of one barren patch. The riot of colour and texture and perfume was testament to her personality — the one which now inhabited Peter's heart as well as his garden. If the garden was destroyed, Peter and she would be destroyed also.

She made her decision and arranged to have everything put to rights. It didn't take long and the following day dawned as only the perfect June one can — early mist dispersing to reveal a benign, caressing sun. Blooms opened their faces to warmth, bees and birds flitted around, undisturbed by anything.

There was no longer a bare patch in Elizabeth's garden. The last rectangle had disappeared under the flags from the original path, their regimental squares reduced to crazy paving to make a patio, dead centre of the garden. Tables, chairs and umbrella furnished the patio and Elizabeth sat in silent, paradisiac contemplation and completely out of view. The sound, when it came, only increased her contentment.

Mulgrew was laughing.

BERT PATON

Burns' Nicht

Kinmorrit wis astir. The day had started wi the dawn creepin in like maist ither Kinmorrit days, but then discrepancies tae normal procedure had done their creepin in tae. The daily routine o the village wis upset. Dresses had been pressed; hair had been permed; trooser turn-ups had been emptied an the legs had been re-introduced tae roond edged creases. Buits had been scraped clear o maist o the fermyaird glaur an violently polished. Some bits o the remainin glaur had been persistently resistant tae acceptin a shine. Wullie Baxter an Davie McKay, Goad save them, had even taen a bath.

In various o the hooses the soup had been prepared an wis bilen, the ordered haggis had arrived an wis bilen, tumshies had been skinned an were bilen, Mairn Ketteridge wis bilen, because the Hall Committee had chosen yellow paper serviettes when she had wanted green anes. Teenie Ramsay had suggested yellow, an there were sae mony Sect on the Hall Committee that Teenie won the day.

Normally, the Sect wis against frivolity, but the day wis the twenty-fifth o January, the Day o the Presence, the day the Bard ruled, OK. Rabbie Burns could not be denied.

Noo wis the day an, even mair important, noo wis the hoor, an a' paths led tae the village hall. In through the doors traipsed folk fae faur an near, firmly clutchin their admission tickets in their freshly laundered haunds. Through the nairrie lobby they grimly trudged their wey, ignorin the Ladies an Gents cloakrooms set on either side, for ye kept y'r coat on meantime as the hall widnae be proper heated up yet. Connie Smairt wis sittin at a whist table that had on it a cash box, beside which wis a wee pile o new admission tickets an an increasin pile o tickets haunded ower tae gain entry. Connie smiled a welcome tae everybody that cam in an kept up an enlightenin commentary on hoo cauld the wither wis.

The peyin guests gien appreciative looks at the three rows o trestle tables lined fae the door tae the stage at the ither end. Pleased they should be, for it wisnae withoot effort that a' the places had been set wi their yellow serviettes, a job Mairn had refused, an the cutlery an crockery. The glesses, hired fae the supplier o the booze, were set oot on anither table, an salt an pepper, sugar an milk set at intervals.

The folk already in had set themsels in dispersed groups in the early birds positions under the overheid heaters. At the end o the hall in front o the stage, Snecky the Beard wis sittin stiff bodied at the middle o the tap table. This wis the table whaur a' the V.I.P.s sat. It wis set across the hall so that the audience could see the performers by twistin their necks either richt or left. Auld Ecky Simpson, a plooman fae ain o the ootlyin ferms, aye had tae sit so that he could see them by turnin his neck tae the left. Years o plooin in the wettest o wither had gien him a rheumatic an he couldnae but turn his heid in that direction.

Maist o the seats were noo occupied. The women seemed tae be a lot freer an mair comfortable than the men, no that the women werenae as well decked oot as the men, but it wis the collars an ties that were garrin the men gaun a bit red in the face. They were accustomed tae open necked shirts in the fields an they aye fund it hard tae draw air doon their thrapple against the pressure o the collars. It wis only twa or three times a year it happened, an this wis ane o the times, like funerals, that it wis worth the discomfort.

A single trestle table stood at the side o the stage an wis covered wi glesses. Sharon Keith wis poorin whisky intae ae lot an Mr Pillets-Mayler wis daein likewise wi the sherry. The twa of them were jokinly swallyin aboot ane in every fower. The mair they swallied the funnier the joke goat an, afore a' the glesses had been filled, the twa o them were almost helpless wi laughin.

Alison Heggie an Mairn Ketteridge were among a wheen ither women that were in the kitchen. This wis ahent the stage and it wis whaur a' the dollops o fuid got served up. Alison wis diggin awa at Mairn for bein taen in wi a double barrelled name. A'body kent that Sharon Keith couldnae be let loose wi the drink, but Mairn had insisted that Mr Pillets-Mayler's presence wid sort o daur her fae imbibin. Instead o stoppin Sharon, though, Pillets-Mayler seemed determined tae get a guid skin-fu' afore her an that taen some daein.

Mairn wisnae botherin tae defend her position. She wis too busy coonter-attackin, "Wis it you, Alison, that wis put in chairge o the fuid?" If there wis ae thing Mairn kent, it wis that Alison had been gien the responsibility for arrangin the supply o neeps and tatties an, abune a', the haggis. Mairn went on, "The haggis is late and nuthin can start athoot the haggis."

Alison wis in quick, "It wis a Committee decision tae get Fiona Carswell tae dae the haggis. Ah wisnae for it, though ah didnae say onything at the time."

There were nods o general agreement. No at what Alison had said, but at what she hadnae said. If there wis ae person could sink the stuff quicker nor Sharon Keith, it wis Fiona Carswell. Fiona's hoose, she wid hae ye ken, had a bar in it. A wuiden contraption staundin aboot elbow hight, an fower elbows, her's an her man's, were placed on it in a nichtly ritual. They stuid there until Algernon, aye, that wis her man's name, until Algeron goat violent. This wis the time when Fiona goat knocked a' ower the hoose an, sometimes, oot ontae the drivewey whaur she wid lie greetin an ca'in for her mum. If ye wanted ony sensible activity fae Fiona ye had tae get tae her afore this critical period. Consequently there wis reasonable cause for Alison's concern.

In the optimistic days o summer when the duties were delegated, decisions were made that widnae hae been made in the caulder reality o winter. Giein Fiona the honour o being Poosie Nancy, on tap o the responsibility o bilen the haggis, didnae look near sic a guid idea at near seeven o'clock on the twenty-fifth o January.

As this dungheap o doobt wis pilin up, there wis a kind o general relief when Connie Smairt seemed tae show true genius. She said, "Could we no mebbe send Mr Pillets-Mayler for Fiona? That micht speed up the haggis an it will stop the drinkin."

Noo there wis an excuse for Connie, she wis young and inexperienced, but it's hard tae pardon the ither women. Age wis wi them an, presumably, they had the experience which Connie lacked. Nevertheless, despite expectations, that's what they did.

Mairn put it nicely tae Pillets-Mayler that he should rescue them by bringin Fiona Carswell an haggis. Pillets-Mayler proved willin an awa he went. Ance he wis awa, the women descended on Sharon, bent on separatin her fae the table o booze. Sharon, hooever, proved a mickle uncooperative. In fact, she threatened tae brain them if they sae much as tried. She stood, balancin hersel against the table, wi her fingers wrapped roond the neck o a half-fu' bottle, pendulummin it slowly back and forrit. Every wee while she laughed intimately tae hersel.

Connie wis fu' o innocence an she stepped nearer tae Sharon tae reason wi her. The ithers stuid rigid, haudin their breath. For some reason Sharon fund Connie's movement hysterically funny an she swung the bottle in an ellipse that missed Connie's heid by aboot twa inches. As Connie jerked back wi her een flabbergasted wide, Sharon doubled up, she wis laughin that herty. Mairn cam forrit, put her haund on the back o Sharon's neck an leaned on it. Sharon couldnae dae onything else but lose her balance an, as she toppled heidlang, Alison caught the bottle an quickly stepped clear so that Connie widnae be hindered fae fa'in on her face. Flet ontae it she went. Puir soul, she tried tae keep on laughin, but every time she pushed hersel up wi her airms, they splayed oot an her face banged back ontae the wuiden boards..

Hamish Ketteridge wis aye the man tae deal wi an emergency. He cam tae Sharon's rescue. He wis well uised tae heavin bags o tatties an bales o hay an it wis nae bother tae him tae lift up Sharon an cairt her oot the emergency door an intae the fresh air. Sharon must still hae been guid-humoured, for her giggles, laughs and gasps could be heard comin oot o the darkness. Hamish must hae been awfy tolerant wi her for the twa o them were oot there for an awfy lang time.

They were, in fact, barely back in the hall when the bagpipes struck up. Saundy Broon wis a young ploomаn. He'd been learnin the pipes for the past three years an this wis his big day. He'd graduated fae the back-gairden o his hoose, that stuid awa in the middle o a wuid, tae pipin in the haggis for this year's Burns' Supper. The pipes wailed their wey up tae fu' volume an there wis the soond o activity the ither side o the hall doors. Saundy had been telt that as suin as Fiona appeared wi the haggis he wis tae pipe it in. That, obviously, wis what wis aboot tae happen. Alison smirked a satisfied look at Mairn. Pillets-Mayler had done the job.

A' een were on the twa swing doors past which the music wis swirlin its way. The doors sort o trembled, swung open a wee bit, then settled back intae place again. The pipes quavered, weakened in their volume, but then, bravely, goat gaun again an the doors were bashed open.

Saundy Broon appeared in a' his glory, his cheeks puffed oot like a big clootie dumplin. His tartan looked sae fine it made his mither's een spring tears. He strutted slowly an importantly through the doors an, at the back o him, shyly, cam Poosie Nancy. Ower her lang black frock she had a peenie. It wis a' stairched for the occasion. On her heid, almost coverin a' her face she wore an auld-fashioned white mutch. Ower her tap lip there wis a braw black moustache. Baith Alison's an Mairn's een rivetted ontae it. Fiona Carswell didnae hae a moustache. Whaur had she goat it? Wait! The truth dawned. That wis Pillets' moustache. Ye couldnae mistake it. It wis a guid ten inches fae tip tae tip. Momentarily confused, Alison wondered hoo Fiona wis wearin Pillets-Mayler's moustache. Then somethin aboot the walk made her suspicious. Fiona Carswell didnae walk like that. Richt enough, wi a skin-fu', she wis apt tae swey juist as unsteadily, but, naw, no like that. That wisnae Fiona, that wis Pillets-Mayler dressed up like Fiona. Naw, no like Fiona — like Poosie Nancy.

Pillets sweyed a' richt. He maun hae had nae ear for music. His sweys didnae keep time tae the piper ata'. They goat mair unbalanced the closer he cam tae the tap table.

It wis Mrs Dawbey, the wife o the Lancur meenister, wha wis tae address the haggis. She wis up on her feet wi the big gully knife at the ready, pointin up taewards the ceilin, as if impatient tae trench the entrails. Saundy passed in front o her an let his pipes skirl a diminishin moan o pleased accomplishment.

Pillets sweyed left, sweyed richt, sweyed le-e-eft, sweyed too faur tae the richt o his centre o gravity. Instead o keepin a grip o the platter, he relinquished it for the mair solid table. The haggis shot up in the air in a parabola an homed in on the point o the gully. Pierced clean through its middle, the haggis gien a last moan o protest, then effortlessly slid doon the blade an wrapped its scaldin skin roond the delicate haund o the meenister's wife.

There wis ain o they intervals when there is total an absolute silence. Juist everybody went stiff, except for their heids movin in sympathy with the parabola. Efterwards, auld Joe Moyce, wha's kind o deef, swore he heard the daith rattle o the haggis as it slipped doon the blade o the knife. That would hae meant that it had survived the bilin, so it wis awfy doobtfu'. What wisnae in doobt wis that as the hot haggis hunkered itsel doon on the haund o the meenister's wife, everybody heard her girn oot a startled, "Bugge-e-er!" a second afore Pillets Mayler's clutchin haunds caught haud o the tablecloth — a proper ane for the tap table — an yanked it agley, sendin a' the dishes clasherin ontae the flair. The meenister's wife, say what ye micht, wis the real heroine o the nicht, because she held ontae the knife, switchin it fae haund tae haund, an saved the haggis fae fa'n ontae the flair amang the shards o broken dishes. Remarkable strong wrists that woman must've had. Some said it wis due tae the practisin she did for the day she wuid strangle Auld Dawbey.

Snecky the Beard uised twa pairs o glesses for special occasions like bein chairman at the Burns' Supper. Ae pair lay aside his watch on the table. He's aye thocht this looked awfy impressive. He's been aboot tae perform his impressive act o changin them ower, fae uisin the ae pair tae read the programme wi, tae uisin the ither pair so that he could see Saundy Broon tae haund him his nip o whisky, which wis the piper's due for leadin in the haggis.

Weel, the change-ower wis in the middle o its execution when Pillets-Mayler's stramash took place an Snecky wis left no bein able tae see a thing. He stuid there immobilised, like a statue, haundin up a gless o whisky. It wisnae for nuthin that Saundy Broon had practised ower an ower again a' the operations o his big nicht. He kent what wis supposed tae come next. He reached ower tae Snecky's haund an disengaged the whisky fae it, downed it in ae throat-burnin gulp an inflated the bag o his pipes wi seventy proof fumes.

Tryin his hardest no tae cough he screwed the pipes an gart them skirl tae the rafters in a wey he'd never managed afore an mairched roond the ootside tables wi as bonny a swagger as ye've ever seen, an he didnae care whither Poosie Nancy wis at the back o him or no.

Poosie kent things had gone a bit wrang. For ae thing his left fuit had torn its wey through the bottom o his skirt an this kind o hamstrung him, so that, when he had scrabbled aboot on the flair until he'd fund the biggest bit of the haggis dish an then goat back ontae his feet, it wis only wi the utmaist difficulty that he hobbled his wey oot the hall wi ony sense o dignity at a', haudin the bittie plate oot in front o him.

Back at the tap table Snecky had at last managed tae latch a pair o spectacles ower his nose. He saw the steamin haggis impaled on the knife an he clucked awa' tae himsel, "Silly woman, she shouldnae hae cut it afore she said the addreth." Decidin tae rectify things as faur as he could, he leaned doon tae the wee wifey an leered at her, his massive halitosis made her heid reel as he said tae her, "Ye should addreth the haggith furtht."

Gie Mrs Dawbey her due, sinfu' she micht be, uisin sic a word as she had uttered this nicht, nevertheless, she performed her duty nobly. The only bit hesitation she had wis when it cam tae, "The groanin trencher there ye fill" an that wis understaundable seein as hoo maist o the trencher had depairted wi Pillets-Mayler.

As suin as the last line o the address wis finished Alison Heggie wheeched the haggis ontae a big plate an vanished wi it intae the kitchen. Three ither helpers surroonded the tap table an goat it tae richts. A wheen o women started roond the tables wi plates o soup. They offered a choice — broth or pea — an nane o the auld haunds asked for broth because that had been made by Mairn Ketteridge. Kennin what her hoose wis like they werenae keen on samplin what had come oot o it. Phil Fraser plumped for pea soup, tae, but his wife, kennin what he wis like efter takin pea soup, changed his order tae broth an he kent better nor argy.

Mr Dawbey wis a'maist caught oot, but he got in juist in time wi the Selkirk Grace, "Some hae meat and cannae eat, and some wid eat but want it. . . " The last line wis punctuated wi slurps as Jake Robertson siphoned his soup oot o his spoon.

There wis aye a lang wait atween the soup an the haggis an neeps. It taen a while for the women in the kitchen tae get a'thing sorted oot ontae the plates. The Committee had got wise tae this though, an tae fill the gap they ca'd in the Queen. At least they uised the Loyal Toast tae dae it. A'body stuid while Snecky asked, "Are y'r glesses a' chairged?" There bein nae denials, he cairried on, "The Queen." He clicked tae attention an sipped his whisky like a truly loyal subject, then his haund, like twa score mair haunds, clawed intae a pocket tae produce a packet o fags. Bein loyal subjects they couldnae smoke afore that toast, so a'body wis agreed it wis a guid idea tae hae the toast earlier in the proceedins so that the interval atween the soup an the haggis could be occupied wi a sair needed cigarette.

The fags were a'richt for the grewn-ups, but the bairns couldnae very weel be quietened wi ain. Teetsie Ketteridge goat a sair pinch fae ain o her ain brithers an her howls shimmied the smoke that wis risin amang the crossbeams o the roof. No tae be ootdone, anither three or fower o the wee tots jined her in sympathetic cacophony. Before ye could say Jake Robinson,the whale section whaur the bairns had been put wis in an uproar.

Craigie Ketteridge wis the auldest o Mairn's fower. He wis awfy like his fether. Tall for his thirteen years, he had a noticeably wee heid an his face looked gey glaiket, but weel enough able tae stride alang at the back o the coos, whangin them wi a long stick. He threw a punch at his younger brither, Adam, for nippin Teetsie. Adam wis genius material compared tae Craigie an faur mair supple. He deuked the punch easy an Craigie's big fist cairried on an hit Bingie Watson on the side o the heid. Bingie an Adam were inseparable an afore Bingie's heid cracked intae Ernie McIntyre's heid, Adam wis flailin awa at his brither. Puir Bingie felt that his heid wis squashed flet ae second an then that it wis balloonin oot the next. He tint his reason an went for Craigie Ketteridge like a ferret. Under the combined onslaught o the twa pals, Craigie wis knocked flet on tap o some o the wee bairns that were sittin at his side.

Ernie McIntyre wisnae sure what wis gaun on except that Bingie Watson had gien him the heid. He wisnae takin that fae onybody an he started scrabblin awa at Bingie. It wis a real dust-up. There were bodies a' place an the noise had tae be heard tae be credited. The menfolk, smilin tolerantly, had a fine time unravellin legs an airms an settin them back on their seats.

The redd-up coincided wi the arrival o the dismembered haggis. The women trotted oot the kitchen wi a tray o plates, fower tae a tray, an laid them in front o the various folk an then hurried back tae get mair. In a wee while the only soond wis the clickin o forks against the plates and the squeakin o knives as they scraped the last grain o haggis, balanced it delicately on the blade, an lifted it tae a safe storage atween the teeth an the cheek whaur it could be manipulated like a cud o baccy.

Ance the haggis an neeps were disposed o, ae lot o women wheeched away the empty plates an another lot brocht on wee dishes wi jeely trifle an the meal ended wi the cups gettin filled wi tea an mooths wi the inevitable fags.

Snecky the Beard goat gravely tae his feet as befitted a man o importance. He positioned his watch an inch tae the richt o the place he had spent three minutes choosin juist previously. He took the pair o specs that wis on his nose aff it an laid them on the table in exchange for the ither pair. He lifted them ower his nose, fixed them ahent his lugs an looked roond at the assembled Kinmorrit folk. "We noo come tae a' the talkin." His voice wis high pitched, even at that time afore the foxhoond damaged him when he wis swingin fae a branch. "And maitht o it will be worth lithenin tae."

Snecky wis clear what he had in mind. He wis a fanatic o the local Sect, an it should hae been his responsibility for arranging for that Sect's preacher tae gie the address tae the lassies. Ah! but what had happened? Because Teenie had gotten her wey ower the serviettes, he had been forced tae ask the Kirk o Scotland meenister.

The Rev. Dawbey looked like a Toby Jug. On initial acquaintance he seemed moderate enough but, efter a minute or twa, ye began tae see him different. He had nae time for initial misconceptions on this occasion an he waded richt in. "Robert Burns was obviously a sex mad fiend. Nothing in his poetry can ever make us forget that, or indeed, forgive that. It is the truth that he no sooner saw a cornfield o any height, but he grabbed the nearest woman an shoved her into it. I am not here to make excuses for him. I am not goin to make excuses for him. I am here to warn all you lassies of the dangers of sex." Toby Jug turned oot tae be an expert on the dangers o sex — a kind o male Mary Whitehoose.

The chairges were levelled against Rabbie Burns richt enough, but it didnae hinder Hamish Ketteridge fae lookin gey uncomforable when Mr Dawbey looked richt at him. Toby, though, wis only singlin him oot because he wis a fermer, an they werenae daein enough researchin tae produce a dwarf size corn.

Snecky ponderously got up on his feet again at the end o Mr Dawbey's diatribe, an he ca'd on Teenie Ramsay tae gie the reply tae the toast. Hoo she'd come tae be chosen tae reply wis ane o the peculiar happenins that occur on committees. They'd been hashin names aroond for likely speakers an somebody had jocularly suggested Teenie. There had been sniggers an comments, but the thing had worked on them an the ootcome wis Alison had asked Teenie tae dae it, never expectin her tae say "Aye". Teenie had said "Aye" and here she wis.

She went for Toby Jug richt aff. She agreed wi him aboot Burns and as faur as she wis concerned a' the lassies in Kinmorrit had already been ower the cornfields. For reasons best kent tae hersel, hooever, likely because he wis Kirk o Scotland, she took umbrage an she said oot plain that she had tae reply tae an address what dotted the Is an stroked the Rs in sic intimate detail. The women broke intae applause at this, an that helped tae droon oot the howl o laughin fae some o the mair ignerent o the men.

It's best no repeatin here exactly what Teenie said, for what ye'll get awa wi in an address at a Burns' Supper micht get ye taen up for libel if ye pit it intae print. Accordin tae Teenie though, Toby's mither's morals wid hae embarrassed a Ketteridge coo, an his fether had aye taen longer tae hervest a field of wheat than onybody else.

It wis a rare barny an a'maist everybody enjoyed it. Toby, af-coorse, classed Teenie wi Burns efter that, an ye widnae hinder him fae gettin tae his feet tae reply tae the reply. Wi deepest voice an maist ominous tone, he said that certain women had been fired at the stake in the past an that the time wis overdue for the restartin o the practice.

Snecky had goat mair an mair agitated as the barny went on. He wis switchin the glesses aff an on his nose an he wis smilin an lookin seek turn aboot. He grabbed the first brek in Dawbey's harangue an announced the next item. Dawbey rebelliously looked as if he wid ignore him, but even he submitted when he saw the eldritch look shaftin its wey fae Teenie, a look that made him feel like Tam O'Shanter must hae done when the first witches cam whooshin oot o Kirk Alloway chasin him.

Snecky's announcement wis that the Immortal Memory wid be gien by Alasdair McIntosh. Alasdair wis a local poet wha had gotten a national reputation for his work. What he didnae ken aboot poetry wisnae worth kennin. In particular he wis an expert on Burns. Inside five minutes o talkin aboot Rabbie's work half o the listeners wis giein crackin yawns, the ither half had either juist finished ain or wis gettin ready for anither. Alasdair became painfully aware that he'd lost his audience an he no only cut his talk in half, he cut his sentence in half. The Burns enthusiasts that filled the hall never even noticed. They cam oot their dwam when his voice ceased an efter a second or twa's hesitation started clappin their haunds like mad. As Wullie Baxter said, "He wis short onywey."

Snecky stuid smilin, fumblin wi his watch an glesses until the applause deid doon. "Noo we hae Mrs Prendergast to render 'Tam o Shanter'". He waved his left haund tae a stoot woman that sat three chairs awa. She acknowledged his introduction an pushed her wey past the further oot sitters. She climbed up intae a corner o the stage an sorted oot some sheets o paper.

"Tam of Shanter," she recited, "As chepmen Billies leave the street; And neighbours thirsty neighbours meet. As Market days are wearing late; And folk begin to take their stroll. We think not of the long Scots miles. . . " Mrs Prendergast wis a visitor fae London that Snecky had roped in because he wis fair taen wi her big posh car. He never missed a chance tae mak himsel kent tae the nobs. Mebbe it wis his simperin an kowtowin that goat her tae agree, but mair likely, it wis because she thocht it richt that she should fraternise wi the natives.

Onywey, ten minutes tryin tae mak sense o the gibberish that Burns had written convinced her she wuid need tae dae somethin aboot it. Wi the help o Doreen Molure, wha she wis bidin wi, she spent three days sortin it oot intae decent English. There's no mony folk wid hae taen a' that trouble an though, mebbe, she wisnae muckle guid at poetry, wi the words at the end of the lines no haein the same soond as the previous ains, it's tae be hoped the Scots appreciate the painfu' lengths the English'll gaun tae sort oot their literature.

Alasdair McIntosh sat goggle-eed, haudin his breath. It wis the maist remarkable Tam of Shanter he had ever heard. The Kinmorrit adults sat wi their een glazed an when the Kinmorrit bairns started actin up in their boredom, Mrs Prendergast reached up half-a-dizen decibels an let a threatenin note burr its wey intae their lugs an they subsided intae a kind o mesmerised stare.

Snecky started clappin his haunds when she finished, but she wis doon aff the stage an pushin her wey back tae her seat, afore onybody else joined him.

The next item wis 'Speed the Ploo', an it wis the turn o Saundy Broon the piper. Bein active in the Young Fermers he wis weel informed an he spent quarter o an hoor lamentin aboot the low price o meat, pork an mutton. Them that could afford tae buy the stuff were feelin gey guilty in nae time ata' for robbin the fermers. His conclusion wis that though Rabbie an his fermin fether had had hard times, they were lucky they were deid. Ae thing wis certain, if conditions had been as bad then as they were noo, Rabbie Burns widnae hae been able tae waste his time sittin lookin at daisies, or writin pointry aboot onythin else. He sat doon tae the soond o Hamish Ketteridge thumpin the table an roarin, "Hear! Hear! Encore! Encore!"

Isa Hendry wis ca'd on tae gie 'The last rose o summer'. The first twa lines she kent aff by hert, then she got confused, hummed awa tae hersel wi her een glowerin at the ceilin, but, at last, conceded defeat. She announced wi a giggle that she'd forgotten tae bring the bit paper that had the words written on it. Hooever, she wis prepared tae hae a go at 'Comin through the rye'. Toby Jug goat awfy fidgetty when she said this, but he neednae have worried. She couldnae mind it either. She admitted that the only sang she really kent wis Garry Glitter's latest, written by himsel. Isa wisnae much on the singin but that sang goat the maist enthusiastic clappin o the whale evenin.

Noo, that micht tend tae gie Isa mair nor wis really her due, for it happened she wis the last o the formal verbal offerins o the evenin an it opened the wey for the pleuchs tae offer their informal vocal an physical assaults. Stevie Lawson on the accordion an Frankie Lowe on the fiddle were auld haunds at giein license tae the juggernauts. Straichtawa' they started reelin them ontae the flair. There wis a momentary reluctance an then the traffic clattered in a' directions. Wi naebody being on point duty there wis bound tae be collisions. Wullie Baxter an Dod Little goat intae gear fae opposite ends o the hall an met heid-on in the middle. Dod's stature wis like his name an he rebounded flet ontae his back. Wullie couldnae brake in time an he ran richt ower him.

Dod wisnae tae be written aff, though, he gien his heid twa or three shakes an in nae time at a' he wis swingin big Suzie aff her feet tae the mortal danger o ony passin participants.

Roond an roond an roond the pleuchs swung the lassies an even efter only the first dance, ane or twa o the lassies were that dizzy they birled richt oot through the hall doorway an, it wis said, the fact that a' the corn had been hervested lang since didnae prove ony impediment ata'.

A novel improvement wis introduced at this stage. The Ca' Inn sent oot a satellite programme. Hitherto, alcoholic beverages hadnae been allood intae the village hall, but this year, despite Teenie Ramsay's frenetic opposition, a licence had been obtained, an noo booze wis freely available if ye had money tae buy it.

Enough folk had enough money, an glesses an their hallowed content were conveyed north, sooth, east an wast an a' points in atween.

What had been a din became uproar, an dance steps were invented that were never seen again. Big Suzie started swinging Dod Little roond an roond an roond. The flair, replaced late last year, vibrated as if it wisnae gaun tae last oot this year. Dod Little's feet were ceasin tae touch the flair; stour wis startin tae cloud doon fae the rafters; Dod Little's fleein body wis a'maist parallel wi the flair; coats were fa'in aff the hooks on the wa's. Big Suzie let go Dod Little's haund; Hamish Ketteridge wis staundin busy in the Gents when Dod joined him through the double plaister-board wa'. "Christ! You must hae been desperate," said Hamish.

"It's a' that beer," replied Dod.

The pandemonium wis at its hicht when the law, in the shape of Tammas Walsh arrived. It wis his duty tae investigate, for report back tae the Cooncil, whether the probity o the licence had been observed. Broadminded though he wis he thocht it necessary tae hae a strict word wi the Beard wha wis gawpin, in a paralysed state, at the scene. P.C. Walsh thocht that it wis Snecky's Sectish morality bein sae mortified that had lost him the pooer o movement, but a look at his glazed een an a whiff o his breath informed him itherwise.

Steppin intae the breach yet again,the constable announced the last dance, a waltz, ladies choice. There were nae inhibitions on the pairt o the ladies tae gaun choosin pairtners. Big Suzie went seekin hers, an dragged him back through the hole in the wa' by the hair o his heid, wi him yellin blue murder.

Hamish said tae his depairtin feet, "Oh, y're awa' then. Ye didnae need after a'?"

Wi the dance finished, an the band packin up, P.C. Walsh had them a' hustlin intae their coats an wavin guidbyes in minutes. Ane or twa o the Committee women were for bustlin roond an lockin up, but Tammas ordained, "Ass to that, there iss no need for you to be going to all that trouble. What iss a policeman for but to attend to such things." An richt he wis.

Suin the last soond o the last car had diminished tae silence; the last whisper o a shouted cheerio had been lost in the nicht air; the last dark shape had vanished intae the darkness; an then, the last lichtit windae wis obliterated tae merge wi its surroondins; an a complete quietness settled a' atour the village. Anither Burns' Supper wis at an end. . .

Or wis it?

For a licht suddenly streamed fae ane o the hall windaes an disturbed the black o the nicht. Occasionally, bodies could be seen movin back and forrit an then the curtain wis drawn tae leave juist a suspicion o licht within. Onybody gettin aff their horse an peepin through the chink wid hae seen mysterious presences engaged in nefarious activities. At that time o nicht the presences could only be taen tae be ill-forebodin. Wha but sic wid hae daured tae flout the strictures o the hall's licence? Wha but sic a laithsome getherin wid hae cairried on for nigh on anither hoor-an-a-half?

At that time the maist horrendous noises ever heard by human ear rose ever higher and higher in volume until it seemed the very heavens themsels wid be shudderin wi dread. Nae ee in Kinmorrit wid hae daured noo tae put itsel tae the crack in that curtained windae.

The bedded souls o the village, wha's blighted minds becam aware o the noise, pu'd pillows ower their heids tae muffle it oot o hearin. The very horses in the next field looked roond anxiously at their tails afore whinnyin an racin tae the faur fence.

Wilder an wilder grew the soond until, it seemed, the hall door burst open like a release valve. . . an oot walked P.C. Tammas Walsh. He took up a position in the middle o the road whaur he gravely held up his haund tae stop ony passin traffic, then signalled clear exit for the noise.

Intae the open air it gained its freedom, an its source wis illuminated by Saundy Broon's glowin face puffed oot tae twice its size. The bags o his pipes had never been intended tae withstaund sic pressure, an the reeds vibrated in discordant protest.

Ahent him, in staggerin disarray, cam Hamish Ketteridge, Wullie Baxter, Billy Allan, an, wi his mutch collapsed ower the back o his neck, Pillets-Mayler. Each wis singin his individual sang, but not a note wis heard abune the shriekin o the pipes. Tammas, satisfied that his convoy had the freedom o the highway, stumbled forward tae walk alangside Saundy an so tae gie him protective escort.

The horses in the field milled in terror at the approach o the demented catterwaulin an the fence gien wey under their combined wecht. They took aff as fast as their legs could cairry them awa fae the noise. A', that is, except Nellie, Hamish's auld mare. Decrepit an deaf as she wis, she wisnae sure what a' the excitement wis aboot, but, nevertheless, she goat caught up in it.

It had been mony a day since she had frisked her heels in the air, but she did her best, so it is understaundable that when she wis on the road an the ither horses turned awa' fae the soond, Nellie turned tae the richt an galloped taewards it. She hadnae covered three quarters o the distance tae the men when she ran oot o steam. She stuid there, her flanks heavin, her forelegs splayed oot, an her heid hingin so's her nose a'maist touched the grund. As the wind hoarselled intae her throat an oot atween her lips, she cursed hersel for bein an auld fool an wondered what the hell had goat intae her.

Saundy, completely engrossed in producin his fearsome soond effects, walked richt intae Nellie. Fortunately his followers were somewhat dispersed, so it wis only Wullie Baxter that banged intae his back, even so, his added wecht shoving the bagpipes' moothpiece against the immovable Nellie wis enough tae jam it doon Saundy's windpipe.

Dark though it wis, P.C. Walsh wis able, vaguely, tae see what the problem wis, an wi some heroic tuggin, he freed Saundy's throat fae its blockage. His tuggin wis accompanied by the deein wail as the deflatin bag, wi its last whisky fumes, emptied tae a wheeze and then silence.

Tammas wis sae awfy upset at onything obstructin the Queen's highway, to wit, the road oot o Kinmorrit, that as suin as he had removed ae impediment he arrested the ither.

Auld Nellie had never been in the haunds o the law afore so she wisnae up on procedure an, truly, she wisnae muckle interested in onythin at the minute ayont gettin some air intae her tortured lungs. Despite a' P.C. Walsh's remonstrations, Nellie wis determined she wisnae takin anither step till the pain in her sides subsided.

Hamish crawled oot o a ditch that he had sort o wandered intae an he saw Tammas haein this conversation wi Auld Nellie. He wove a circuitous route tae whaur the twa were staundin an he said, "Ah didnae ken you twa had met afore. Nellie, ah hope y're no talkin tae this man withoot a proper introduction."

"I haf arrested her for obstructing the Queen's highway," Tammas explained solemnly.

"Arrested Auld Nellie? Ye cannae arrest Auld Nellie. She's mah horse an she widnae dae onythin that wid cause trouble tae the Queen." Hamish put his nose intae Auld Nellie's lug an said, "He's a nashty man, that. You come hame wi me."

Nellie wis gettin her second wind, noo, an wis mair than willin tae be guided back tae the gate that led intae her field.

When Hamish goat back tae the group, they were gethered roond Saundy, commiseratin wi him. He wis lamenting wi a hoarse voice that he wid never be able tae play the bagpipes again.

"Noo, noo, there's nae need tae be feelin like that," said Wullie Baxter, "Onyway, Billy here'll mak ain o they iron lung things for your pipes if need be. He's awfy guid at things like that."

Tammas said, "You are back, Hamish. You realise that you haf interfered in the administering of the law. That iss a serious charge."

Hamish wis ignorin Tammas. His lugs were cocked tae a soond that wis gettin louder as it cam nearer. "Horses!" he exclaimed.

An horses it wis. When the skriechin wail had subsided, so had their panic an wi the silence cam a strong longin tae be back in the field they'd left in sic a hurry. An unerrin instinct guided them tae the collapsed fence an aff the hard tarmacadam that reverberated their hoof soonds an they galloped on tae the saft, soond insulatin turf.

P.C. Walsh had become aware o the hoofbeats an he wis intent on cairryin oot his duty. The Queen's Highway must be kept clear at a' costs. He stuid in the middle o the road wi his haund upraised darin them tae pass.

Hamish, Wullie, Billy an Saundy left him tae his fate and heided fu' pelt for the ditches.

The clatterin o hooves became sudden silence wi nae interval atween.

Slowly Tammas lowered his haund, starin as if he wid manage tae pierce the darkness. He spoke, "It iss an uncanny thing that hass happened." He turned tae the ither men tae emphasise his statement, an they had disappeared as weel. Momentarily, even he wis irresolute, but nae earthly bein could make quicker decisions nor he could, his highland superstitiousness cast the fear that mebbe he wis mixed up wi unearthly creatures, an for siccan things, distance wis the best preserver. His legs took a life o their ain an he heided back tae the village, homin in on his bicycle.

Gradually, ane by ane, the heids o the ither fower men emerged fae the ditches. They had left him on the roadwey in solid flesh, but noo he seemed tae hae been gethered up by the ghostly horses an Hell kent whaur he would end up. Each man had his ain thochts an it wisnae wise tae voice them in these surroondins. They were still tryin tae come tae terms wi events when a shadowy somethin whooshed past them, its presence felt mair by the disturbance o the air than by scent or sicht or soond. In the darkness they didnae recognise P.C.Walsh on his bike hell-bent on gettin oot o Kinmorrit an its unchancy environment an hame tae the dependability o his rowan tree.

Happenins were gettin on tap o the men, sort o fa'in oot o their control. The age auld remedy in sic circumstances wis tae get intae bed an hap the blankets ower the heid. Bein o ae mind they didnae discuss it, juist stuck their haunds in their pooches an started aff in the direction o Kinmorrit, that is, a' except Hamish, for he lived at the tap o the hill in the opposite direction.

"Hey," he yelped in a whisper, "What aboot me?"

The three o them stopped. Hamish's plight had been nigglin at the back o their minds, but wi no haein a discussion, it had remained a niggle they were prepared tae ignore. It didnae tak a medium tae realize that someplace atween them an Hamish's hoose there wis a pit o mystery.

Hamish's plaintive voice cam again, "Ye cannae leave me. Ah've goat tae get hame, tae. There's three o youse."

Reluctantly, first Billy turned, then Saundy, an then Wullie, realisin he wis gaun tae be left on his ain, turned as weel. So, ance again soondless, the fower o them cautiously put ae fuit in front o the ither, until, wi audible sighs o relief, as Hamish darted along his path an in through his hoose door, they were able tae heid hamewards themsels. Mind, ance they were surroonded by the hooses o the village, they gained confidence enough tae speak oot loud an agree that they wid hing thegither until they were a' equidistant fae their ain hoose doors. The Deil tak the hindmaist efter that, they wid a' mak a bolt for it, fairly certain their strategy wid win at least ane o them safe hame.

The Bard, they felt, wid hae some answerin tae dae for this nicht's wark.

GRAHAM FULTON

Sceneries

Sheep dog trials are erupting
nearby
and I go and watch country dancing.
The occasional girl
consulting her map
and sandals on her pink small feet.
She calls BONJOUR,
I call HELLO.

A lumpy big island. Bicycles,
a blue ceiling
over flat blue bays
smudging into Atlantic chill.
Water and scenery, I gaze

at Flora Macdonald's seaside grave,
and water and scenery.
A scenic drill stabbing the tar.

Play pool, play jukebox
deep in some dream-pub
and watch the World Cup,
drunk mens of the world,
the occasional girl
buffing her dust
from her strawberry skin, buzzing
with sun, stroked.
She calls HELLO,
I call   as well.

Wet Wall

East Berlin 1987

Shanty stalls are hawking
wool balls
and horrible jewellery,
thin socks and pottery.
Hunters cluster
around the tables
dripping little
brittle bargains.
Napkins.
Dolls and chocolate.

A tourist bus zooms by,
Nikons clicking
at flags
flags
a fountain
of proud uniformity.

Oblivious to the master plan
the fat jazzmen band
is striking up
another number
written fifty years
before.
Sweethearts spin
on the slabs,
palms smack until
they are hot.

The joint is jumping
and diluted orange
is drunk
in great quantity.

Man I Never Saw

above
the flat
the sound
of him
crossing the floor,
rhythmic bumps
of crutch
the vicious
clearing
of throat

window
heaved open
the release
of contents
down past us,
to the weeds,
but now
he is dead,
and that was
a while back

Margaret

Mascara tears
slow
and black.
The jangling hangers
in the wardrobe.

A holy bible on the shelf
beside the sachets of sugar and tea
the souvenir book of matches.

A Kleenex wipes them
away
as the kettle begins to noisily boil
as if they never existed at all.
"Go back to sleep" she says
so I do

or try to.
Helpless
naked
counting sheep.

Counting the towels I know I won't steal.
Listening to
the painful stir of the spoon in her cup.

ELISE McKAY

Old Diaries

They lie in cupboards, holding more
than anyone should know;
tight-clasped and slightly stale.
A sense of mustiness pervades
their secret place, as though
some confidence too heavy for hard backs
to bear, leaked out and spread
a slow contamination on the air.

Guarding the years, were they true friends,
those books that held their silence,
never answered back?
The writer thought he told
what he had seen. Did he deceive himself,
produce an artifact, and shrug away
the truth he could not bear?

Or did he stop to wonder
what was real, and let it surface once,
to be pushed down again?
His version of the version that he knew.
Truth, inexplicable as any dream,
cannot be grasped, but slips away
as all the days and years
that hold their secrets pass.

JANE O'HAIRE WHAMOND

Against Crystal

Goldfish need
A clear bowl

I told them
Mouthing against crystal
But they didn't listen

Isn't he cute they said
Turning out the light

When the morning came
The sunlight
Lacerated my eyes
Cut burns into my gold flesh

Cut glass cut me to the quick
Incarcerated in the bowl of light

Mouthing against crystal.

WILLIAM HERSHAW

Guisin

Sune eftir tea the lift was daurk and starny,
Syne oot tae play ablo thon thrummlin carry
Sae muckle abune oor heids. Blent'rin sprites
Wha taen the shape o aulder human gytes.

Forbidden adult warlds a' aroonds us,
Ettlin tae be groun-ups in guisin duds,
Like bairns we thocht mair freedom was tae cam,
Unkennin that we held it a' alang.

It's queer, ma hert ay aches this time o year,
Ettlin tae win tae be a bairn aince mair.

November In Celtic Fife

November morn —
The seasoun heids tae hell's mirk mou'.
Laich, the sun ligs lanelie in the lift,
Fresh, the bree is frae the reid Firth blawin.
In bare birks the druid rooks kaa oot o tune
Tae bless ane mair day's gowden dawin.

CATHERINE MOWAT

A Last Word On Winter

At last the thaw.
Sooty gangs of starlings
Swarm against a grudging sky,
Lusting for virgin fields
Now laid bare. Untouched,
The bird table stands
Like a wife deserted.

JAMES GRAHAM

Schoolboy

Leading the file of boys, the black eyes
came to class. The oil-black,
deep-sea eyes that seemed to make
a twilight in the room, were turned
toward me always as I moved

Until, stared out, uneasy, I
attended to some paper. A rich
and resonant fat-man snore declared itself
out of some caverns that his tiny frame,
packed with thin bones, could not contain.

The face was in repose,
pale as the daytime moon. I met the open
eyes again, and saw much more
than facile innocence — a temperament
I could not name, not only vulnerable,
not only wise.
                                        And when he spoke, he lied
as if to say the sun is warm, and rain
gives blessing to the flowers, and life
is brief but precious.

He eclipsed
my understanding daily after that.
He was not Hansel at the mercy
of the wildwood and the witch, nor quite
that other woodland boy, young Siegfried,
unschooled in fear.
In thirteen years
he had learned to face the world's
amalgam of false words and true
without obliquities: with No
defined as Yes.
I wondered when
the Devil had apologised to him, restored
him to an Eden where no apples grew;
or whether Jesus having turned his wine
to water, had once made him sick.

He was not born beneath a silver sky
whose stars were black. I had not thought
the school-bus ran where shadows,
coruscating, cast
dark figures. Yet the field
of those unfathomable eyes was where
light gravitated, and was lost.

MARGARET GILLIES BROWN

Legend

My mother lived a legend;
Dark haired, vivacious,
Vivid as November's morning star,
She claimed to be a hark-back
To the French — (the other half
Of that old 'Auld Alliance')
One of those twins snatched from the roaring seas.
She did much to make this myth come true,
Brought foreign thought to young parochial minds,
Inspired us with French stories.

Her imagination lit our lives;
Our garden, dull at the back,
Plain grass, grey walls
And spindly trees, thin in their moving shadow,
Became for us
A cool French courtyard,
Giving it charm and mystery
Where it had none.

She travelled once to France
Before our birth,
Told us of feeling at home
The moment foot touched land,
And talked of places,
Strange marbling to the tongue,
Versailles and Sacre Coeur.

Once we saw her weep,
The day France fell
And for a while
Light vanished from the courtyard
Yet after the first strong shock
Her faith returned —
"One day!" she'd say, "One day . . ."

Wars fought and won
She never made for France,
(No money and no time
were her excuses),
Looking back it seems,
For her, dreams were enough —
Wishing was the Mother of invention,
Believing was becoming.

Ruth In High Places

Ruth, living on top of the world
Back from the Caribbean
and a faded love,
Starting life fresh
In these high valleys —
Alone but not lonely

Ruth, in a shepherd's cottage
Perched on the lip of the hill
Facing east, looking through high curves
To the far spiring city,
Straight down to the river
A blue ribbon running through
Green shot silk of barley,
Past gaudy yellow aprons of rape-flower.

Ruth among the clouds —
Can be reached by a rough track
Winding up through a forest of green light
Skirting a dangerous ravine
A black lamb dancing in the pasture. . .
Through her beckoning eyes.

High in these windy places
Where sun chases shadows,
Rain draws across her long skirts,
She waits —
For the next throw of the dice —
He who will come.

Contentment at Autumn

I wake, the raining has stopped,
the stars are still hiding.
No sound but the draw-in,
let-out breath close beside me,
rhythmic and calm.

Early we'd laid
back on green pillows,
eaten sweet grapes
brought by our daughter.
You laughing, feeding me, sometimes,
The juiciest fruit
(like a bird I once saw,
in far Tenerife, feeding his mate.)
The window was open.
The night air was warm
and smelt of burnt stubble.
The sound of the rain's continuous purr
(with the grain gathered in)
made soft music to me.
I heard it fall on the grass,
on the gravel,
the leaves of the trees.
Close, in the orchard,
the apples and plums,
held by thin stalks,
would be running with raindrops.
'Tomorrow I'll make plum jam for the winter,
for tall hungry sons,
apple pies for the freezer,
rouged with ripe brambles.'
Planning beside you, I fell fast asleep.

Now, the silence outside,
the calm of your breathing,
the musical chimes of the very old clock
counting the hours.

VALERIE CUMING

Sheep in a Field of Brussels Sprouts

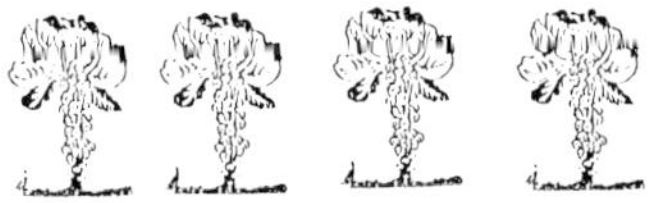

Black-faced sheep in a field
Of December-frosted sprouts
Gaze like Victorian maidens
Stitching at samplers while
Dreaming of a wider world.

The ordered rows of stalky Perthshire
Vegetables proffer good animal feed
Not worth a human's gathering.
Stems yellow with a sun-giving warmth.

One black sheep stares, unblinking
As a movie starlet, disturbing symmetry.
Sombre thoughts of a different flock
Shadow the wintry field.
Lambs to the slaughter come Easter.

LILY MORRISON

The Spare Room

The spare room is beautiful, white and red,
Cheery big poppies adorn the bed.
There's a book for the guests,
which has never been read.

The spare room is cosy, somewhere to sit,
Watch telly, play records, or just read a bit.
A hand holds a lamp,
which has never been lit.

The spare room is modern, the furniture stacks,
A good place for someone to sit and relax.
Some playing cards lie there,
still in their packs.

The spare room is thoughtful, a warm dressing-gown
Is waiting for someone, coming from town.
It hangs there neatly,
not taken down.

The room is for children, who may want to stay,
For a week, or a weekend – even a day.
They promise to come,
but still stay away.

The spare room is beautiful, red and white,
Cheery big poppies – a sorry sight
On the uncrumpled bed,
each lonely night.

MARTIN SULLIVAN

Pardon

Pin my shadow to this prison wall
And hook my conscience to that jet
Flying north;
While gulls mock progress
And sparrows impress the lawn
With harmonious neglect
Of man's apparent genius,
Looking up only to check the flock
Before bouncing furiously
To the next patch of clover
Swallowing as it does,
As they do,
The squirming remains of chrysalis.

INA FOTHERINGHAM

Grief In Our Time

I remember again
And want to howl
Like a wounded dog.
I want to twist and drag
My hair from its roots;
I want to scrape and tear
The skin from my flesh;
I want to rock mindlessly,
To wail out my grief
Till my body is empty
And at peace.
But I smile and pass the sugar.
Yes, it is cold for the time of year.

LIZ NIVEN

Dressing Up

I remember pink frosted plastic shoes,
Stalactite heels, unstable like our memories.
Mother young, hair still black,
Her lineless face smiled as we pranced
In flowing dresses she once wore.
Her inky coloured perfume bottle now
Brings thoughts of dressing-up time.
Remember how she always said her faith
Was more to her than clothes?
Evening in Paris the scent is,
The bottle dark as a French night sky.
She'll never go now
And if she does, it will be with
A slow measured step
In sensible wool and careful shoes
Her only beads her rosaries.
She's left behind her finery, her youth;
We took them all.
Ungrudgingly she gave us what she had
And we were kitted out for life.

We've dressed up many times since then
In graduation gown and wedding veil
And she has come and looked on all,
Owning still the one possession that we didn't want —
Her faith.
Without a thank-you we said no and gave them back
And it has always grieved her.
Education is to blame, she said,
'They've lent you borrowed robes I don't approve of.'
This thought she wraps around her like a great cloak of Sorrow.
I fear this is how our dressing-up will end
When all pretence is stripped away.

DOROTHY WHAMOND

Swaley's Wife

What her name was, I never knew. She was never called anything but Swaley's wife, even at her funeral, even that day after the funeral, when the smoke plumes from Swaley's yard swirled across the Gallowgate in dark belching clouds.

Swaley was the biggest dealer in the district. He dealt in fish, coal-briquettes, carpets, but his main trade was horses. A proud man, who spoke little, he was bearded, with the hollow cheeks and snapping black eyes of the true-bred gypsy. He always dressed well, in a neat dark suit and shining laced boots. But his shirts were collarless, topped by the knotted handkerchief that was the hallmark of his trade. His was the most prosperous among the warren of yards in the sprawling back streets of the Gallowgate. There were dozens of them — low-doored and low-ceilinged, dark and windowless, dating from the days when horsemen believed that fresh air and sunlight ruined the sheen of a horse's coat.

Each stable housed twenty or thirty horses — horses from local markets, from Ireland, from the islands, from the famous Appleby Fair. Heavy horses, vanners, hunting horses, trotters, they were all there. You saw one, you made your bid, and that was that. It was yours — your word was your bond.

Swaley bought one from our yard once, but the next day it went down with colic and had to be shot. When we told him, he looked at us steadily.

"Dead or alive," he said, "it's mine. I bought it. My word's my bond." He pulled from his pocket a wad of notes and tossed it to us. We didn't argue. Some months later we heard he had married, and we sent the money, the same wad of notes, to him as a wedding present. Next market day he came over, shook hands and smiled. He didn't often smile.

Swaley's wife, like her husband, spoke rarely. A tall strong woman, untidily-dressed in shabby jeans, she had the dark-eyed look of a Spanish gypsy. Her tied-back hair was waist-length, her skin had the rough tan that suggested, not sunlight, but a lifetime spent in smoky caravans. Like all gypsy women, she worked. She was out in the street selling fish at seven in the morning, she hawked coal-briquettes, she fed the horses, worked them, and drove the trotters on the race-track.

"She does a man's job in the yard," Willie told us. Willie was the yardman. Small and wizened, when he wasn't mucking out or racking hay, he was bent double over his brush, sweeping the yard. No droppings, no mud, no bits of straw. It was always bare and tidy, except on that day, the day of the fire, when it was covered in black soot, ash, and wisps of charred satin curtains from the burning caravan.

The first time I met Swaley's wife was in the secretary's office at a show. A crowd of us were waiting to enter horses. She looked awkward and out of place in her faded jeans and man's shirt, with a knotted handkerchief at the neck. An ancient threadbare velvet cap was jammed low on her brow.

"What classes did you say?" The secretary didn't bother to hide his amusement as he handed her a schedule — it was obvious that she couldn't read it.

I was so angry I couldn't speak. I took her arm, pulled her aside and filled in the entry form. In silence she handed it in, her cheeks dull red, then gave me a quick nod, and smiled. You could sense she didn't smile often. Her smile was strange, wide and hard, with no laughter behind it. Her teeth were big and square, all the same size, like a horse's teeth. But out on the track, she was in a class by herself. The best moment in a trotting race isn't the finish, although that's when the crowd roars. It's when the tape flies up and the horses know the moment has come. Their heads go up and they set sail as if their lives depended on it. Swaley's wife felt it too. Her face would light up, her eyes burn, and she looked alive and free.

After the race she was always white and drained. If she won, she showed little interest in the trophies and prize money. Swaley would come forward to receive them. But she loved driving the lap of honour with the winner's rosettes on the bridle, the many-coloured ribbons streaming in the wind.

Swaley loved it all — the victory, the cheering crowds, the photographs in the local papers. He was a big man by this time, in the motor trade, with heavy lorries on the road. He had shaved off his beard and wore a collar and tie with his checked tweed suits. At Appleby Fair he made history by the huge price he paid for a colt by the legendary Hurricane — a big bay colt with, unfortunately, its sire's bad temperament. It took six men to unload it on arrival and get it into a loosebox. Swaley warned his wife to keep away from it.

No one knew exactly how or when it happened, but she began to be seen in its box, rubbing its ears and talking to it. Then she was grooming it, tacking it up, and lungeing it every morning on the waste land behind the stable. Six weeks later it was broken and going well in the sulky.

To everyone else the colt was still aggressive — no one was safe from the bared teeth, or the vicious side kick. Only when it heard the footsteps of Swaley's wife in the yard it stood still, listening, ears pricked and nostrils wide, waiting for her hand on the door. The blacksmith refused to shoe it unless she was there to hold the halter.

We had struggled once for hours with a young horse which refused to go up the ramp into the horsebox, and in despair we asked her help. She didn't put a hand on it — just said, "Come on, lad!" and walked up the ramp. It followed her and stood quietly, waiting to be tied up.

Inevitably she became something of a legend. People told tales about her that grew with each telling. They stared at her in the street, they whispered about her, they sought her advice.

Swaley began to feel resentful. A proud man, he saw her as a threat to his status. It was at Appleby Fair that he saw, beyond all doubt, what the horse world thought of the woman he called his wife.

They came from everywhere to Appleby. The rough bowtop wagons parked up on the hill. Down below, in the long meadow where they ran the horses, were the long luxury wagons, mobile homes deeply carpeted, with refrigerators, television sets, the windows filled with silver and fine china. Swaley's wife sat at the window of their caravan, against curtains of rose-pink satin tied back with clasps of fretted silver. Her hair was loose on her shoulders and her face glowed tanned and golden against her pin-tucked blouse of fine lawn.

Each man who passed looked up and doffed his cap. Swaley was furious. He knew the reason for their respect. He had known it for some time but had refused to recognise it. His wife was a horse whisperer.

Down the ages there had always been horse whisperers. They had the word, the power, the presence. It was a secret thing, a gypsy thing, known but not discussed. Swaley's face darkened and he retreated into silence that was at once watchful and menacing. His wife no longer drove the trotters. She still went to the race meetings, but drank heavily and was often brought home slumped insensible on the back seat of her Mercedes. She developed a taste for haute couture, jewels and exotic dogs. Sometimes, passing the yard, we saw her, in a Puccini shirt, feeding the horses, accompanied by six or seven chihuahuas.

People passing at night told of shouting and arguments, the sound of running feet and breaking windows, and furniture hurled across the yard.

I lost sight of her some some time, but one day, in the impeccable elegance of McDonald's in Buchanan Street, I saw her. Even against that background she stood out, in her pale mink coat with matching hat, tall cream suede boots, and ring-heavy fingers. She turned and smiled when I touched her arm. The years had not been kind — her face was dry and seamed, like the faces of old women in hot countries, her eyes were bloodshot and infinitely weary. She carried a tiny long-haired chihuahua, pale gold, with flaring fronded ears and a mink collar round its neck. She gave me the chi to hold while she collected her parcels. It sat upright, watching her every movement with its huge dark eyes. Close at hand, the eyes were not black, but deep ruby. Chihuahuas had been the temple dogs of the Aztecs, and were burned on the funeral pyres on the death of their owners. So the ruby eyes were greatly prized — they were supposed to have the power to light the journey of the soul into the next world. As Swaley's wife took the dog from me she put her hand on my arm and I felt her quick breath against my cheek. Then she smiled and was gone.

Watching her go, I felt curiously peaceful, as if I had come to terms with life. Her breath had a faint sweetness, a warmth of meadow hay, like the breath of a horse.

A few weeks later I heard that she was dead. An accident with a horse, they said — her skull had been shattered by a heavy blow. My first thought was of the Hurricane colt — he would be a stallion by now — but I couldn't imagine him attacking her. Or any horse, for that matter.

The day after the funeral I passed Swaley's yard. Shadowy in the smoke, Willie was sweeping busily. He jerked a thumb at the blaze.

"Swaley ransacked the house," he told me. "Everything she owned is in there — the caravan with its satin curtains, silver, the lot. All her dresses, and her mink coat. He kept saying, 'it's our custom'."

"What happened to her chihuahua?" I asked. "The little long-haired one she carried with her?"

"Can't tell you," he answered, not lifting his head.

"Strange people. They have their own ways."

He swept the debris into his barrow. "Look!" he said suddenly. "There's the wee dog's collar. At your feet."

I bent down to lift it, but he stopped me.

"Leave it, for God's sake! Wait."

With a hay fork he tossed the collar onto the fire.

"Better there. It's bad luck."

As he walked away with his barrow the smoke blew across in gusts. Perhaps I only imagined in it the faint whiff of burning flesh.

The ruby eyes.

Dear God, I prayed, let them light her journey.

RONALD McNEIL

Waken Yourself Up

First, there's the usual knock, loud, impatient as ever, then up goes the flap on the letter-box. Nan sees Barbara's eyes dart here, there and all-ways. The eyes fly away and her mouth appears. "Nan," it calls in, "are you there?"

Nan's in the lobby half-in, half-out of a too-tight dress.

She knows fine it's too tight. Somehow she manages a hand to the lock, trussed though she is.

"I thought you'd be ready," Barbara says, stepping in, seeing her there with the dress rucked over the midriff and only one of her stockings on.

"I tried to be, Barbara," says Nan. "I got up early. But, uch, one thing and another." The usual cry. But it's obvious Barbara's pleased to see the state she's in.

"Come here till we fix you up," she says. "What are we going to do with you, at all?"

Nan lifts her arms for the dress to be tugged down and yawns. She can see it's always going to be like this between them.

"Is there not something else you could put on?" says Barbara, cramming Nan's flesh into the gusset. "Something that would let you move about." She draws the zip up quick.

"This dress cost me a lot of money."

"That's neither here nor there. You want to be able to move about."

Nan feels her mouth go that firm way. She isn't going to be bullied into anything. She likes this dress. It corsets her where she needs it. She feels dressed in it and she likes to feel dressed, even if that means hurting a wee bit. She runs her hands all down the silky material. Crepe de Chine, in actual fact. Today reminds her of when she was a wee girl and her mother would stand her on a chair in the kitchen and dress her up for church. She can remember those clothes, how uncomfortable they were. Coats with collars that chaffed her under the chin, shoes that pinched her toes and made them bleed. At one stage she thought the discomfort she suffered had something to do with the church: some decree that said she must suffer as the Lord suffered. She'd sit there right on the edge of the pew, imagining the spear go in, shivering for all she was worth.

Already she can feel the dress cut the circulation to her arms. She doesn't have to do this to herself. She could turn up at Barbara's church dressed like a rag picker and nobody would bat an eyelid; it's that sort of a place.

But Sunday is Sunday and she likes to feel dressed.

Barbara, though, is still at it trying to get people to do her bidding. "It's a scorcher of a day, too," she's saying. "You're going to be absolutely melting." She starts wheeling round and round in the lobby, her white skirt fanning out. "Take that stocking off at least. I've mine's off, see?" She hitches the skirt up her short brown thighs, and — "Blillum, blillum, blillum," — wriggles her toes.

"Uch, you can't sit in a church bare-legged," says Nan. She turns towards the kitchen slowly. "That's just going over the score." She doesn't know why she's bothering to say this. She could save herself the effort. She'll be taking off the stocking, sure as guns.

Barbara's behind her now, prodding her in the back, bustling her into the kitchen. "Over the score nothing," she says. She goes straight to the window and rips back the curtains. "You, Nan, you're that staid," she says as the light bursts in on them. "What is it the Bible says? 'Awake,' doesn't it? 'Loose thyself from thy bands.'?"

So Nan rolls down the stocking. Surprise, surprise. There was no coming or going with Barbara at all. And when she looks up Barbara's standing there, ogling at her. She can feel her face go red.

The dirty plates on the dresser have begun to smell the place up.

This is what Nan does, you see, she lets things lie. Barbara has ducked beneath the sink for the rubber gloves. "This is the last time I'm doing this for you, Mrs Woman," she says. "If you were as pernickety about your house as you are about your looks you would do okay."

Nan draws her a dirty look. She's getting hell of a brave, this weather. Barbara doesn't see her, though. She's catching air in one of the gloves. She pops out the fingers, an udder. "The last time," she says, "remember."

Nan allows herself a wee laugh. How many times has she heard Barbara say this? Nan hopes to God she'll be saying it for a long while yet. She's standing with the stocking in her hand wondering what she aught to do next. She decides to make herself up. She thinks this thought, then Barbara says, "You should leave your skin alone, let it breathe," as though she has read her mind. This is a thing that happens between them. It's not as unusual as you'd think.

Barbara's whole body seems to quiver as she scours the plates. "You'll have to waken yourself up," she tells Nan, looking at her over her shoulder. "Give yourself a shake. The food's stuck to these plates like limpets."

The room they're in is L-shaped. Nan calls it the kitchen, but she doesn't know if that's exactly correct. The tail of the L is the bed recess. Robert whipped out the bed that was there to make a scullery. He put in her cooker and built her a lovely cabinet with sliding doors. The carpet's from the factory where Nan and Barbara work. Doesn't beige get dirty awful quick? Both the fireside chairs are littered with clothes, some are laundered and some are rumpled up. Nan tucks the stocking she's just removed underneath one of the cushions. The fire has been set since February, March. Scrapings out the pots are all over the coal. What a mess. There's too much clutter on the mantlepiece. It would be nice to get a letter; she could put it in the letter-rack. The Dutch boy and girl, the clock. It chimes as she looks at it. She looks in behind it and there's Robert's insurance account. 'The Shepherds' Friendly Society'. She wonders why they call it this. She'll have to see about getting it cashed. There's something like thirty pounds in it and thirty pounds is thirty pounds.

At the end of the mantlepiece is her Bible, the one she's had since she was so-high. She takes it along with her, but she doesn't know why. She never seems to use it. Brother whatever his name is'll start to read, then inspiration will call and that'll be that. Close the book. And the hymns they sing are from something called 'Praise the Lord!'

Yet most of the ones there take their Bible. Barbara takes hers. It's in the pocket of her cardigan; Nan can see the bulge. Fay gave it to her as a sort of keepsake. Miss Wonderful. There'd been a brooch, too, but Barbara lost it. Sort of leaf made of copper. Big. Not a very nice brooch. Nan thinks she would have lost it, too.

It's funny, she knows next to nothing about this Fay, yet she's never done hearing about her. 'Me and Fay used to do such-and-such.' 'Me and Fay used to do such-and-such else.' But what sort of sweets did she eat, for instance. What did she like to watch on the television? And as for the truth about what happened, well, about that she knows even less; only the odd thing Barbara's let drop. So what does she know, exactly? She knows that Fay came up from England. To visit her father, apparently. She knows that she liked it here, decided to say. That she found herself a job as an auxiliary at Ayr County Hospital. And really that's about all she knows. She doesn't know why she left her job, or why she moved back south, although she's a good idea. Tongues had started to wag; that's her theory. And what lassie could cope with that? It's the thing she most dreads herself. Imagine it all came out in the open and you had to leave your job under a cloud. But maybe that wasn't what happened at all. Maybe she's got it all wrong.

She only saw Fay twice, at least, that she can remember. She looked kind of thin. That was the thing about her you noticed most. Barbara probably nagged her all the time to eat more. Barbara would. 'You'll need to put some flesh on those bones.' You could imagine Barbara saying something like that.

The first time she saw Fay was in Woolworth's. She was along with Barbara. They were going from one counter to another, lifting and laying things. Bars of soap, things like that. Then Barbara started plonking this toy piano, the sort of thing Barbara does, and Fay pulled her by her scarf to make her chuck it.

That was the first time. The second time, she was visiting Robert. She'd gone out to the corridor to find a nurse — she was in one of her states; she was excited — and Fay came round the corner carrying this tray. There was a glass of water on it and she had her head down looking at it, at the glass of water on the tray. Nan just let her pass on.

Fay moved back to England in the same week Robert died. Barbara says this is no mere coincidence.

For a long time they didn't really know one another, she and Barbara. It's funny, that. Even though they worked together at the same loom. It was only really their misery that brought them close. Barbara would go on about Fay and she would go on about Robert. They were given this beautiful carpet to work on during that time, she can remember. The pattern was based on a garden somewhere. They were told where. It wasn't Culzean Castle. She can remember its lovely colours, all the reds and greens, the way they sort of merged into one another. It was a lovely thing. And she's only really known Barbara since then.

She can't say she's ever been keen on this church carry-on. But what can you do? Nothing. She was actually quite scared the first time, the way people would just get up out their seats and start gibbering away. It isn't so bad now, right enough, but she can't really say that she likes it.

And the other thing, she's never been keen on that either. But that she just likes to put right out of her mind, not to even think about it. She knew it was bound to happen and now it's happening and she's only got herself to blame.

There's a stack of soapy dishes on the dresser. Good old Barbara is peeling off the gloves. "I'll leave you to dry them," she says. "Surely you'll be able to manage that?"

Then she asks Nan if she's got sandals.

"Sandals?" says Nan, acting thick.

"Aye, like these," says Barbara, holding up her foot.

"I should have somewhere," says Nan. "I had quite a nice pair with red bits going across, but I can't mind now whether I threw them out or not."

"Well, away and see if you can see them," says Barbara. "They'll likely be kicking around. Then give your face a bit rub with the sponge. You're awful kind of seedy looking," she says.

Sandals. With a Crepe de Chine dress. But she doesn't bother to say anything, just goes through to the bedroom like a good wee girl to look. She gets to her knees — it isn't easy — and hunts along the line of shoes beneath the dressing-table. She finds one sandal, then the other. She sits on the edge of the bed and straps them on. Church bells start to ring somewhere. Clang, clang, clang. She shuts her eyes and she's back in her mother's kitchen, standing on a chair.

SUSAN CAMPBELL

Fuck

It was Festival time. We went to this bar which was very dark and full of famous writers. Famous in Glasgow anyway. One of them started talking to me.

"Do you know what I am?" he said. "I'm a fucking good writer."

He went on to tell me about all the things he'd written. They were all to do with real people, who spoke in real language. He was an International Socialist he said. He talked a lot, and I could hardly hear him, so I just nodded at intervals.

"You know," he said, "you wouldn't be half so interesting if you were plain."

To save me thinking of a reply, all the guy's pals just then converged on us. They were all writers. One had a big beard, another had pale eyes and a croissant shaped face like the man in the moon.

"Come on back to mine for a wee dram", said the beard. He'd been talking to my friend Angus, and their faces were glowing. We got into two cars, and drove to a douce curving Edinburgh terrace. Up a close, we squeezed into a small cold living room. Angus said something in Gaelic. The man with the pale eyes said:

"Just relax son, for fuck's sake. Think that stuff makes you look good?"

The beard tried to defend him.

"I don't think Angus meant . . ."

"Don't try and fucking patronise me, that's all. Don't be cheeky and you'll be all right Angus."

"I'm only learning," said Angus.

"Aye well . . . " He rearranged his feathers like a hen. Everyone was poured a large whisky.

"So what do you do yourself Susan?"

I said that I was trying to write. There was a stir of disbelief, as if I had said I was a coalminer.

"Do you use the word fuck in your writing Susan?"

"Eh, no."

"How no?"

I said that I didn't use it much in spoken language, so it seldom occurred to me to write it.

"What's wrong with the word fuck?"

"Nothing."
"Offend your fucking middle-class sensibilities does it?"
"No. It's just . . . "
"You think BBC English is the only valid language don't you? I suppose you want to write for TV."
I said that I had thought of it. There was a howl of derision confirmed. I tried to make my position clearer.
"It's not that I mind bad language . . . "
"Bad! Bad! Did you hear that? Fucking . . . "
Angus tried to save me.
"She didn't mean bad. You can't help using the language you're used to."
"We can't what!"
"Not you, one, us, anyone."
"You patronising little shit."
"Fucking establishment invalidation."
Angus continued through the shouting.
"What if people insisted you use Gaelic words, even though they're not part of your vocabulary?"
"Fucking wise guy. You know two words of fucking Gaelic and you think you're more of a Scot than me eh?"
"It's just the way you're brought up isn't it?" I said, faintly. "I mean one."
"You've got a fucking nerve coming here to tell us the way we write is wrong. Who the fuck do you think you are?".
"You think you can oppress any language that's not your fucking RP. If you've not been to University you shouldn't open your mouth eh? Listen darlin I spent ten years on the yards, and seven years on the dole, and I'm a fucking good writer . . . "
After what seemed like a long time of this, I sank down onto the carpet, but the atmosphere was no better there, and I got up and went out. I didn't really want to go to the bathroom. I stepped over someone who was sleeping in the hall, opened a door and found myself in a study. I pushed the door to. I could still hear the argument, but muffled. I sat down at the desk and rested my head on my arms.
I looked up to see the beard standing in the sliver of light at the door. He closed it behind him and came and knelt on the floor in front of me. He

rested his head, which was covered in corkscrew curls, against my knee, and leaned there, companionably. He had not said anything during the argument.

"Never mind", he said now.

"They're so hard."

"Och I know. They're drunk that's all."

We stayed like that for a while, neither of us saying anything. There was a picture of a pretty woman on the desk in front of me.

"Is that your wife?" I said at last.

He caught my hand, and, not seeming to know what to do with it, placed it on the top of his head, which was soft and springy. I stroked it experimentally. He got up on his hind legs and kissed me. He had a nice warm mouth, but it hardly seemed appropriate, and I turned my head away.

"Get down", I said.

He sat back down on the carpet.

"Come on," he said, "Let's go and walk the doggie."

"Have you got a dog?" I said.

"Aye."

"Where is it?"

"It's in the bedroom."

"In the bedroom?"

"Honestly. I had to shut her in there. Let's go and take her for a sprint round the Meadows. She'll be bursting."

He was jumping up again, full of enthusiasm, putting his arms round me, introducing his face into mine again.

"Oh for goodness sake". I slid away, got up and went out, leaving him lying dispiritedly on the carpet.

Back in the living room, more whisky was being poured, and a writer had put on a cassette tape of him reading one of his own works. I sat down beside Angus.

"A strange thing happened to me out there", I said to him in a low voice.

"LISTEN!" roared the first writer. "If you don't listen you won't learn, Susan."

I shut up, intimidated. I could not make much sense out of the reading. The beard came shambling back in, blinking in the light, and sat down behind me. He picked up a strand of my hair and began to twirl it above my head like the Bellman with his crew. I kept twitching to shake him off, but he would not be discouraged.

Angus was starting an alternative reading, from a book of poetry he'd found on the floor.

'in this cold city slabs
of stone, hard, people . . .
though i touch your hair
i can't touch your heart.
fear and desolation,
desolation and fear."

"Is that poetry or not?" said Angus.

"Didn't I write that?" said the beard.

"You know Angus you're fucking full of shite," said a writer.

"What do you mean I'm full of shite? Give me an example," said Angus.

"No Angus you're not listening. You're not being logical. If he says you're full of shite, you're full of fucking shite, right?" said the other writer.

"What are you talking about? Why can't you be human?" I said hopelessly.

"Can you give me your phone number Susan", said the beard. "Perhaps I could meet you tomorrow."

"I still don't understand your argument, and I don't think you do either," said Angus.

"I'll put you through that fucking window!" roared someone, "and that goes for you too, blue eyes."

"Oh, put me through a window then," I said, unwisely, half to myself. I was suddenly very tired. I looked up to see a large pink fist coming into my face. There was a crunching sound, then silence.

"You asked for that," said the croissant face. "Don't start getting sexist now darlin."

I stood up and went into the bathroom and spat blood. My lip was turning black and swelling up. I looked at it with interest, then started to shake, and sat down on the edge of the bath, snivelling. After a while, I went into the hall and got Angus's and my coats.

Back in the living room, the four men were spinning around, crunching broken glass into the carpet. There was a strong fresh smell of whisky. Angus was holding a broken bottle.

"Fucking cowards", he was yelling.

I caught at his arm and pulled him away. From the door, as we clattered down the stairwell, the beard called, faintly,

"Susan, can I have your phone number anyway . . . "

We walked out of the close into early morning.

"Fucking hell", said Angus.

"Did you break it over his head?" I said.

"No, just on his side."

We walked on a bit.

"It was a forty-ouncer," said Angus thoughtfully.

We walked across the Meadows, holding hands for the first time, though we had known each other since childhood.

PAT GERBER

A Girl's Best Friend

Drips plonked onto the soggy floor of the dungeon.

"Gosh," said Zenobia, one hand deep in a fissure, "they're still here!" She pulled something out and thrust it at Marcia.

"Ugh, it's all slimy you clot!" Marcia dropped the dark package.

Her torch threw marbled pools of yellow on the cracked rock wall. The tunnel breathed an earthen odour like Kelvinbridge Underground at home.

We scanned the ooze under our wellies. In an instant Zenobia found the small bundle of mouldy newspaper. She crouched down and pulled it apart.

Brilliant light bounced millions of rainbow reflections, scattering gleams and glints over the wet rock like some glitterball at a dance.

"You'd never think such a small handful of diamonds could throw so much light," I said obviously.

"Oh shut up, Smells, that's exactly wot you said wen we planted them." Marcia was still so bloody English, you never got an 'h' in what, when where or why. She was O.K. on who.

My name is, unfortunately, Esmeralda. I'm the only one of the Musketeers whose nickname still sticks. You see, twenty-five years ago the three of us were all at boarding-school. We lived in a converted house next to the castle in St Andrews.

Marcia used to have long golden hair and look like a Vestal Virgin. The staff always believed everything she said, so she was useful as our Front.

Zenobia held the diamonds up as if they were holy relics. "Gosh, quarter of a century? And no-one's discovered them. Poor thingies. Poor Stefano." The five-row choker dripped from her hand like a petrified waterfall. She was about to put it round her neck.

"Give it to me, Zen. I'll take care of it." Marcia practically snatched it out of her hands. "We were always sure they were paste anyway, weren't we?"

"Cripes, all, wait till we tell everyone in Sally's!" Zenobia's grin split her face like a gleeful turnip lantern. Her bone-structure had sunk without trace nowadays.

"Wot on earth do you mean? We can't possibly tell. There'd be the most God-awful scandal. Anyway it might not be — safe."

I knew what Marcia meant.

Here we all were, among two thousand respectable matrons and other pillars, assembled like battery hens in the University hostels to celebrate the centenary of our Old School. It was 1975 and a lot of water had passed under all our bridges not to mention other flotsam and jetsam.

Marcia's hair had gone fawn now, crimped into a style she thought suitable to a vicar's widow living in provincial Essex.

She and I had persuaded Zenobia to come with us for the frolic.

Yesterday everyone had been very stiff and formal, still mentally clad in the minks, Bentley's and nannies of home, or the blue-stockings of academic superiority. But after last night's shindig all shreds of dignity had gone to pot. Magically — well through large gins actually — we became again the girls we had been. And the feeling had lasted right through church today. Even the choirboys looked the same as they used to. We were dizzy with youth and irresponsibility.

The same seemed to have happened to all the other age-groupies too. Bunches of neo-gels from octogenarians to those still in their dewy twenties had swaggered round the school slapping each other on the back, reminiscing and recognising slogans still visible on the ancient desks alongside more modern stuff like 'Miss Murgatroyd is gay', which would have been considered a revolting example of sucking-up in our day.

In our day, Marcia, Zenobia and I had wrapped the diamond choker carefully in a sherbet-shandy bag, then in a copy of the St Andrew's Herald.

Sweating with fear and horror and excitement, we'd scaled the castle walls. For the usual fee, Old Groper had let us borrow the key to the dungeon.

Old Groper was the custodian most often doing Saturday evenings in summer. He knew us well. In return for a wee kiss — which included a bit of body contact, Marcia's bum, my thick thigh and Zenobia's lesser bosom — she liked to keep her best one for Stefano– Groper would let us into the grounds.

It was there we met any boyfriends we could sufficiently interest. Mine was usually an acne-ridden cigarette-bearing choirboy called Norman. We exchanged passionately meaningful looks all through Sunday sermons and had an elaborate system of notes left in an arrow-slit of the castle wall.

Marcia was actually keener on the junior gymn mistress but put up with one of Norman's mates for decency's sake. Zenobia of course was really mature. She slept regularly with Stefano, an Italian medical student from Sally's which was conveniently just across the road from our House. A useful shrubbery lay against the wall in our grounds providing cover for her weekly excursions.

Occasionally he'd meet all three of us there before smuggling Zenobia up the fire-escape to his room. Being Italian he was very passionate. Zenobia said you couldn't control a man like that, it was bad for him. So you had to Give In.

In the end Zenobia got expelled for being engaged to Stefano — and pregnant.

She was on her third marriage, and a converted Jewess now. Stefano and Catholicism hadn't worked out. And after he got done in by his godfather or someone she decided to make a change. She'd left a trail of six children before landing back in Edinburgh with this jeweller. She was quite happy, because Something-stein (I can never remember his name — a little grey-rabbit man) turned an aged and blind eye to her weekly infidelities. She had as much rope as she could use and a good house in the New Town.

Compared to Zenobia and Marcia, my life was fairly textbook really. Children — a boy and a girl and heterosexual as far as one could judge, who only occasionally irritated their father, my husband. He's a workaholic G.P. I play golf and work the antique markets. Edwardian jewellery mostly though I'll try anything I can carry. I want to open my own shop.

Marcia runs a business full-time. It must be pretty healthy though she won't talk about it, because she drives this Ferrari and wears silver-mink to balls. Not like most vicar's widows. But her stepson's a heroin addict.

It had been because of Zenobia that we got the diamond choker.

We'd found it in the bootroom one Saturday, while we were changing for Games. Our school was modelled on Eton, so we had enforced Games every day including Saturdays to mould our characters. It was in Marcia's hockey boot. She stubbed her chilblain on it. While she was screaming in agony I read the note.

'This piccolo gift I offer you for your quiet S.'

"Of course they're only paste," Marcia had said. "But jolly dee. Woolworth's, wot?" Just because it was her boot she assumed they were for her exclusively.

I had pointed out that I too had to be kept quiet — and that if it hadn't been for dear old Zenobia we wouldn't have anything to be quiet about — so the choker belonged to all three of us. At that age I was still naively trying to live up to the Christian Ethic instilled into me every holidays by my father. It usually wore off about the time they stopped taking our temperatures for the pox, three weeks into each term.

The problem was what to do with the diamonds. We couldn't very well wear them. Flash was forbidden in any form, even sleepers. Our things were meticulously inspected every Sunday — each drawer, bag and desk gone through. Everyone was a suspect till proved innocent, even the prefects. You couldn't hide a stick of Wrigley's or a dirty sock with any hope of success.

Shivering along the road back to our House after hockey (I'd been in goal again — two hours of hypothermia as punishment for running in some corridor) I suggested the tunnel. We knew there was one running from a dungeon. And the public weren't allowed in. That was no problem to us, what with Old Groper.

We called in to see him and arranged everything. Because of my lingering Ethic I got Marcia, who lied like an angel, to convince him we were researching the ghost of some bishop who got martyred there. He swallowed it whole.

About a week after the fait was accompli, the Mafia theft splashed the headlines of even the quality press we were allowed to see. Interpol were hunting for the killer of some Italian countess *and* for a diamond choker she'd been wearing to a charity ball in London. I still have the photo I cut out.

Apparently this countess had been on the Mafia's black list for years, having fled to Britain for sanctuary. Her dismembered body still in bits of ballgown had been collected from the branches of trees in Hyde Park. But a section of her neck was missing — and the choker.

Zenobia nudged me back to the present. "Cripes all, what are we going to do with the lovely thing? It's — well — a bit of an embarrassment, isn't it? Remember all the hoo ha?"

"Why don't I take it south to a little man I know in Bond Street?" Marcia slipped the choker into her pocket, extinguishing its fire.

"I say, come to that my beloved could tell us if they're real or not." Zenobia bent, darkening the pool of light.

I grabbed the torch from Marcia. "Shsh, someone's coming. Listen." I shoved her against the wall and in the scuffle dropped it. It shattered on a jut of rock and tinkled blindly into the sludge.

"Oh Smells," giggled Zenobia, "You clot! Now we can't see."

In the darkness the earth-odour seemed stronger and the drips louder, echoing round the dungeon behind is.

"Marcia, feel along the wall with one hand, and hold onto Zenobia's back with the other," I snaked forward.

"Were are you Zen?" Marcia's voice was going high. "Witch way's the dungeon? Oh Zen, I'm scared."

I'd found the dungeon corner. For an instant I hesitated. There was the feel of someone else being there. My eyes were getting better at seeing through the blackness. Where I thought the ladder led up from the dungeon there seemed to be a paler gloom.

Then the whispers started. Sibilant sound wound round the chamber, elusive as smoke. I remembered its facility for behaving like a whispering gallery.

I made for the dimness at the foot of the ladder, quite confidently. Then I bumped into someone. There was a sharp intake of breath. The thick tweed was neither Zenobia nor Marcia. The breath exhaled in a giggle.

"Let go my coat, idiot! Jilly! Let me go! Oh, who is it? Where are the boys?"

I realised that we had probably been neither the first nor the last schoolgirls to make use of the castle. There was no way of knowing how many of them were in the dungeon with me, and I thanked God for the confusion that ensued. From the ladder I could hear old girls and new girls in a confusion of mirth.

My hand found the ladder. The mini was quite discreetly parked beneath the overgrown bushes of the shrubbery over the wall. By the time the girls sorted themselves out I'd be half-way to Glasgow.

The diamonds rattled merrily in my hand. Not bad for an amateur pickpocket, I thought. There would be no difficulty disposing of them through the underground. I knew a little Italian family. They had an ice-cream shop near Kelvinbridge.

It would make a grand site for my antique shop. I'd buy it from them. And continue to work for the underground. Like Marcia, I knew the diamonds were real.

LINDA McCANN

The Bad Thief

"An orange juice," she said as they bundled in through the swing doors, dripping with rain.

"Still rainin Big Man?" shouted a voice from somewhere.

"Naw-naw," he said, making straight for the bar without looking round.

The girl edged herself in towards the wall seat of a small corner table near the door, under the fierce glow of a barred electric wall-heater which seemed merely to swallow each new draught as the doors swung shut.

The pub was almost empty. A discussion programme was playing quietly on Radio Clyde, the American Amens of an evangelist condemning drink and sex, proud of his shame as he told of the evils he had done when he was still a lost sheep, in the days when he preyed on people, before discovering the benefits of praying for them. The radio crackled and hissed along with him.

As the girl sat down, a strange young man was at her side. He put his drink on the table, his burning cigarette in the ashtray, and sat down in the seat next to hers, crossing one skinny leg over the other and folding his arms. She saw that he was smiling at her. She smiled back at him and then stared down at her handbag.

His arms still folded, he leaned towards her and whispered "Opium."

She hesitated and then said "Oh — no, I'm just in for a drink. No looking for anything."

"No," he said, "I mean' Opium'. Yer perfume."

"Awh, I see what you mean, yeah — that's really good."

All the time, he stared and smiled at her, never looking away. "Chanel Number Five in here last week if ye'd been in. A fiver."

"Och imagine that," she said, looking towards the table.

"Aw hullo Big Yin!" he shouted, as her boyfriend arrived and put a pint of Guinness and an orange juice on the bar.

The boyfriend glanced at the girl and sat down opposite them, saying "Aye hello." He had seen their companion in there before. He was known as The Fish because his name was something like Salmon, or Haddock. Several seconds passed. "Did you want the ice in it?"

"Yeah, that's fine," she said.

He looked at their friend.

"D'you want a drink?"

"Naw," said The Fish, unfolding his arms and patting the side of his half-empty pint glass on the table. "I'm no drinkin the night." He folded his arms again and leaned back in his seat. "D'you know what I'm goany tell yeze?" He reached for his cigarette, tapped off the growth of ash, and puffed a quick column of rings which rose like indecipherable signals, then wobbled and spread to hover above his head for a moment in a ghostly question mark.

They shook their heads slightly.

"See that?" he asked. He was pointing up to somewhere high over the bar.

"What?" they said.

"That beam above the bar. Up ther I was sittin last week. Barred me."

He lifted his pint to his lips, lowering it again long enough to add "Let me back in but."

"What were you doin up there?" she asked.

"Nuthin," he said. "Jist sittin. Barred me fir nuthin." He sipped his drink.

"Oh," she said.

A group of people arrived, the men holding the doors open for the women to enter first. Icy air was pouring in as one woman slowed the group down, turning to the men and saying "Aye bit that's whit I'm tellin ye

Davey. That's whit I saze tae them."

"Aye, I know, I know," said Davey, "Now what ur yeze aw havin?" The group moved past to debate at the bar, crossing a few minutes later to a table in the far corner, carrying a multi-coloured assortment of tall and short glasses.

"Aye," the woman was arguing, "It's definitely no real but."

Soon there were enough people for there to be a queue at the bar. They came in stamping their feet and rubbing their hands together as if they were waiting for hot soup to be given out.

An old woman came in with a very old mongrel.

"Heh Fish," shouted a man, "Ye better watch or that dug'll think you're a bone!"

"Aye," said a woman. "A fillet!"

"Quite busy the night, eh?" said the boyfriend.

"Aye," said The Fish, "It's always busy on a Friday night. D'yeze waant a gittaney?"

"A what? Eh, no thanks. We don't smoke."

"Nuthin but the best in here by the way," The Fish said, striking a match, "French perfume. French fags." He beckoned them closer with a jerk of his head. "French sunglasses."

"Oh, aye," they said.

"Three-fifty a perr. It's a sale. A fiver if it wiz the summer."

"Ah well," the boyfriend said, "We're no really needin — "

"It's awright," said The Fish, "Ye kin go intae the changin room an try them on." He nodded towards the door marked "Ladies".

"Let's see them," she said.

By the time The Fish had sold his first pair of sunglasses the pub was filling steadily, a one-way flood that would not overflow until closing-time. Conversations were growing louder to be heard over their own noise. Every now and then the fruit machine rattled wildly and pounded out snatches of tunes according to the skill of the player and the luck of the game, each verdict greeted by a curse or a cheer.

A middle-aged man rushed in and came over to the corner table where the young couple sat. "Heh Jimmy," he said to them all in general, "I waant this fur ma hoose."

"What?" said The Fish.

"I'm havin a party the night," explained the man.

"Aw aye, I see," said The Fish, lifting the ashtray and his pint, "Nae bother pal — on ye go."

They all snatched up their drinks as the man took the table and walked out with it under his arm, people apologising to him and stepping back as he hit them on the legs with it.

A man at the next table said "Aye ther ye are hen," clearing a space and dragging his table towards them so that they could reach to put their drinks on it. He gathered together some used glasses. "Aw come on now — what about clearin some a they empty glasses here, ih?" Turning back round, he added "Whit-kinna bloody pub is this anywey?"

No one heard him and the glasses were stacked inside one another and shoved onto the window ledge, in between the dark burgundy curtain and the bars.

The Fish made his way to the toilet.

"Heh — d'ye see him?" a woman asked. "Away intae the Ladies."

"Aye — kinky bugger he is — he diz that," said her friend. "Did ye see Magrit in here the other night?"

"Naw."

"Aw a bloody sin so it wiz. She kim oot the toilet and she'd tucked a bit ay ir skirt intae ir knickers at the back, right up. Aye. They were aw callin ir Signor Bum. Bloody sin."

"Aye," said the other woman, "I've done that before. Awfa embarrassin."

An old man was walking sideways across the floor, holding onto the backs of chairs as he mountaineered towards the nearest exit. He stopped when he reached the gap between the last chair and the wall, and he stood there like a sleepwalker on a tightrope. Bells rang in the fruit machine as it hammered the opening to 'Bridge on the River Kwai', and people cheered each time the old man moved forwards or backwards as if held up by invisible strings, his feet feeling around for the floor. When almost at the door, he swayed to one side and then swung fast in the other direction, saving himself a few times by bouncing off the wall, until finally there was a deep, sick thud as his head came down on the large rusted hinge that was sticking out at the bottom of the door.

The climax of laughter faltered as the old man lay still on the floor, sawdust reddening around his head. The fruit machine gave a quick jangle of 'The Death March'.

"Ohph — Jesus Christ did you see that?" said a man. "That wiz a dull yin."

"Oh aye, a right dull yin that wiz right enough," said another.

A woman shouted over to the old man, "Ur ye awright?" and there was another burst of laughter all around. "Naw," she said, "That wiz a dull yin."

In the lapping blue of the ambulance light, the barman followed the stretcher towards the door, sprinkling sawdust over the stain, not noticing the soiled white hairs rising up from the hinge when the doors banged shut.

"Come oan!" The Fish was complaining to a woman, "Thir wiz seven perr ther! No six! Wher ur they?"

"Mibbe thir doon the back i the seat," somebody said.

A tall man came over and The Fish said "That's right int it Andy — we goat eight perr."

"Aye," said Big Andy, "How?"

"Ah it's definitely no right," The Fish was saying.

"Okay. Wait a minute," said Andy. "Order please," he shouted, "can we have a wee bit a order please? Right. Huz embdy saw a perra specs?"

Nobody had seen a thing.

"It's hur I'm tellin ye," said The Fish, looking at the floor while pointing towards the smiling woman.

"Prove it ya wee shit," she said.

"Aye," shouted The Fish, "You're a thief! That's whit you ur!"

"Aye, jist listen tae it!" said the woman.

"Right," shouted Andy, "That's enough fae the lot a yeze," then, turning to The Fish, he said, "Christ sake man, jist let ir have thim. Ye don't argue way hur."

"A durty thief ye ur anywey," shouted The Fish, his arm grasped by Big Andy. "Nuthin bit a durty thief!"

"Aw come on now," said a man. "Cool it — ih?"

The barman looked back down to the overflowing pint he was pouring.

The Fish went up to the far corner to watch the darts game and to sulk into a Southern Comfort.

The "durty thief" left.

About ten minutes later a man battered in through the doors and stood panting, his feet on the patch of damp sawdust as if he had been drawn there by the smell of the blood he now stood on. Only his eyes moved, searching all the faces.

The noise broke down to a low discordant hum as a silence spread among people who remembered the man from before his latest, and very long, spell of absence. For the people who recognised him as The Snake, a legend fading to myth was now made reality.

Nobody let on they knew him.

The barman started to pull down the metal screens from above the bar, securing them at the bottom.

There was a sudden clatter of wood upon flagstone as a swarm of men darted past The Snake and out through both exits.

The Snake waited and said nothing.

Soon the pub had emptied apart from a dozen or so who were too drunk to notice, and the people who were trapped at the corner table, their exit barred by the man who now stood calculating.

Then he moved. He butted, booted, threw over tables-full of drink, never accusing, never noticing those who tried to fight back.

When all the people in the corner were either against the wall in submission or on the floor in defeat, he stood waiting, streaming in blood.

A young man emerged from the rubble and approached, raising a pint tumbler with the intention of smashing it in The Snake's face. The Snake easily saw the glass coming, raised his hand and slapped it out of the way to crash on the floor. The young man smiled slightly.

All heads now turned from the challenger to The Snake. The Snake grinned back at him and sighed, raising his arms and placing one hand on each of his opponent's shoulders. The young man stood fixed, fascinated as the face of the Snake came closer and swivelled to the side, the mouth beginning to open.

Several seconds passed before The Snake turned and walked away. The young man's nose was almost off to the bone, with scarlet rows of teeth printed on either side.

The Snake went out the way he had come in, leaving his victim staring at the creaking doors, and smiling.

"Right — come on now ladies and gents," shouted the barman, raising the guards again, "Last orders: please."

The Fish slowly looked round from behind the door of the ladies and then was first at the bar for a double Southern Comfort.

Outside, The Snake crossed the road and was joined by a shadow which slipped out from a hidden close. As they walked, she linked arms with him, and she put on her new sunglasses to cover her blackening eye.

JEFF TORRINGTON

Boag's Gallery

Interrupted at prayer in the locker room Sheridan, down on one knee, dropped his hands and pretended to be tying his shoelace.

His joints creaking he rose so quickly he felt dizzy. The wobbling image before him, that of a short, blue-suited figure with a lugubrious face and restless hands, steadied.

"Yes, Stan," Sheridan asked, "what's the problem?"

When Stan Cutter, the senior stringer, came looking for you there just had to be a problem; tonight was no exception. Although the shift hadn't started yet Cutter wanted a 'rogue body' on the Trim Line subbed. Sheridan took note of the sequence and chassis numbers then the details of the replacement shell.

Producing a cigarette, Cutter tapped it a couple of times on the back of his thin hand. "Oh, and another thing," he said, dipping the cigarette end into his lighter's jittery flame, "the loading bay hoist's knackered. Chain's bust or something."

Sheridan nodded then took a roll of tape from his locker and stooping began to patch a rip in a bulky plastic bag at his feet. Cutter smoking in stressful little bursts watched for a while then his gaze wandered to the photograph taped to the inner side of the greyback's locker. It was of a red-haired girl with vivid green eyes. Wearing a university graduation gown she was posed seated with a scroll between her pale hands. Cutter's cigarette pointed like a piece of chalk.

"Your daughter, eh?"

Sheridan rose and lobbed the roll of tape onto the locker shelf. He nodded. "That's Joyce. She's lecturing in London just now. Doing well."

"Mines does all her lecturing at home," Cutter said morosely. He took a withering draw on the cigarette then, dribbling sparks on the stone floor, nipped it out between his fingers. He sighed. "Well, back to the treadmill."

When Cutter's footsteps had faded Sheridan reached into the locker and took from it a well-thumbed bible. As was his custom he flapped the book open at random and his gaze settled on the first verse it chanced on:

"Be sober, be vigilant," he read, "because your adversary, the devil, as a roaring lion, walketh about seeking whom he may devour."

There was major news that night: the Widow had been sabotaged. Someone had gone into the Transfer Tunnel and lashed an outgoing cradle to an incoming one with a steel hawser. As a result, when the Widow started up, yards of tracking had been wrenched from the roof supports and at least two car shells were on the deck. Substance had been given to this report, not only by the Widow's inertness, but also by the unprecedented level of activity in Zombieland. The Panic Wagon with its acid orange light flashing had already been despatched to the break-down source; harried tradesmen with their mates laden down with tools scuttled in its wake. Several Suits had been seen going in the same direction although the rumour that the Supreme Martian was in attendance had been ridiculed.

Except for the sporadic clatter of a trucking movement (the Paint Hospital was still disgorging shells) things were quiet in the Trim Shop. Operators basked in the silence of the seized-up Widow. They stood along the walls in the smoking areas chatting or sat at tables palled with smoke playing cards and drinking tea. Some men were still at work in the Trim Shop; the roofers and the sill-fixers; and on the line itself, a few operators were working out-of-station so that they could enjoy the break later when the Widow started up. A couple of greybacks gossiped at the top of the estate storage track and there was the usual drift of traffic through the building: the citron garbage truck droning like a heavy insect between bin areas; and stacker-trucks plying to and fro with seat materials.

Sheridan took advantage of the stoppage by getting the Trim Line snagger and the spare man to work-up the 'insert' car Cutter had asked for. Leaving them to this he went out to the loading bay to check the hoist. Obviously a dayshift fitter had been at work on it for the chain lay coiled upon the concrete floor and some of the hoist's parts were spread on a piece of sacking. To be on the safe side he decided to report the fault again. As he passed the Inspection Booth, an aluminium enclosure on the underseal ramp, Jack Boag who worked there called down to him then lobbed a set of car keys which Sheridan caught with a one-handed snatch.

"What's the verdict, then?"

Boag, a tall fleshless man with abnormally long sidelocks and a beard like an arrowhead, leaned his arms along the ramp rail. "Good enough for another thousand," he said.

Sheridan smiled up at him. "I hope you mean miles."

"Clutch, as you know, was knackered, handbrake hanging by a thread, points needed adjusting and the wheel alignment was out of wack. Reasonable nick otherwise, though."

"I'll square you later," Sheridan said.

Dropping the car keys into his overall pocket Sheridan slipped from the building by a side door and crossed to the hunched shadow of a battered looking hut near the water storage tank. Its surface made turbulent by the wind the tank splashed the odd freshet of water onto the hut roof.

The door squealed as Sheridan pushed it open. He poked his head inside the hut. As he'd expected he found it to be occupied by a rasping snore and the sour stench of alcohol.

Sheridan, the tails of his coat overall flying, recrossed the yard. The snorer in the hut was Fogarty, of course. He'd known what was going on for some time. The men were aware of this, knew that he affected not to notice Fogarty's absence from the demasking grid or that the men were covering up for him by sacrificing their own breaks. They were involved in a conspiracy of kindness the aim of which was the hoped-for rehabilitation of a man they all respected. Fire had swept away Fogarty's family and the flame of alcohol was bidding fair to expunge his life too. But there was always the chance that his grief might burn itself out. Their mutual secret unified their relationship. The men, respecting Sheridan's ability to 'turn a blind eye' as far as Fogarty was concerned, often co-operated beyond the bounds of their man-assignments. The very strength of the pact lay in both sides' tacit denial that it even existed.

Back at his desk at the top of the Trim Line, Sheridan entered a couple of memos in the Section Diary. These concerned the loading bay hoist and a complaint received from the Trim Line shoppy about puddles from roof leaks affecting the working areas — a possible safety hazard. With the memos completed Sheridan capped his pen and returned it to his pocket. The repair to the Widow might take a long time so he'd have to keep tabs on the empty-trolley supply to the Paint Shop. He flicked backwards through the pages of the Diary finding a sorry record of lost production, most of it down to human frailty. This business tonight, for instance, what had the saboteur hoped to gain by it? It was madness, sheer lunacy. Last week there had been a spate of headliner slashing then some maniac had walked down a line of Sultans dragging a file or some such tool along the paintwork. Thousands of pounds worth of damage — and for what? To hit back at the System, was that it? You wounded your enemy by cutting your own throat!

Sheridan paused at a Diary entry he'd made about a fortnight previously. It had been a report concerning a minor line stoppage due to a cradle circulator fault. But the entry had not been completed. Sheridan's face tautened: Death had intervened here, had crept up behind him in the grey shape of Ted Bullock to tell him that there had been a phone call, that he must go home at once. And that had been how his old familiar existence had ended, halfway through a sentence, the amputation of an optimism that his marriage would go on untroubled for many a year yet.

He raised his eyes to look at the static lines of cars. In a way his own life was like that now, immobilised, out-of-action. It too had been sabotaged, but not from malice, at least there was that. "But Dad, I can't just throw up everything to come back here. It isn't possible." Joyce's words returned to him from the vault of that awesome day. "I know it's terrible, you being left on your own like this, but it can't be helped." She'd been dressed in expensive mourning and had been generous with her sympathy but she had gone just the same, left with a brief wave from the wheel of her brand new Porsche.

A movement at his side interrupted his musings. Maurice Henshaw from the Inspection Booth stood there. He looked hopelessly lost inside his overlarge boiler suit, an industrial waif with glasses that magnified the timidity of his eyes. When he spoke his dentures clacked and he always seemed to have a boil plaster on his plooky face. A new-start in the Trim Shop, word had got around that he was a scoutmaster and with cruel inevitability he'd been nicknamed 'Woggle'.

"Ah, Maurice," Sheridan said, "I was just on my way to see you." From beneath his desk he dragged out the plastic bag. "Here's the stuff I promised you for your jumble sale." He placed the bag at Henshaw's feet. "It's mostly my wife's things, coats, hats, dresses, and so on. Some shoes, too — hardly been worn."

Henshaw thanked him but in a diffident way, scarcely raising his eyes, a mucky finger rubbing at his boil plaster. He looked nervous, more so than usual, that was. Perhaps he was embarrassed to be seen accepting something from a greyback in full view of the squad, although judging by the racket they were kicking up over the card games they weren't a bit interested. Still, maybe it had been indiscreet. "I'll bring it over later," he suggested.

"No, I'll take it now."

The troubled look remained, somehow bordering on reproachfulness, as if a wrong had been done. "You alright, Maurice?" Sheridan asked. "Not sick or anything?"

Henshaw shook his head then with a startling pulsation of blood into his gaunt features he blurted out a question. Sheridan absorbed it, turned it over in his mind, seeking out the reason for it. "But why d'you want a move? I thought you were doing alright in the Booth."

"I am — I was."

"Well then?"

Henshaw's flush deepened. "I'd rather not say."

Sheridan studied him. "It's not Boag, is it? I know he can be a bit of a wag."

Henshaw bent to take a grip of the bag; it looked as if he was preparing to ditch the conversation.

"Wait, let's talk about this." Sheridan took the pen from his pocket and tapped with it on the desk to emphasize each point. "You want a move — right? Okay, maybe I can arrange it. But I need to know why — so tell me."

Henshaw frowned, wet his wormlike lips, then taking a deep breath muttered, "It's those filthy pictures. I can't stand them."

So that was it! 'Boag's Gallery', a collection of nauseous pin-ups that besmirched the walls of the Inspection Booth, the sordid cullings of pornographic magazines and tabloid page threes. Similar muck could be found plant wide and though Sheridan thought them to be vile in the extreme his fellow greybacks could see little harm in them.

Henshaw's dentures continued their desolate clacking. "It's not only the pictures, it's all those blokes milling around the booth swapping porn magazines and tapes. You can't get moving for them."

Sheridan nodded but for the moment said nothing. Caution must be the keyword here. Diplomacy. In the car industry 'custom and practice' was an emotive phrase. 'Boag's Gallery' had been there a long time; operators came from all over the plant to ogle at it; it was practically a shop-floor institution. To try to tear it down in one go would be asking for trouble. He was well aware that major strikes often arose from trivial causes, an instance of this being the 'Broadmoor Bust-Up' when an over-zealous greyback had stormed in on a card school and ripped their card pack to shreds. That action had caused the Company to lose two weeks production. Yes, caution, the softly-softly approach, was the only way.

"Have you spoken to Boag about this?" he asked.

Henshaw shook his head. "I get enough stick as it is."

"But you're willing to make an official complaint?"

Henshaw took a firmer grip on the bag.

"You see, Sheridan began, "I can't make a move unless — "

"Forget it," Henshaw said with surprising aggression. "I just thought that — "

"Thought what?"

He stood looking at the floor in all his pathetic gawkiness. "Something should be done," he mumbled. "Something . . . "

"Leave it with me," Sheridan quietly said. "I'll look into it."

He watched the round-shouldered Henshaw dragging the bag across the floor towards the Inspection Booth.

An hour passed but the Widow remained motionless. It could be likened to an industrial coronary, the Centaur stricken, down on its knees. Having ensured that the Paint Shop had a bank of empty trollies Sheridan chased up the hoist repair job again. But soon he was unable to put it off any longer — the business with Boag.

Stan Cutter who had gone through to assist in a sequence change had granted Sheridan the use of his office and he sat there now behind a table cluttered with specification tallies and model plates. There was also on the table a small transistor radio with its back removed to reveal its Japanese innards. Cutter had obviously been fiddling with it for a screwdriver, a loop of solder, and a soldering iron lay nearby. Sheridan stared into the radio, looking in vain for the fault, the loose connection.

The Boag problem which Henshaw had raised was just as intractable. He couldn't very well read the riot act or cut up nasty with him. There could be no recourse either to a fiery diatribe against the evils of pornography. No, what he was going to use was a gambit that contained perhaps just a pinch too much of compromise, a ducking of the real issue. He lifted the screwdriver and drummed its blade on the table. Was he about to 'tie his shoelaces' again? A little clot of shame slid through his system as he remembered the incident in the locker room when Cutter had barged in on his prayer. "Be sober, be vigilant", the Good Book had warned him and nor should he forget about the devil who was himself on the prowl, "seeking whom he may devour".

Floating up the passageway between the storage lines, his head and shoulders visible above the shining roofs of the car shells, came Boag. He had hitched a ride on a 'firebug', one of the battery-driven runarounds used by the plant firemen on their inspection tours. Sheridan, still fiddling with the screwdriver, now placed it firmly on the table. What was he feeling so jumpy about? They were going to have a straight man-to-man talk, that was all. Nothing drastic, nothing too heated. He saw the scarlet snout of the 'firebug' emerge from amongst the stored lines of car shells and watched as it approached the office.

Boag dropped from the vehicle as it passed the door and he padded in on his canvas boots. He scraped a chair towards him by hooking a foot around its spar. He slapped himself down, one leg rising to straddle the other. The usual smirk was scribbled along his mouth as he leaned back, seeming to appraise the discomfited Sheridan. The lightly flexed lips and sardonic stare seemed to be saying: "Don't get on your high horse with me, pal — I knew you when you rode a donkey."

Sheridan began his rehearsed speech. Boag, spotting the transistor radio and the screwdriver on the table, leaned over and lifted them. His shrewd eyes raked over the instruments workings then the screwdriver began to probe various locations. Sheridan had begun to feel like a wireless himself, one that was only being half-listened to. Boag continued to probe with the screwdriver.

Sheridan paused, awaiting some response. None was forthcoming. Instead, Boag who seemed to have located the fault, rose and taking up the soldering iron plugged it into a wall socket. Sheridan turned to him in exasperation. "Am I talking to myself, or what?"

Boag balanced the soldering iron on the table's edge. "I heard you, alright."

"And?"

"Seems in case some virgin from the Sewing Room (that's a laugh!) comes to work in the Booth and finds out she's got tits I've to strip all my stuff off the walls, right?"

"I didn't put it as crudely as that."

Boag grinned. "You know me, John, never call a tit a mammary gland if I can help it."

"You'll do it, then?"

"No chance." Boag's smirk, if anything, had deepened. "By the way," he added, "I forgot to mention, I'd to replace your cylinder-head gasket."

Sheridan frowned, then lifting a model plate flicked at it with the nail of his forefinger. "I was hoping we could sort this out without any hassle."

Boag tested the soldering iron tip and seemed satisfied that it was hot enough. "You haven't the right to ask," he said as he positioned himself with the soldering iron above the transistor's entrails. "I mean," he went on as he homed in on the loose connection, "there I'm stuck in that biscuit tin for the best part of a ten hour shift. Try it sometime. Never a minute. You've to send for a snagger if you want to scratch your arse. So I stick a few dolly birds up and — "

"A few thousand."

"So what? I've a taste for erotic wallpaper." A globule of solder dropped where he had evidently wanted it to. "There, that's got it." He turned the transistor over and pressed a button. There was an immediate burst of music. He switched it off then taking up the cover replaced it and screwed it down. As he went over to unplug the soldering iron Sheridan said: "They're coming down, Jack, one way or the other."

Boag went across to the fire bucket in the corner and jabbed the hot iron into the sand. He sauntered back to the table and leaned on it with both hands so that he was looking down on Sheridan. "Tell you something, John, I've no respect for you. Why should I? You couldn't drive a hot nail into butter. You're letting that grey rag on your back fool you, kidding yourself on you really amount to something. Well, you don't. And morals? Think you're big in that department too, eh?" He leaned closer. "I could tell you something that'd blow that dog collar of yours clean off."

"What're you talking about?"

He walked to the door but as he grasped the handle he turned to look over his shoulder. "They're staying put, John. And you can tell that fucking monk-in-a-boilersuit, Woggle, that I said so . . . "

The door crashed shut with a glass jarring crunch then, almost immediately, both office phones began to ring.

Vic Logan, the underseal shop steward shook his head in disbelief. "I don't get it," he said. "You mean for a bunch of tit-fodder you'd risk a — "

"A what?" Sheridan demanded. "A walk-off? Credit the punters with some sense."

The discussion was in progress at Sheridan's desk. Logan, who'd at first been treating the matter as a joke, began to look more serious. "You never know what way the men'll jump. Boag's popular. Anyway, what's wrong with a few pin-ups — they're all over the place."

"I want that muck off the Booth walls tonight."

"You're having me on!"

Sheridan sensed that he was pushing too hard. Stupid setting a time limit like that. He was beginning to lose the place, could feel the nonsense gathering momentum. Boag's remarks had upset him, no doubt about that, but for the moment he still had the initiative. How many punters getting paid for doing nothing would support Boag when the chips were down? They'd be the laughing stock of the plant. "The Dolly Bird Dispute" that's what they'd call it. Imagine telling your wife you were on strike over a bunch of tatty porn!

Logan must have been thinking along similar lines for he said: "Listen, how about this? If, and when a female comes to work in the Booth we'll call a meeting and consider what you're after — right?"

Sheridan decided it was time to get off the hook. Yes, he was compromising himself for the moment, saving face, but maybe sooner than later he'd be able to wangle a female inspector into the Booth. He was on the point of conceding to the shop steward's proposal when a burst of laughter and handclapping from the underseal area made him turn quickly. The men were cheering a grotesque figure who, wearing a floral dress, beige felt hat, and with feet half-crushed into high-heeled shoes, was posing on a flap of cardboard on the ramp. It was Boag. To claps and shouts of encouragement he gyrated his hips then began to perform a mock striptease, lewdly raising the dress to show his rolled-up overalls beneath it. Every cell in Sheridan's body began to vibrate with rage. The dress Boag was so obscenely flaunting was the one his wife had worn to their daughter's graduation ceremony. The hat — it flew from Boag's head as he performed a rumbustious can-can — was the one she'd always worn to church.

"Tell'm to stop it," Sheridan hissed through grinding teeth.

"It's only a bit of fun." Logan was as amused as the others. The smile, however, was abruptly swept from his face when Sheridan leaned forward and said viciously in his ear: "You can tell Boag if he's not got that muck off the walls in ten minutes — Fogarty's for the high jump."

"Fogarty!"

"That's right — Fogarty. I know, and you know, he's lying blitzed in the tank hut!"

The men watched in silence from their tables as Boag cropped his 'Gallery' from the Booth walls. Naked ladies fell at his feet like rancid snow. Boag's face was expressionless. The rip-ripping sound went on and on. Sheridan stood with his back to the desk. The 'den of iniquity' was being cleansed but this brought him no joy. For who was going to rip the moment from his mind when Logan had called the squad together to inform them of his threat? It would remain there, clinging obscenely, that glowering look the betrayed squad had fixed on him. He stood now on the edge of their contempt, his blood winding through his body like a slow poison.

The ripping sounds in the Booth stopped. Boag appeared on the ramp. He came down the steps with the men's eyes on him, crossed to confront Sheridan. "Been saving this for you, Squire," he said, taking a piece of paper from his overall pocket and passing it to him. It was a page from a glossy magazine. Sheridan slowly unfolded it. His eyes flinched as if they'd been stung with acid.

"Great thing education," Boag said gruffly. "I suppose you'll notice that's not a scroll she's got in her hand?"

There arose a loud shout from the operators as with a rapid series of jerks the Widow began to move. In the general scramble of men making their way to their assigned positions Sheridan walked unnoticed across the floor and went out onto the loading bay. He crossed to where the hoist parts lay on the piece of sacking then, bending, began to gather up the chain; he laid it in clanking hoops over his arm. Bearing the weight of it he now moved towards the door and went out into the darkness of the yard.

Fifty paces would take him to the water tank.

BIOGRAPHICAL DETAILS

Donald Adamson is a member of the Dumfries Writers' Group. Having worked abroad for several years, he now writes and edits EFL textbooks. In 1985 he won the Radio Clyde Poetry Prize. His work has appeared in GLASGOW MAGAZINE.

John Brewster is Chairman of Fife Writers' Group, has edited SCREIVINS and has work published in magazines and anthologies. Married with two children, he currently lives in Glenrothes.

Margaret Gillies Brown is a member of Dundee University Writers' Workshop and her work has appeared in many magazines. She has had a fiction collection published by Blind Serpent Press, Dundee, has had three collections of her poetry in OUTPOSTS and one published by Akros.

Elizabeth Burns was born in 1957, lives in Edinburgh where she works in a bookshop, is a member of the School of Poets and of Waves, a women writers' group.

Ken Campbell has lived most of his life in Clydebank. He is a member of Clydebank Writers' Workshop and has contributed to the group anthologies.

Susan Campbell was born in Glasgow, brought up in Skye and now lives in Glasgow. She has written for EDINBURGH REVIEW, ORIGINAL PRINTS, STREETS OF GOLD, Radio 3 and Channel 4. A story collection will be published by Polygon in the autumn.

Valerie Cumming was born in London, brought up in Havana and is a member of Dundee University Writers' Workshop. Her work has been published in GALLIMAUFRY and BLIND SERPENT.

Maud Devine is a mobile librarian with Glasgow District Libraries. She is a member of Glasgow University Writers' Workshop and has had poems published by the GLASGOW HERALD, NEW WRITING SCOTLAND, WEST COAST MAGAZINE and ORIGINAL PRINTS.

Joe Farrell was born in the east end of Glasgow and has had an address there ever since. He joined the merchant navy at sixteen, has sailed on freighters and liners working from cabin boy to cook and was shipwrecked off Gibraltar. He is a member of Glasgow East End Writers' Group, has contributed to their booklets and written two unpublished novels.

A.D. Foote is a member of Dundee University Writers' Workshop, and has had numerous poems in magazines as well as publishing one book THE HOUSE NOT RIGHT IN THE HEAD (Blind Serpent Press).

Ina Fotheringham lives in East Kilbride and is married with five children. She trained as a teacher when her youngest son started school and now teaches locally.

Barry Fowler is 27, married and lives in Glasgow where he works in housing. His work has been published in THE SCOTSMAN, QUARTO, NEW EDINBURGH REVIEW and LONDON MAGAZINE. He is presently trying to publish his first collection.

Graham Fulton lives in Paisley and is a member of Paisley Writers' Workshop. His work has appeared in IRON, THE ECHO ROOM, LA VACHE, EDINBURGH REVIEW and TOWER OF BABEL. A booklet of his poems The EIGHTH DWARF was published earlier this year. A collection called HUMOURING THE IRON BAR MAN is to be published by Polygon.

Janice Galloway was born in Ayrshire, lives in Glasgow, has had stories in EDINBURGH REVIEW, RADICAL SCOTLAND, CHAPMAN, MARGIN, WEST COAST MAGAZINE, AURORA,

GLASGOW HERALD, ORIGINAL PRINTS, NEW WRITING SCOTLAND and anthologies published by Women's Press, Serpent's Tail and Sheba. Her first novel will be published this year by Polygon.

Pat Gerber writes every morning and teaches two creative writing classes for Glasgow University's Adult Education Department. She has been vice president of Glasgow Writers' Club, has written for SCOTTISH FIELD and SCOTTISH AMBASSADOR and has stories in NEW WRITING SCOTLAND 3 and 4.

Jim Glen is a freelance English tutor and a member of the Central Writers' Group in Edinburgh. His poems and stories have appeared in CHAPMAN, TEACHING ENGLISH, NEW WRITING SCOTLAND and GRAFFITI.

John Glenday has been a member of Dundee University Writers' Workshop and the Dudhope Creative Writers' Class. His poetry has been published widely in Scotland, England and Canada and his first collection THE APPLE GHOST was published this year by Peterloo Poets. He is an editor of the Blind Serpent Press.

Susan Goodship is a former member of Falkirk Writers' Circle. She is the editor of EVERGREEN, an anthology of poems about gardens, and is currently working on a book about Rett's Syndrome, based on the life of her daughter Bethany and a series of lectures she has given to Rett Association Conferences in Vienna.

James Graham was born in Irvine and teaches at a local school. He is a member of Ayrshire Writers' and Artists' Society and has had "some dozen or so poems published in small magazines".

Ishbel Gray was born in Bellshill, lives in Bothwell, works in Blantyre and is a founder member of Hamilton Writers' Workshop.

William Hershaw is a member of Fife Writers' Group, and has published three collections of poems GLENCRAIG, HIGH VALLEYFIELD and MAY DAY IN FIFE. His work has appeared in most literary magazines and he has edited a collection of poems by Fife English teachers for the Arts in Fife Association.

Tom Hubbard is Librarian of the Scottish Poetry Library. He is co-founder of the Fife Writers' Group, its magazine SCREIVINS and SCOTS GLASNOST. He and William Hershaw are two of FOUR FIFE POETS: FOWER BRIGS TI A KINRIK (Aberdeen University Press, 1988)

Robert Johnstone was born in Glasgow, brought up in East Kilbride, studied art at the Central School and Goldsmiths College, London, now lives and teaches in Ayr and is a member of Ayr Writers' Club.

A.L. Kennedy was a member of Dundee University Writers' Workshop before moving to Glasgow Her work has appeared in BETE NOIR, THE DEVIL AND THE GIRO, ORIGINAL PRINTS 3, EDINBURGH REVIEW and STREETS OF GOLD.

Brenda Leckie was born in London, lives in Glasgow and has attended the creative writing classes run by the Adult Education Department at Glasgow University for a number of years. Her work has been published in magazines AKROS, POETRY REVIEW, NEW WRITING SCOTLAND and in the anthology NEW POETRY.

Sheila Lewis has lived in Glasgow all her life. She has been a member of Glasgow Writers' Club for fifteen years and is a member of the Romantic Novelists' Association, Scotland.

Henry Longmore is a native of Paisley who now lives in Howwood and is a member of Johnstone Writers' Group. He is an unemployed shipyard worker whose poetry has been published in SOME SAY, IMAGES and ACORNS.

Linda McCann is a graduate of Glasgow University and has published poetry, short stories and reviews. She is currently Creative Writing Tutor at Maryhill Resource Centre and is editing an anthology of the work of her group.

John MacColl was born in Oban, attended school in Stirling, graduated from St. Andrews and is an assistant librarian at Glasgow University Library. He has been a member of Falkirk Writers' Circle and Glasgow Writers' Group.

Gail McGarva is a member of Onthank Writers' Workshop in Kilmarnock where she has lived most of her life. She is unemployed.

Philip McGrade is twenty-nine, lives in Cathcart and teaches in Lanarkshire. His last published work was A DAY IN THE LIFE OF A SUITCASE in Primary Six.

Ruth McIlroy was born in Wales, spent her early childhood in Jamaica and was educated at Edinburgh University. She lives in Edinburgh, designs computer systems for a living and is a member of Waves Writing Group.

Elise McKay is a member of the School of Poets whose work has been published in OUTPOSTS, AQUARIUS, WORDS, LINES REVIEW and other poetry magazines as well as the Stirling Gallery anthology TREES. She has published one book UNRAVELLING KNOTS (Outposts).

Alex McLaughlin is a member of Linwood Writers' Workshop and his work has appeared in IMAGES and ACORNS.

Ellen McMillan has written for pleasure since primary school. Her stories have appeared in ORIGINAL PRINTS and THE SCOTSMAN.

John McMurray started writing stories instead of sitcoms when he joined Johnstone Writers' Group. His story 'Two Characters in Search of a More Intelligent Author' won the 1986 Radio Clyde – Glasgow University Short Story Competition.

Ronald McNeil lives in Gourock, has had work published in EDINBURGH REVIEW and is presently at work on a novel.

Rosa Macpherson is a Project Officer at Alloa Arts and Crafts Workshop, tutor of Alloa Writing Group and a member of Stirling Library Writers' Workshop. She won the Radio Scotland Short Story Competition in 1985 and has been published in EDINBURGH REVIEW, NEW WRITING SCOTLAND, THE DEVIL AND THE GIRO and SCOTTISH SHORT STORIES (Collins).

John Morrison was born in Kuala Lumpur and educated in England and Scotland. He is a member of the School of Poets. His work has appeared in GRAFFITI and a poetry card has been published by the School of Poets.

Lily Morrison was born and lives in Glasgow. Her work appears in print here for the first time.

Catherine Mowat founded Bo'ness Writers' Workshop in 1983. Her work has been published in THE SCOTSMAN, EDINBURGH EVENING NEWS and SUCCESS.

P.S. Murray recently graduated from the University of Stirling which she attended as a mature student. 'P.C. Graham Fraser' is her first attempt at story writing.

Liz Niven was a member of the Dumfries Writers' Workshop and recently established a writers' workshop in Newton Stewart. Her work has been broadcast on Radio 4 and Radio Scotland and published in LINES REVIEW.

Janet Paisley joined Falkirk Writers' Circle six years ago, has published numerous short stories and poems, and broadcast on Radio Scotland, Radio Clyde and S.T.V. Poetry collections include IMAGES (Moray House) and PEGASUS IN FLIGHT (Rockbook).

Bert Paton's work has appeared in a number of magazines and has been broadcast by the BBC who "thought it was imaginary, found it wasn't and promptly refused further efforts".

J.N. Reilly lives in Glasgow. His work has appeared in EDINBURGH REVIEW, NEW WRITING SCOTLAND, WEST COAST MAGAZINE and the anthology WORKERS' CITY.

Brenda Shaw is a New Englander, currently living in Oregon. She was a member of Dundee Writers' Workshop, edited SEAGATE II and had her first collection THE COLD WINDS OF SUMMER published by Blind Serpent Press.

Morelle Smith was briefly involved with the School of Poets and the Scottish Writers' Co-operative and has had stories and poems in various magazines and anthologies.

James P. Spence is a member of Leith Writers' Workshop and has recently been involved in setting up the Joined Up Writers' Inc. His first collection THE FATAL TOUCH was published last year.

Nan Sprott is a member of Paisley Writers' Workshop. Her work has appeared in IMAGES and four other Library publications. She won last year's Paisley Writers' Competition and Motherwell Bookfest Competition.

Jane Struth is a member of Strathaven Writers' Group. One of her stories was included in ORIGINAL PRINTS.

Martin Sullivan is a member of Fife Writers' Workshop, and appears with Bert Paton in THE THEY AND THE THEM.

Jeff Torrington was born in the Gorbals, lives in Linwood and has attended many writers' workshops. He has published short stories and articles.

Janette Walkinshaw started writing five years ago when she joined Paisley Writers' Workshop. She has had several stories published and a radio play broadcast.

Jane Webster was born in Edinburgh in 1956. She was a member of the Wester Hailes Women Writers' Group and more recently has attended the Stirling Writers' Workshop. She has had stories included in NEW WRITING SCOTLAND and SCOTTISH SHORT STORIES.

Dorothy Whamond is a member of Falkirk Writers' Circle, and has had poems, fiction and articles published in STIRLINGSHIRE GAZETTE, FALKIRK HERALD, SUCCESS and MY WEEKLY.

Jane O'Haire Whamond works as a schoolteacher and lives in Denny.

Katherine White is a member of Dundee University Writers' Workshop. Her work has appeared in CHAMBERS JOURNAL, THE LADY, CAT WORLD ANNUAL, BLIND SERPENT and GALLIMAUFRY.

Jackie Whittet has written and recorded quite a few songs but no hits, has worked as a compère, singer, disc jockey and managed groups until illness stopped him working. Joined Johnstone Writers' Group to learn about scripting and started writing short stories.